DARKNESS RISING

VOLUME SIX: EVIL SMILES

Books by L.H. Maynard & M.P.N. Sims

Shadows at Midnight
Echoes of Darkness
Incantations
The Hidden Language of Demons
Moths
The Secret Geography of Nightmare
Selling Dark Miracles

As editors

Darkness Rising
Enigmatic Tales volumes 1-10
Enigmatic Novellas volumes 1-6
Enigmatic Variations volumes 1-5
Enigmatic Electronic online
F20

DARKNESS RISING

VOLUME SIX: EVIL SMILES

Edited by L.H. Maynard and M.P.N. Sims

PRIME BOOKS
Canton, Ohio

DARKNESS RISING
VOLUME SIX: EVIL SMILES

Published in the United States by **Prime Books, Inc.**
P.O. Box 36503, Canton, OH 44735
www.primebooks.net

ISBN: 1-894815-39-4

CONTENTS

Introduction to "Ha! Ha!" by Hugh Lamb

Social reformer and best selling author **George R Sims** *(1847—1922) is now almost forgotten. Yet over a century ago he featured in the Strand Magazine's monthly portraits of celebrities, the modern equivalent of a photo feature in Hello magazine. The Strand said of him (May 1891) 'at sixteen he was already a keen observer of life and character. At twenty four he was writing for several magazines and papers, and six years later he became a member of staff of* **The Referee** *under the now celebrated non de plume, 'Dagonet' . . . (his play) The Lights O'London has now been running for ten years.' Sims wrote a series of letters to the* **Times** *on the plight of the poor, which prompted a Royal Commission to investigate the appalling conditions of those in need in London. And yet he is now hardly mentioned. His neglect is all the more peculiar as he wrote some real little gems of weird fiction, tucked away in his many books of short stories. 'Ha! Ha!' overlooked for over a hundred years, comes from his collection* **The Ring O'Bells** *(1894). It has been in my pile for 30 years; it was smmarily ejected from one anthology of mine by the publisher, and was lined up for another book cancelled at the last minute. It is only fitting that a namesake of the author should see it into print at last.*

Hugh Lamb, Surrey 2002.

HA! HA!
G R Sims

'Good Heavens! Peyton, what have you been doing with yourself!'

The exclamation was forced from me by the extraordinary appearance of my friend Charley Peyton, the popular young comedian of the————Theatre.

I had been absent from town for a couple of months, and had not seen Charley since I shook hands with him outside the Junior Garrick, the night previous to my departure for the Continent. Then he was a good-looking, bright-eyed young fellow, full of life and unusual spirits, and with a complexion that would put a Devonshire lassie's to shame. Now—I hardly know how to describe his appearance, it was so extraordinary. He was thin, and he had been stout; he stooped, and he had been upright as a poplar; his eyes were sunken and glassy, his face was deeply lined, and his skin was of that dull unhealthy tint so common to people suffering with nervous diseases; deep violet circles were round his eyes, his lips were pale and blistered, and as he held out, his hand, in response to my startled question, I noticed that it trembled. I clasped it, and found it burning hot. Peyton drew his hand gently from mine, and in reply to my eager question as to what was the matter with him stammered out:

'Oh, nothing; I'm a little out of sorts.'

I was not to be put off in this way, for Charley Peyton was a great favourite of mine, and I was really distressed to see him looking so dreadfully, ill. I slipped my arm through his, and strolled with him along the

Strand. I plied him with questions, and cross-examined him with a pertinacity worthy of an. Old Bailey barrister. I tried every art of which I was master to coax the comedian's secret from him, but he parried every attempt, and at the corner of Wellington Street left me hurriedly, saying he had some business to attend to.

Wandering back towards my chambers, I met a couple of Charley's friends, and in the course of conversation I referred to his strange appearance. They had noticed it too; in fact they told me it was the talk of the profession. None of them could say what was actually the matter with him, but everyone agreed that mental distress had a great deal to do with it.

Peyton was in the bill of the———— and having an 'off-night' I determined to drop in that evening, and see how far his acting was affected by his condition. Being one of the, I am afraid, small class who never ask to be passed into a theatre, however well known to the management, I put down my two shillings at the pay-hole and strolled into the pit, just before the curtain rose on the comedy in which Peyton played a principal part. The house was full, and I had to stand up at the back—a position the playgoer, whose theatrical digestion is too weak for `the first farce,' generally has to occupy, if he selects a successful piece for his evening's entertainment.

The first act went off smoothly. Charley was capital; he made all his points, was perfectly at ease, and got a call at the fall of the curtain. He seemed full of life and spirits. I could hardly believe he was the same melancholy individual I had met in the morning.

Half-way through the second act occurs the best situation in the play. The hero, to test the affection of a girl for his friend, has to make love to her. His own sweetheart, unnoticed by him, is in a position to overhear every word he says. The interest is worked up splendidly to this point, and although what is about to happen is obvious, the attention of the audience is focused and there is a dead silence.

Charley came gradually to the climax with the finished care of an artist. The audience watched his every gesture; they seemed to feel the consequence to him of the words he was about to speak, and there stole over the spectators that strong desire to call out and give warning of the impending danger which now and again is provoked by the realism of a situation and the art of a performer.

It was just when all nerves were strained, and the hush was deepest, that there came from the centre of the pit a clear and distinct `Ha! Ha!' It was over in a moment, a few heads were turned impatiently, and then every eye was fixed upon the stage again.

But the effect upon Peyton was remarkable. His whole demeanour had changed, his hands trembled, his voice was husky and indistinct, he seemed suddenly to have lost his self-possession. I saw clearly that he had gone utterly to pieces, and that the situation was irrevocably marred. He stumbled through the scene, missed his cue, flurried the other performers, and seemed only in a hurry to get on and quit the stage. The audience noticed it; they fidgeted, and whispered, and grew inattentive. The spell was broken; the second-act was utterly spoiled, and when the curtain fell there was not a hand given except by the girls at the refreshment bar, and the programme-sellers, who applauded as usual.

I was so disappointed myself that I did not wait for the third act. I went over to the Gaiety, lit a cigar, and read the evening paper till I knew the play would be over. Then I went back to the theatre arid waited at the stage door till Peyton came out. He did not notice me, and I tapped him on the shoulder as he passed. He gave a little scream, and turned hurriedly towards me. The lamp-light fell full upon his features, and I in my turn started back. His face was ashy white, his sunken eyes were staring as though some midnight horror had riveted them, his lips were wide apart, and he breathed in a painfully gasping manner.

'Charley, old man,' I exclaimed, really frightened at his appearance; 'what is the matter with you?'

'Nothing.' He shook himself from my grasp, and would have passed on, but I took his arm and held him.

'Nonsense—you are seriously ill. I saw you tonight in the comedy.'

'Ah! You were there. Did you hear him?'

'Him who?'

'My murderer.'

He hissed the words into my ear, and his hot breath burned my cheek.

'Listen, old fellow,' he continued, speaking hurriedly; 'I've never told a living soul before, but I'll tell you now. The fellows would have laughed at me and thought me cracked—you won't. I'll trust you. Where can we go where no infernal spies are listening?'

He gesticulated so violently, he spoke and glared about him so strangely, that I felt convinced his reason was affected.

'Come to my chambers,' I said; 'we shall be quiet there.'

He never spoke a word till we got to the Temple, and I did not question him. I had some experience of mental excitement, and I know in such cases the talking should all be on one side.

When we reached my chambers and the door had been shut, he flung his overcoat onto the sofa, thrust his hands in his pockets, and commenced to pace rapidly up and down the room.

'It's been going on for a month, old man, and I can't stand it any longer,' he said, suddenly facing me. 'Some night I'll leap off the stage and strangle the scoundrel where he sits.'

'But what is it he does?—who is the scoundrel?'

'You saw me change in the second act?—you heard that 'Ha! Ha!' through the dead silence?'

'Yes.'

'Well, that same 'Ha! ha!' has come every night at exactly the same moment. At first I did not notice it; now, I listen for it. As I get near the cursed line that brings it, I burst into a cold perspiration. I know it's coming, and I'm powerless to stop it. It comes and drives me mad. By Heaven!' he cried, bringing his trembling hand down violently upon the table, 'it's murdering me by inches. Look at me!'

I had no necessity to look at him. I had watched him intently during the whole of his narrative, and I saw the truth of what he said. A highly sensitive temperament was being acted upon by certain circumstances to such an extent that physical and mental health were alike being slowly undermined. Even the thought of what he had gone through was too much for him, and the perspiration was streaming down his hollow cheeks now, and his lips trembled with suppressed rage.

'If I had him here now I'd kill him like a dog!'

He brought his heel down with terrific violence on the carpet, then flung himself into the chair, and breaking down, sobbed hysterically.

I poured out some brandy, and he drank it eagerly. Then I sat down beside him and endeavoured to calm him. I knew the condition of mind and body in which he was required the greatest care and attention. I told him that, whatever might have been the cause of his illness, it was apparent that he was seriously unwell, and that he ought to go out of the 'bill' at once, and go away for a time. Rest and quiet would brace him up, and he would be all right.

He would not listen to it.

'NO,' he answered petulantly. 'I will not rest till I know why I am being murdered, and by whom.'

'Have somebody to watch in the pit.'

'It doesn't always come from the pit. One night it is in the gallery, the next in the boxes, then in the pit. One evening I swear it came from the wings, but it is always the same voice, the same 'Ha! Ha!''

'But have you tried to find out who it is?'

'Yes. We had people watching all parts of the house, and they have never been able to say who does it.'

'Do you suspect anyone?'

'No.'

'Then why bother at all about it? Let the idiot laugh, and take no notice.'

'How can I help taking notice? I tell you I listen for it, and—it is the agony of suspense, the wondering if it is coming or if my persecution is over, the doubt as to where it will come from—these are the things that are driving me mad, and not the laugh itself.'

A few minutes later he put on his overcoat, and shaking hands, went off hurriedly, refusing to let me accompany him.

* * *

The next night I went to the—— theatre out of curiosity. I was determined to see if I could not detect this extraordinary individual who went every night to the same theatre, and persistently laughed at the moment when everyone else was silent. I selected the pit as the likeliest place, and stood at the side near the orchestra, where I could see the occupants of every row from back to front. After the overture there was a little bustle at the corner of the curtain, and presently the stage-manager stepped onto the stage, and there was a hush. He regretted to say that Mr. Peyton was suddenly and seriously indisposed, but another gentleman had kindly undertaken the part at a moment's notice, and claimed their kind indulgence. I had guessed the nature of the announcement directly I saw the manager's shirt-front at the wing; but I determined to stay and see where the laugh came from. The second act was reached, the silence came, the line, which Peyton had told me was the signal for the laugh was spoken, but no laugh came. The curtain fell on the second act without a sign of it. I saw at once that Peyton was right in his surmise. The laugh was intended solely for his annoyance. It was too late to call at my friend's lodgings that night, but the next day I went up directly after breakfast. I was not allowed to see him. The landlady told me his mother was with him, and he was to see no other visitors. 'He was quite off his head, and was raving that awful about murder, and a giving 'Ha! Ha's!' as is enough to curdle honest folkses bloods.' I ascertained that my poor friend was in good hands, and that his doctor was an able man, and I left. For a month I called continually, and received varying accounts of him. I had to leave town later on for a fortnight, and when I returned I heard that he was much better, and that having been recommended a sea voyage and total change of scene, he had accepted an engagement in America, and had set sail the very day I came home.

It was about six months after the departure of Peyton for the States that, chancing to be at the East End of London one evening, I turned into a local music-hall for an hour, just 'to study character.'

The entertainment was of the ordinary kind. There were the usual comic songs, the Sisters Thinga-my-jig, and the dancing dogs. There was one thing on the programme, however, which was a little out of the beaten track. A Signor Thomasini gave a lecture on ventriloquism, accompanied by illustrations. The native skies of the Signor were evidently those which are distinctly visible from any part of Whitechapel, but in spite of his foreign name he gave ample evidence of native talent. One of his tricks particularly struck me at the time as excellent. Standing on the stage, he flung his voice, now into the centre of the hall, now at the back, and now up in the galleries. The phrase he used was, 'A pot of beer, please;' and this order he gave so naturally in each place that the waiters instantly answered, 'Yessir!' The entertainment made nothing but a passing impression on me; and in a week I had forgotten it.

One evening, on my arrival home, I found a card in my letter-box, 'Charles Peyton;' and underneath it was written in pencil, 'Back again. Shall be at the club to-night.' I found Peyton a different man.

The voyage and the complete chance of life and scene had completely re-stored him. Still, when he told me that he was going back into his old part at the——Theatre, I thought I noticed a nervous twitching of the lip.

'You've quite got over the old nervousness,' I said cheerily. 'You can snap your fingers at the 'Ha! Ha!' man.'

'He won't come,' answered Charley, filling his pipe: 'I've made up my mind that's over. For heaven's sake, don't set me thinking of it.'

I turned the conversation at once. I saw that the old sore was not healed, and I confess I trembled for the result. The idea took possession of me that the 'Ha! Ha!' would be heard again. I tried not to think of it, to pooh-pooh it; but, somehow all, that evening at the club, and half the night as I lay awake at my chambers, I pictured that second act and listened for the mysterious laughter.

The night of Charley's rentree at the——Theatre came. I saw him for a minute as he went in to dress. He looked well, but was evidently nervous. The few words he spoke to me showed me that he was preoccupied. I was certain that the old terror was coming slowly back. As I turned from the stage door he caught my arm, and said in a low tone.

'If I don't hear that to-night, old fellow, I'm cured. If I do—God help me!—I'm a ruined man.'

I shook his hand and bade him not think about it; that silly business was all over. The first act went off admirably. Charley played with all his old animation and grace, and got a big call. The second act commenced, and I felt myself growing hotter and hotter. As the situation was neared my hands trembled, and I expected to hear my teeth chatter. I didn't know what to do with myself. At one time I felt I must rush out of the house. I conquered the feeling, and, gripping the seat in front of me, watched the stage. The line came. Peyton had begun to tremble. I saw his eyes wander fearfully round the house. He stumbled at a word, and seemed dazed and awkward. The line was spoken amid a dead hush. Suddenly over the silence rang a loud and mocking 'Ha! Ha!'

I sprang up, horror-stricken. Peyton gave a shriek. Then his mouth twitching convulsively, and his eyes glaring, he rushed down to the foot-lights and tried to speak. His hands extended towards the spot where the sound had come, he hissed out some indistinct word, then, clutching at the air, fell down upon the stage, moaning. The curtain was lowered; the people rose terrified from their seats, and there was a movement towards the door. The manager, with great promptness, came before the curtain and begged them to keep their seats. Mr. Peyton, he explained, had been seized with a fit, and was being medically attended. With their permission, however, the play would be continued. Mr. So-and-So, who had understudied the part, would play it. There was a little chatter and confusion, and after an interval the curtain was raised and the comedy proceeded.

* * *

For over two years Charley Peyton has been in a private mad-house. His reason never returned. His health had long been undermined by the previous torture he had endured, and this sudden shock, at a time when he hoped the persecution was over, inflicted a blow from which he will probably never recover. It was only lately that I have been able to fathom, to a certain extent, the mystery of that murderous 'Ha! Ha!'

By a mere accident I discovered that one of the attendants at the theatre had the gift of ventriloquism, and that he had taken to it as a profession, under the name of Signor Thomasini. Careful inquiry led me to the discovery that on the night of poor Peyton's re-appearance Thomasini had been among the audience. He was recognised, and chatted with two of his old confreres, and I am forced to the conclusion that he had practised his art on poor Peyton in a sheer spirit of mischief, never dreaming the effect it was having. Hearing of Peyton's re-appearance, he doubtless thought it would be a lark to treat him to one of the old 'Ha! Ha's!'

I afterwards ferreted the man out and taxed him with the trick. He strenuously denied it, and I have no means of bringing it home to him. I am, however, convinced that he has heard of the serious consequences of his experiment, and fears to tell the truth. I cannot in any other way account for the 'Ha! Ha!' which brought my poor friend Charley Peyton to such a terrible fate.

CRY HAVOC!
Paul Finch

Considering it had been England's bloodiest battle, there was remarkably little now to indicate it had even happened. Penrose took stock with his guidebook and his folded map. Yes . . . there was no mistake. This was the spot . . .

He closed his eyes, put the two or three groups of locals picking sloe berries from the hedgerow at the edge of the meadow from his mind, and let his imagination wander . . . tried to imagine this place as it had been all those years ago: rivers of knights in their flowing, multi-coloured livery, pouring against each other, battle-lances levelled, heraldic banners billowing, behind them, rank upon glittering rank of steel-clad infantry; the sky turning alternately dark and light as showers of barbed goose-shafts rattled back and forth; the swoop and hiss as edged weapons sliced the air, their crash and clatter on shield and buckler; the shrieks of horses; the guttural war-cries of men . . .

The author was already writing, scribbling avid notes in his margins. What a momentous engagement. Fought on the Palm Sunday of 1461, it had signified one of the great turning points in English history. And how fittingly epic in size it had been. For over six hours, two armies, thirty-thousand strong apiece, clad in the heaviest mail and plate-armour, equipped with the most brutal weapons of the age, from longswords and double-bladed battle-axes, to mattocks, flails and razor-edged billhooks—had mercilessly hammered each other on the snow-swept plateau of Towton Moor. As large in physical scale as Waterloo, and costlier in lives than the first day of the Somme, this had been the medieval battle to end them all, and, unusually for that era, one that would later boast an epoch-making outcome: the doughty Lancastrian army shattered on the Yorkist anvil; the fiery Edward, Earl of March, wounded but victorious, sent galloping for London, to claim the English throne and found a new dynasty . . .

Yet now—Penrose glanced up again, suddenly stricken by the rural silence—there was no evidence that so cataclysmic a thing had ever occurred. Castle Hill Wood, where the Lancastrian commander Somerset, had concealed crack-troops and, during the height of the battle, ambushed the western flank of the Yorkist army, almost turning the course of the action, was now a gentle, thinly-treed slope, from which pleasant views of quilt-work farm-land could be had. The point where the Lancastrian army had finally broken under the onslaught of Yorkist reinforcements, lay beside a lonely country road, and was earmarked by a single stone cross, cracked across its pedestal and bearing a few paltry inscriptions now faded to illegibility.

Even this exact spot, Bloody Meadow, where the author now stood—where the fighting had reputedly been thickest—was a simple sweep of grassland at the western end of Towton Dale, not far from the peaceful River Cock. It was churned up here and there by the passage of cattle, but otherwise undamaged. Clumps of gorse made it pleasant to look upon—complemented the pastoral scene, so to speak—but that wasn't why Penrose was here. The guidebook advised him that should he walk west from this point, then turn north along the river, he would eventually come to grave-mounds still visible after five centuries. The author had tried it, however, and hadn't seen anything except locked gates and 'No Ramblers' signs.

It took him only ten minutes to stroll back along the quiet B1217, passing more arable land and occasional stands of ash and alder. The air was ripe with the autumnal scent of leaves. Overhead, flocks of rooks gathered in the branches, ready to migrate, cawing madly. Beyond the trees, dusk settled in a dim, grey blanket.

At Saxton village, Penrose came to the small but atmospheric chapel that was Saxton Church, and stopped to explore further. In its yard, he found himself examining the criss-crossed stone that marked the grave of the famous campaigner Lord Dacre, who had been buried along with his horse. In retrospect, it seemed odd to Penrose that the Lancastrian general's corpse had been laid to rest here, perhaps ten minutes' walk from the main scene of the fighting, but then, like so many medieval battles, Towton Moor wouldn't have been confined to the actual 'tilting-ground,' as it was known at the time. Parties of horsemen, in particular knights, would have ranged far and wide around the circumference of the action, circling and counter-attacking, pursuing other parties, and in the process, ravaging crops and orchards, trampling pasture to ruin; while coarser men—the free companies of mercenaries and men-at-arms—would have hunted up their booty, seizing livestock, sacking and burning cottages, cutting down anyone who tried to stop them. In truth, the battle would have engulfed and devastated this entire district, probably for miles in every direction. As always, Penrose couldn't resist a small tremor of excitement that he was actually standing on such historic ground.

He glanced round one more time, before crossing the narrow lane to his car. This was only the outskirts of the village, and as such was very quiet. To the left of the church there was a small green, and beyond it a line of eighteenth-century stone cottages, with handsome rose-gardens laid out at their fronts. Penrose glanced beyond the roofs of the houses to the rolling uplands that made up this southern fringe of the verdant North-Yorks dales. The setting sun now burnished the higher crests, turning the meadows red and gold, throwing crimson shadows through the lower coppice. Penrose was a Londoner by origin, and had grown up in the city, but the beauty of this scene was not lost on him; it made a perfect picture of the English wold, he supposed; in truth, it was probably the very thing they had been fighting for all those years ago . . . this peace and fertility, this richness of land and culture.

That was when he spotted the bookshop.

The author was just about to unlock his car when he saw it. It occupied a most unlikely place . . . was the end-terrace, in fact, on the row of cottages. He stood gazing at it, a little bewildered. He'd noticed it as a shop earlier of course, but had thought it an off-license or newsagents, something of use to the local villagers and farm-folk. But now, quite clearly painted across its black lintel, in archaic gold leaf, were the words:

Battle Books

A moment passed, then Penrose was crossing the road towards it, shoving his keys back into his slacks' pocket. Now that he thought about it, it seemed obvious there'd be a gimmicky shop somewhere in the area; a tourists' place hoping to exploit the glorious follies of the past. And Penrose, for one, could hardly blame them. But . . . here?; with Saxton and Towton the only habitations in walking-distance, and both of them tiny hamlets, populated by folk to whom the battle of Towton Moor was nothing new?

He'd now come right up to the shop, and found himself staring through the front windows. It was close to half-past seven in the evening, so the place was obviously closed; it was dark inside, its solid, nail-studded front door firmly shut. There was a faint creak from above, and Penrose glanced up. A shield, rather like a pub-sign, only cut in an authentic shield shape and bearing the quartered insignia of the English lions and the French *fleur-de-lys*, swung from a short yardarm. The author gazed at it for a moment. It looked like it was metal laid over a base of timber, though it had been severely battered . . . probably by time and the elements, both.

He glanced back at the shop. As visitor-centres went, it wasn't especially attractive. Though the exterior was smart enough—very olde worlde, all black timber and white wattle—there was a thin film of grey dust on the inside of the widow, and the display it revealed was singularly unappealing. A succession of materials—many torn, drab, odiously stained, and bearing ancient heraldic devices that were poorly sewn—provided the backdrop to three leather-clad books on low stands. The historian understood what the cloths were all about, of course; they were a rather amateurish attempt to create the impression of surcoats or knightly cloaks, but whoever had put them together had lacked both imagination and finesse.

They were soiled rather than colourful, primitive rather than sumptuous.

The books surmounting them followed a similar line, being fat, bare, lumpy. There were no illustrations on their covers, and the wording visible was again in a crabbed, arcane hand. **The Kings' Evil**, one read. **England Under the Hog**, said another. **The Breaking of Spears**, was the third. Penrose had never heard of any of them before, but was a keen enough student of his subject to be disappointed that he couldn't now enter the shop and investigate further. No authors' names were visible on either the front covers or spines, though that wasn't entirely unusual in very old editions.

That was when he heard the horses . . . approaching fast over the open countryside behind him.

He turned abruptly. It sounded like several-hundred were coming at least. It was a deep rumble, a hacking, booming cacophony. The ground literally vibrated, the thunder of it rang in the otherwise calm September evening. The historian wondered if he was about to see a hunt come dashing through the evening gloom, or maybe a herd of cows being moved en masse from one paddock to the next, though he couldn't work out which direction either would come from.

Seconds passed, yet he saw nothing. The narrow green lay empty, only the odd leaf spinning in its gentle breeze. Beyond the rock wall that bordered it, the blue-grey dusk continued to settle. Penrose gazed around, increasingly bewildered. A vague chill began to creep along his spine. The sound continued, rising steadily and furiously as it drew closer . . . ratcheting, pounding, like a miniature earthquake, and then, just as it reached an ear-splitting crescendo, it seemed to break, seemed to crack apart in the evening air, and then it was nothing more than faint, falling echoes, descending swiftly into damp, muffled silence.

The author shivered. He realised he had backed right up to the window, that his mouth had gone bone-dry. Even though he stood there alone, he felt he needed to make some comment. He probably would have done, had somebody else not done it for him.

'Not to worry, sir,' came a soft Yorkshire voice.

Penrose looked sharply to his right. A man, presumably the shopkeeper, was standing in the now-open doorway, smoking a pipe.

'Just the Leeds-Harrogate railway,' the man said, with a friendly smile. 'Often has that effect. Strange acoustics round here. Regularly catches visitors unawares.'

'It certainly caught me,' Penrose replied, now feeling a little foolish.

He realised that his forehead was pin-pricked with sweat, and suddenly yearned to dig his handkerchief out and dab it all away . . . but no. Self-consciousness forbade it.

Not that the shopkeeper seemed amused by the stranger's disquiet, or even that he had noticed it. He was only a shortish chap, about five-foot two, and in his late-fifties at least. Thin, white hair was combed across his brown scalp like a crisp napkin. He wore grey tweeds, and underneath his jacket, a thick, woolly cardigan, a collar and tie. He smiled again and nodded. Even the slight squint in his left eye did nothing to detract from his generally homely appearance.

'I, er . . . I was just admiring your shop,' said Penrose, feeling that some form of conversation was necessary.

'Oh yes? Interested in books, are you, sir?'

Penrose patted the haversack that contained his guidebooks and notepads. 'I ought to be . . . I write them.'

'Oh!' The shopkeeper's sudden interest seemed sincere. 'Anything I might've read?'

Penrose ventured one or two titles: '*Sceptred Isle* . . . ? *Age of Honour* . . . ?'

The shopkeeper puffed on his pipe as he considered.

'The name's Penrose,' the author added.

The shopkeeper now took his pipe out. 'Not Christopher Penrose?'

'That's right.'

The shopkeeper's eyes seemed to light up. 'Well . . . how do you do, sir.' He offered a knotty old hand, and Penrose shook it. 'I can't say I've read all your books, but I certainly know about them. And very spectacular pieces they are too, if I might say.'

'Thanks very much.'

'So what brings you to our neck of the woods?'

'Well . . . I'm working on a new one.'

The shopkeeper smiled knowingly. 'To do with Towton Moor, no doubt?'

'Towton Moor's in there, certainly,' Penrose replied. 'It'll actually be called *Tides of Steel: Twenty Classic Battles of the English Feudal Host.*'

The shopkeeper drew on his pipe again. He seemed genuinely impressed. 'Course . . . being England's biggest battle and all, Towton's been covered a few times, but to have a colourful and exciting wordsmith like you on the job, well . . . that'll be one to read, right enough.'

'I hope so.'

The shopkeeper stepped aside. 'Perhaps you'd like to come in? Have a look at some of the stock?'

The author was surprised. 'You're open?'

'Oh . . . **Battle Books** is always open, sir.' He gave a crafty wink; either that or his squinting left eye was playing up. 'Can't afford not to be, if you know what I mean.'

'Er . . . yes.' Penrose zipped his bag and made to go in. 'Silly question perhaps, but I take it you specialise in books about battles?'

'We do indeed, sir. Like yourself.'

'Medieval?'

'Predominantly.'

There was only one sales-room inside. It was small and pokey, and had the dull, grimy atmosphere of a junk-shop. Though it wasn't visibly dirty or especially cluttered, there was a vague smell of must, and Penrose felt discomforted the moment he entered. He'd been incorrect before—the light was actually on, but it cast such weak illumination that it was barely noticeable. A single doorway led through into the back-area of the shop, but was covered over by a dingy curtain. There was no sign of a desk or till; of course, that wasn't entirely unusual in second-hand stores in remote areas, though in this day and age Penrose always found it eccentric and irritating.

The books themselves—of which, it had to be said, there were a great many—appeared to have been packed haphazardly into crude cases made from twisting, black wood. The author sampled one or two straight away, picking them down from the shelves, but only gingerly . . . up close, there was something off-putting about their clammy, leathery covers; they were cold and greasy to the touch.

'Of course, Towton Moor was pretty dreadful by any standards,' declared the shopkeeper, behind him. 'You know between thirty and forty-thousand poor lads got butchered here?'

'Yeah . . . I heard that,' said Penrose distractedly.

'And many more must've died later . . . from wounds and what-not.'

Penrose made no answer. Each book he flicked through was dusty in the extreme, its pages old and yellow. Again, without fail, they were titles he didn't recognise: **Horsemen from Hell; Built on Blood**. In most cases, the authors' names were noticeably absent.

'Savage,' the shopkeeper added, almost to himself. 'Neither side would give in, you see.'

Penrose turned, puzzled. 'Pardon me for asking, but how do you, er . . . how do you make this little business of yours pay? I mean, with you being so isolated and all?'

The shopkeeper took his pipe out again. 'Well . . . I suppose the truth is that if we were a little business, we'd struggle, but we're not you see. There are branches of **Battle Books** all over the country.'

'There are?' Penrose couldn't conceal his surprise.

'Oh yes . . . we're a busy chain.'

For a moment, the author wasn't sure what to say. He didn't believe it for a moment . . . mainly because he'd never heard of such a franchise. But then again, why would the chap lie?

'You don't seem to be selling anything well-known,' Penrose finally pointed out.

'Not much from the modern age, that's true,' the shopkeeper agreed. 'We mainly stock the authentic voices of the past.'

Penrose glanced again at the crammed and crumbling shelves. 'You're telling me these are first editions and such?'

'Oh absolutely. Quite a few are the only editions.'

'Are some of them very valuable then?'

The shopkeeper shrugged. 'Well . . . I suppose that depends on the individual shopper, and what he or she regards as valuable.'

'It's just that I've been in plenty of London shops that specialise in eso-teric books, and . . . well, their stuff tends to be behind glass.'

The shopkeeper nodded. 'I think we prefer our inventory to be more accessible.'

Which loosely meant, Penrose decided, that they couldn't be bothered taking expensive protective-measures because hardly anyone came in here anyway, and the books rarely got handled . . . though this thesis didn't sit comfortably with the story that Battle Books was a widespread operation. The author found the whole thing rather confusing.

'Seen anything that takes your fancy, Mr. Penrose?' the shopkeeper asked.

'Er . . . ' Penrose glanced down at the book he was holding—a stodgy ,chocolate-brown tome called **Traitors All**. Hurriedly, he put it back on the shelf. 'I have to tell you . . . no.' He gave a regretful sigh. 'No offence, but I'm on a research trip at present, not a buying trip.'

'I see.' The shopkeeper nodded again, as if he understood completely.

'Don't like to mix business with pleasure.'

'Of course not.'

Penrose moved to the door. 'It's a marvellous-looking collection, all the same. And I'm glad that you're doing well. Perhaps, one of these days, you'll have a couple of my books for sale here?'

The shopkeeper smiled through his pipe-smoke. 'I'm sure that's very possible, sir.'

Penrose strode out into the fresh night air, relieved, then quickly made his way back to his car. The truth was the place hadn't been his cup of tea at all; it was hard to specify why, but there'd been something oddly grim about it, something almost forlorn. Was that the right word . . . 'forlorn'? He supposed it was as good as any, though of course being forlorn didn't mean there was any real harm in the place. The chap had seemed pleasant enough, and keen . . . in a small-town, armchair-historian sort of way. And anyone who helped foster an interest in Penrose's beloved Middle Ages was to be applauded, not criticised.

A few moments later, the author had forgotten it. He drove away into the gathering darkness quite content that, while he hadn't gleaned a great deal of value from his field-trip to Towton Moor, some of its atmosphere had seeped into him, even though so much surface detail had changed. No doubt the moor had been a wilder, more desolate place back in 1461, far from any source of salve or succour. He couldn't imagine there'd have been much of that for those left dying on the banks of the River Cock—their limbs hacked off, their throats slashed; or those on Bloody Meadow itself—at the very bottom of the slaughter heaps—blinded, disembowelled, being slowly compressed into the torn, gore-soaked grass by the sheer weight of dead flesh and dented arms, unable to breathe, agonised by their own wounds, weeping through their crushed, broken helms . . .

Penrose couldn't resist a shudder. That had been an odd line of thought. What had brought that on, he couldn't imagine. Sure, war was Hell. Wherever and whenever. But there was no point in making a big issue of it.

Then he wondered where he was.

He stared hard through the windscreen as his small Allegro toddled gamely on down the narrow country lane. He'd assumed he'd followed the B1217 towards Garforth, from where he intended to take the A1 south to Pontefract. But surely he should have passed Lotherton Hall by now, and gone under the M1 motorway? All he saw, though, was the blue-back night falling continually away before his headlights, and to either side of his vehicle, the vague outline of trees and tangled undergrowth. Getting lost, of course, was the last thing he needed. He'd hoped to be back at The Royal Alms well in time to spend a good hour knocking his day's notes into comprehensible form, then enjoying a leisurely bath before dinner. Still . . . this part of Yorkshire might be lush and agricultural, but it wasn't exactly vast and trackless. If he had managed to get lost, he doubted he would stay lost for long. He drove on steadily, maintaining an easy thirty-five miles-per-hour, happy that at any moment he would come to a junction or turning and see a signpost to some place he recognised. The probability was, of course, that, at this speed, on so narrow and winding a road, he hadn't even travelled very far yet. Almost certainly, he was still on the battlefield.

Then the Allegro's engine cut out.

With a single, rather daunting clunk, it simply ceased to rumble . . . fell totally silent.

Penrose felt the power die beneath his feet. He sat there stupefied as he suddenly realised he was freewheeling, that all he could hear was the hiss of the tyres on the unmade road.

A moment passed, then warily, determined not to panic or get himself upset—he was under strict orders from his doctor about that—he touched his foot to the brake-pedal, and slowed the Allegro down until at last he came to a halt on one of the grass verges. Instant silence descended. The deep blackness of night swam up to the car on all sides.

Penrose tried switching the ignition off, then switching it on again. Nothing happened. The engine didn't even turn over. Seconds went by as he sat there, pondering. He didn't know the first thing about cars, or about anything else mechanical for that matter, so there wasn't much point in him going under the bonnet. It could be that he'd run out of petrol, he surmised, but looking at the gauge on the dashboard, he saw that he had over half a tank left. The fact that he could see the gauge, of course, and the speedometer, and the digital clock—all still brightly aglow—meant that the battery hadn't died either. Which was something.

Penrose glanced up again. Out front, the headlamps were in working order too. They showed a dense thicket of hawthorn, its small leaves hanging limp and withered, and below those, an unsightly clump of warty, reddish toadstools. It wasn't an ideal place to be marooned for the night, he supposed, though doubtless in daylight it was less sinister, probably a local beauty spot or a scenic lay-bye on some quiet lovers' lane. Not, he imagined, that it would really come to him being marooned here all night. This was England, for Heaven's sake, not the back roads of the Balkans. There was a better-than-even chance that somebody—even if it was only a bumpkin on a tractor—would come past in the next half-hour or so. All Penrose needed to do was wait. At the worst, he could cadge a ride to the next inn, and sort the blessed car out in the morning.

So he did just that. He sat there and waited, and to while away the time, he dug out his notebook and assessed what information he'd thus far assembled for his new project. **Tides Of Steel** . . . what a title! And what a book it was going to be! Granted, it wouldn't be massively different in subject matter to the thirty others he'd previously written, but he already had a firm readership and their interest wouldn't change, so why should his?

As he thought on this, he took a pencil from his jacket pocket and began to make amendments to his notes. He scanned again the list of battles he intended to detail in the book, each one a martial 'blockbuster' in its own right. Some of them were well known, of course. At Hastings, for instance, William of Normandy had smashed the Anglo-Saxon host and given birth to a new era of history. Ten thousand had died in that one. It beggared belief when you thought about it . . . ten thousand in a battle that lasted only one day. The same could be said for Falkirk, he supposed . . . when Scottish hero William Wallace was finally outmanoeuvred; in a single afternoon, Edward I of England slew eight thousand Scots, losing nearly three thousand of his own men. Horrendous!

Suddenly Penrose laid down his pencil. Again, he wondered what had possessed him. This was proving a much gloomier exercise than normal. Hells bells . . . where was the courage and prowess, the medieval splendour, the chivalrous gestures even in the heat of the most brutal and merciless combat? That was what his audience wanted.

What they specifically didn't want was the horrible slaughter at Jaffa, when the streets of the city lay strewn with bloated, rotting corpses as a besieged force of crusaders fought it out, day after day, against awesome numbers of Muslim warriors. He could picture it easily: Every building burned or burning, the sky filled with smoke and black with vultures' wings. The fortress itself stood battered by missiles, scorched by Greek-fire; its water and food had long since run out; its cellars were stuffed with dying, gangrenous men; in every fly-blown corner of it was the mingled stench of heat, dust and roasted, melted flesh. Yet still the madness raged on, the

Christians emerging repeatedly in a storm of slashing, hacking blades, repelling the Saracens with maximum carnage, laying out carpet on carpet of gutted, shredded carcasses, their heathen innards left exposed and festering for days in the infernal temperatures . . .

Of course, in war, horror knew no limits. He could also have crawled like a rat through the great heaps of torn, desecrated bodies on the blighted plain near Shrewsbury, seeking those he knew who still breathed but who were so broken and mangled, so trampled by hooves, so mutilated by axe or mace that they'd never know another moment without unbearable pain . . . and then finishing them; a swift thrust with the misericord, a twist and crack of neck, praying all the time in abject terror for his own worthless soul, the hot tears streaming on his filthied, wounded cheeks . . .

Worse still, he might have slaved through the seething, grey miasma in the Agincourt hospital tent, stifled by the stink of sweat, bone and open, running bowels, working frenziedly with fingers and pliers to uproot the cloth-yard arrows that pinned plate metal to the writhing torsos of uncountable wounded. Many of those arrows were sunk to their feathers; in most cases the steel casing would not be removed, the blood spurting from every chink or join in it, the horrific screams affrighting the very air, so that outside, crows and ravens, drunk on carrion, swarmed over the fallen standards and broken spears, a new, voracious plague just waiting to descend and devour . . .

Penrose awoke from the hideous dreams in a feverish sweat, groaning aloud as though he himself was being tortured. Several moments drifted by as he slumped there, panting, struggling to regain his composure. He tugged at his collar, loosened another button, then mopped the moisture from his brow with his sleeve. Only then did it strike him that it was a lot darker in his car than it had been before. Still disorientated after his impromptu sleep, it took the author several seconds longer to make sense of this. Then he noted that the illumination from his headlamps—prior to his snooze a bright curtain of reassurance—had now faded to a dismal glow. The same could be said of the various gadgets on his dashboard. His eyes flicked confusedly from one to the other, before finally coming to rest on the digital clock. Penrose was stunned when he saw that it now read: 1.48 a.m.

His hair prickled. The shoulders went rigid inside his green corduroy jacket. He'd slept for over five hours! Was that feasible? He glanced wildly around for some confirmation, or hopefully something that might disprove it, but of course there was nothing. Suddenly, it was hard to breathe in the cramped interior of the Allegro. Penrose was under strict medical orders not to get himself excited; he wasn't on a daily dosage of warfarin for nothing—his heart was way too fatty. All the same, he was so shaken by events that a monumental panic now overtook him. He scrabbled with his seat belt, yanking it loose, then fought his way out of the car, literally, kicking and punching the door, forcing it hard into the crackling, snapping hawthorns.

The moment he climbed from the vehicle, his suede shoes plunged onto, or rather into, sodden, mushy ground. The deep grass was drenched with dew; chill mud spattered up over his ankle-socks. He cursed aloud, then blundered his way around the car, snagging his clothes and even his skin on twigs and thorns, tottering out into the middle of the rutted lane. His breath was still coming in gasps, and now visibly pluming in the much colder early-morning air.

For several moments, that rasping breath was the only thing he could hear . . . that and a faint breeze in the surrounding trees. He was alone, he realised . . . miles from anywhere. He turned in a tight circle, desperately seeking a light, but there wasn't the faintest glimmer visible. The author gazed upwards. In a sky as dark as Halloween crepe, Orion's jewelled belt was clearly visible. Not far to the east, the rigid pattern of The Plough could also be distinguished. But there was no moon . . . not even a sliver, which meant that when the battery of the car finally gave out—and that couldn't be long now, after he'd left it on at full-power all evening—he'd be in total darkness. Penrose was already unconsciously shivering with the cold, but this thought set him shivering all the harder. Total darkness. All the way out here, where he couldn't put one foot in front of another without fear of disaster.

But of course that was nonsense. He tried to shake the ludicrous idea from his head. For God's sake . . . he was a modern man, wasn't he? Well . . . yes, he was a modern man, and there, perhaps, lay the problem. Modern Man, as oppose to Penrose's hardy Medieval Man, had been softened by centuries of easy living and civilised idyll. Where Modern Man was concerned, a casual stroll in the benighted park might as well be a trek through the ancient wildwood for all that he could deal with any problems that might arise.

Whhsss . . .

Penrose started violently, involuntarily ducked.

What . . . surely that couldn't have been . . . ?

Dear God, had some maniac just fired an arrow at him!

The author glanced frantically left to right. He could have sworn he'd just felt its swift passage as it sailed by. There'd even been an accompanying thud a split-second later, as if to indicate it had stuck in the bole of some tree.

The author backed up in fright. For a moment he held his breath. Then he tried to chuckle, thinking again about his recent dreams. It just showed. Even a professional writer like him should never take-for-granted the power of the imagination . . .

Whhsss . . .

Another one flew past . . . or rather over, almost parting Penrose's hair.

He fell into a crouch, instantly petrified. Desperately, he scanned the surrounding landscape. His eyes were now attuning to the faint starlight, and he could just see that to the right of the road, it rose up into a low embankment, while to the left, beyond a low wall, it sloped away. He also saw them. For the first time. Melting slowly out of the blackness like figures cut from anthracite.

In the hollows among the thickets.

On the open acreage where the mist now spilled.

In the deep, oily shadows at the heart of the spinney.

And he saw that they were armed . . . with longsword, with ball-and-chain, with brutal spike-headed mace. No fine-detail was visible, just the crude, flat outlines of those ancient, barbarous weapons . . . but the outlines were enough.

Penrose gave a low, keeping whimper.

Wordlessly, they began to advance. There wasn't a clink of steel or a creak of leather, but they came all the same, marching towards him through the shadows, in the aggressive, determined manner they had probably marched to the battlefront.

With a choking scream, he turned and ran, charging along the muddy road in the direction he had come from. Within moments, however, his flabby heart was beating a burning tattoo in his chest, his untrained legs wobbling like rubber. Below him, his uncoordinated feet started to slip and trip on the impacted dirt. In less than no time, it seemed, he was set to collapse, but new levels of terror were to spur him on, for now he heard hooves come thundering behind, many sets of them . . . iron-shod, ploughing up the ground with their war-horse ferocity.

Penrose tried to scream again, but lacked the breath or strength. Sweat poured off him in rivers, his clothes were soon sodden rags serving only to hamper his middle-aged frame. At one point—he wasn't sure where or why—he veered off the road, fighting his way through the undergrowth, then barging between the trunks of trees. Perhaps he was seeking cover, perhaps he was following some instinctive sense of direction . . . but it did him no good, for the heavy pursuit was maintained, vegetation smashing and tearing under its onslaught. In his mind's eye, Penrose saw red fire and mountains of corpses. His nostrils were filled with the mingled stenches of blood, bandages and foul grave-dirt. All he could think, over and over, was that he didn't want to be hewn and pulverised, he didn't want to feel the bite of the battle-axe in the middle of his cranium!

He was still thinking this when he came stumbling out from the cover of the trees, fell over a low stone wall and found himself facing a road, an open grassy area and beyond that, a line of vaguely familiar buildings—the cottages in the village—with an open doorway beckoning. There was no light beyond it, but any kind of shelter was desirable now. Penrose made straight towards it, gasping hard, the wind working in his lungs and throat like a saw. He didn't dare look round to check whether or not they . . . those things, were still chasing him. The blood beat in his ears, the world seemed to caper around like a mad beast, but at last he'd crossed that remaining fifty yards, and the doorway loomed.

He stammered for help as he threw himself through it. Nobody responded. Penrose didn't expect them to . . . it was late. Mind you, this place had been left open. Even in the midst of his terror, the author had time to be fleetingly baffled by that. He glanced around breathlessly. Through the must and shadows, he saw walls lined with thick, leather volumes. So he was back in the shop. That didn't entirely surprise him, though neither did it relieve him either—because there was no denying it, this place had seemed odd as well, and certainly it should not be standing unlocked at this late hour.

Then he heard the sounds from outside; the harsh, guttural whispers . . . the clip-clop of hooves coming quietly over the road.

Penrose was jolted into frantic action again. This time he backed through the drab curtain into the shop's rear room, where complete shadow and an even denser, dustier atmosphere now enclosed him. He continued to retreat until he came to the far wall, where he slid down into a sitting position. Silence fell. The author hugged his knees to his aching chest, and waited. His body was wracked with pain, strained, fatigued, cut and smarting all over. Sweat continued to pump from his flesh, soaking through his clothes, which now were heavy and freezing cold. He ignored it all. The only thing he could do was listen . . . strain his ears for any sign that those horrors might be coming after him.

If they intended to enter this shop, however, they didn't do so straight away.

A timeless period passed. Eventually, he began looking around, trying to penetrate the gloom with his eyes, trying to work out exactly where he had run to. He fancied there were stacks of old books on either side of him, but imagined them tatty and disordered and sheathed in dust-webs. Up above, perhaps, there were low beams, and on top of those a mass of straw and thatch. If there was any furniture in the tiny room, he couldn't imagine what it might look like. And was the floor beneath him beaten earth? Had it been strewn, maybe, with dried grasses, which had now turned rank and noisome? The faint scritch-scratch he could hear in the corner was possibly a rat, the fluttering between the roof-beams, birds nesting, or moths, or bats.

When the figure stepped out of the darkness beside him, Penrose was almost expecting it.

It was the shopkeeper, his hair now mussed and matted, his thin body clad in a sackcloth shroud that stank of mildew. When he crouched down beside the author, Penrose saw that the man had removed his false left eye, which had probably been a painted stone or marble, and now exposed a deep raw wound, much larger and more circular than the original socket must have been.

Penrose tried to swallow his revulsion, but when he spoke, his voice was little more than a subdued wail: 'I'm still writing my book,' he said. 'And I'm writing it the way I want to.'

The shopkeeper mused, then nodded. 'Of course, you must. It's your book, after all. But I can't answer for what will happen to you if you do.'

'But why me?' The author was shaking violently; he felt ready to swoon. 'I'm ... I'm not the only writer to do this, not even the only person who feels the way I do about the mythology of the Middle Ages. It's not fair.'

'War never is,' the shopkeeper replied. 'Take this, for instance. A Yorkist lance went clean through, even though I was trying to surrender.'

He leaned up close to Penrose, so that his shattered face filled the author's vision. There was no option but to gaze down into that torn, bloody chasm . . . that black, bottomless tunnel to grotesque agony and mind-numbing madness . . .

The author tried to look away, but he couldn't. Instead, he began to scream, to scream so hard and hysterically that eventually he thought his lungs would give out.

* * *

'Just relax, sir . . . try to relax,' said the gruff Yorkshire voice.

When he opened his eyes, Penrose found himself looking through a grey haze of pain and exhaustion. At first he thought he was paralysed, but then he realised it was the seatbelt holding him firmly in his seat. Not that moving was much of an option . . . for some reason, the author was too weak even to turn his head.

He could just see enough to identify a police officer in a luminous yellow slicker and white Traffic Department hat, standing by the open door to his Allegro. The cop now noticed that Penrose was awake, and leaned in again, putting a reassuring hand on the author's numb shoulder. 'I'm not an expert, but I think you've had a minor heart-attack,' he said. 'Looks like you came off the road some time last night. Anyway, listen . . . the ambulance'll be in here in a minute, and then we can get you to hospital. Okay? So just keep still. I'm sure everything'll be fine.'

Penrose did as he was told, and it wasn't too difficult . . . he didn't think he'd ever felt as physically tired as he was at this moment; he was too tired to question the nightmarish events he still remembered so vividly; too tired even to be concerned by them. Instead, he glanced wearily at his surroundings. Watery sunlight now filtered into the Allegro through the hawthorn thickets encircling it. For the first time, he noticed the white-and-orange Range Rover pulled up on the road, the North Yorkshire Police insignia visible on its nearside flank.

For some reason, this was all rather restful.

It was several minutes before the paramedics arrived, but when they did, they wasted no time hooking Penrose to a drip, and feeding him oxygen as they lifted him out and laid him on a stretcher.

'You look like you've been in the wars, sir,' one of them joked, as he took the patient's pulse.

Penrose would have roared with laughter at that, had he been able to. Instead, he scrunched his grey, sweaty face into a grimace of glee and shook his head from side to side.

When they placed him in the back of the ambulance, he did manage to speak. It was in reply to the Traffic cop, who climbed into the vehicle after him and asked him if he wanted to keep hold of 'this manuscript'. He then offered Penrose his notepad, saying the author had been clutching onto it for dear life when he'd first found him . . . wouldn't release it even while first-aid was being applied.

'It's . . . it's a book I was writing,' Penrose tried to explain, his voice cracked and weak.

The cop shrugged. 'You can take it with you, if you want. I mean, we'll send everything else along of course, but if this is something special . . .'

Slowly, Penrose shook his head. He smiled. 'It doesn't matter. I think . . . I think I'm going to write a different one . . . different title too.'

And with that, he laid his head back on the pillow and allowed the paramedics to replace the oxygen mask. The cop climbed from the ambulance and tossed the notebook back into the Allegro. A moment later, the ambulance had gone, a few twists of leaves blowing about behind it. He took his own pad and pen from his pocket, and began to detail the position of the Allegro and the angle it had come to rest at. It seemed like a pretty cut-and-dried case, but paperwork was paperwork in the modern police service.

Only then, for a very brief moment, did he fancy he heard something; hoof-beats . . . slow, receding hoof-beats. An image stuck in the officer's mind, though he wasn't sure where it had come from . . . of a horseman, slumped sideways in his saddle, as though injured somehow, drawing slowly away along the other side of the hedgerow, his animal walking aimlessly, perhaps hurt itself, its handsome skirts hanging in bloody tatters.

It was so startling a vision that it made the cop wander off the road and up through the coppice to the undulating pastures on the other side, just to see for himself. There was nobody there, however. The ancient battlefield lay still and empty in the mellow autumn sunshine.

The cop glanced around, then shook his head, cross with himself. It wasn't like him to be overly imaginative . . . wasn't part of his remit, so to speak. And putting it firmly from his mind, he turned and made his way back through the woods to the road, where his job and his duty awaited.

AT THE MERCY OF THE METAL DRAGONFLY
Andrew Roberts

Johnny Dane liked helicopters. They were probably the only form of distance transport where you didn't have to worry about someone offering you a blowjob.

The band bus was out of the question, of course. The band bus was practically dripping with blowjobs (collective noun: a gobble?). You couldn't even get up to take a leak or flex your knees on the band bus without looking down and finding some girl with too much make-up and too short a skirt fastened on the end of your dick. Aah, stardom.

It was the same with cars. The record company always sent some vanity mobile that might as well be painted with the slogan 'Hey, girls, here is someone famous—fellatio welcome'.

Trains. Trains would probably be the best bet. Late-night trains. Anonymity. But no record exec worth his or her salt was about to send the lead singer/guitarist of their Single Biggest Act! Travelling astride a jolting, rattling piece of standard gauge. Maybe it was the policy—modes of transport were allocated/employed according to their blowjob factor. Only when you were above such things as sex of the oral variety—when you were an artist—did you (pardon the expression) rise above such things. Literally. The order of merit went something like this: bus, car, limo, helicopter—cheap blow, easy blow, high-class blow, no blow.

He hoped the pilot wouldn't offer.

The pilot didn't. Johnny knew he wouldn't. He didn't have the same starstruck-starfuck eyes as the eighteen- and nineteen-year-olds that stared up at you for ninety minutes and then begged their way backstage and knelt for the belt.

'Hi.'

The pilot nodded. There was a slight curl to his lips that might have been a sardonic grin and might not. No blowjob here that expression might have said. Do I look like a teenage slut? Besides, the radio mike would get in the way.

Johnny made a mental shake of his head. He hadn't touched anything hallucinogenic in fifteen months and now he was having paranoid delusions about mind reading helicopter pilots. Rock and fucking roll. He pointed to the seat in front.

The pilot shrugged as if to say whatever and Johnny climbed inside and dropped his bag beside him.

'I'm Johnny,' he said and held out his hand. A real rock and roll greeting. Celebrity. I'm famous. So fucking famous I'm gonna grin my paid for pearly-whites and tell you my name even though you'd have had to be on Mars for the last twelve months not to know who I am. Las fucking Vegas, here I come. Quiz show to follow.

The pilot nodded again. Strong silent type—that was okay. He tapped a finger on the clipboard that hung beneath the instruments in front of him. 'Yep, that's what it says here.'

Johnny noticed that semi-grin hadn't left the man's face yet. It was the kind of smirk that had probably got the guy beaten up as a kid. The kind of grin that took a pummelling and still didn't disappear. Still grinning, huh? Let's see you grin at this, fucklips! People just hated grins like that. Grins that said, I know something about you. You wear your wife's underwear, don't you? Slept with someone of the same sex in college, didn't you? Eat snot from the end of your fingernail when you think no one's looking—gotcha!

The shame of it was about half the people who owned grins like that had no idea they were walking around that way. It was just the way their faces had been made. Of course, the other fifty per cent were fully aware how discomforting the little twist on their lips could be and played it for all it was worth. This guy looked like one of those.

Johnny clipped his belt together. That was the unsettling thing about helicopters. The occupational hazard aspect. He didn't think any rock 'n' roller—no matter how successful—had ever stepped into a helicopter without being unable to resist seeing their own tragic end. Crash and burn. Another too-soon-too-stupid death. Weather. Fuel. Incompetence. Bad luck.

God. It didn't matter. They all added up to the same thing—more gold discs, more airplay. And the downside? A distinct lack of personal appearances, that was all. Fuck that—what good was immortality if you weren't around to see it?

Overhead, the blades started to chop and whirr. How come in the movies they were always already going round? Wasn't it supposed to take five minutes for them to warm up? But he knew that wasn't true. It was like saying a car wouldn't take you where you wanted to be unless you sat in the garage with your foot on the accelerator for sixty seconds. It was just something that looked good in the movies. Hell, he stood up and wiggled in front of fifteen thousand people every night—he knew about things that looked good in the movies, even if those movies were only the ones inside people's heads.

Besides, the important thing was not that they worked while you were on the ground; the important thing (the crucial thing) was that they went round while you were in the air. As long as that happened, they could paint the blades blue and pink and use them as toothpicks as far as Johnny was concerned.

A little voice spoke up inside Johnny's head then. It sounded a little like his mother, a lot like his father and at least something like himself—the himself that was a deep, cool well of doubt and negativity. That well had a bucket with holes in and the bucket was called self-worth. Isn't it a little early, the voice said, to be worrying about your own legend? Do you really think anyone will give a fuck if you die young and beautiful? Are you River Phoenix? James Dean? Or are you just the schmuck whose record company almost dropped him before that vital third record?

That was true. After the initial splash (let's be honest—ripple) of new act/first record activity his career had come to a bright and glorious shuffle and halt. Twelve months later the record-buying public had greeted album number 2 with a hale and hearty no, thanks. Johnny had tried to buy that record in five different stores in his hometown. Not one of them had stocked it. Two said they could track it down if he wanted to place an order. The rest had frowned and shaken their heads. Not a good sign.

Even the rest of the band and management had resigned themselves to the inevitability of having their option passed over. They had entered the recording studio for what they assumed was a third and final time on a fourteen nights no budget mike-'em-up and knock-'em-out deal and waited for it all to end.

For the first three days that was what had happened. The rest of the band weren't talking to Johnny; Johnny had resisted the offer of outside songwriters, Johnny was an asshole. Johnny wasn't talking to the rest of the band; the rest of the band could go fuck themselves. The management wasn't talking to anybody, because the management was out somewhere blowing what was left of the minimum expenses account. Only the producer had plenty to say to all concerned. But then the producer was speeding his tits off on amphetamines twenty-seven hours a day. The rest, as they say, would soon be history.

On the fourth day, Johnny walked into the lounge area with an acoustic guitar, told everyone to shut the fuck up and then perched his backside on the edge of a chair and played them two brand new songs he had been up all night writing. And the band had shut the fuck up. They had shut the fuck right up. By the end of the day those two songs were in the can and Johnny had written another that was almost as good.

It was like he had suddenly found his own voice, stopped trying to sound like anyone else. Of course, that wasn't entirely true. This was rock 'n' roll, after all. But Johnny thought there might be enough in those songs (and the others that he hoped to God were still inside him) for people to actually start talking about a Johnny Dane feel and style. They were good these songs. They were honest and true. Moreover, they were his.

There was a band meeting the following morning. Band meeting. And didn't that just take you back to the good old days when you were seventeen and one beer and a hand under the shoulder strap was enough to get you buzzing? The outcome of the meeting was twofold: a) the management team could (as soon as they came back, of course) go right to hell; and b) Johnny should give serious consideration to staying up every night until they had enough songs to fill the album.

Johnny didn't stay up. Not much past three, anyway. He only wrote one song that night, but popular opinion said it was the best of the bunch so far.

By the end of the fortnight they had ten new songs and only two of the original ones they had come here to record remained. Even those two didn't sound so bad hidden away among the others. It wasn't perfect. It had been recorded in fourteen days, for chrissakes. But it was good. Damn good.

When it was over there were pats on the back and a few more cigarettes and beers. Not that that was any indication—that stuff happened at the drop of a hat. It was easy to convince yourself you had done better than you had when you were living in your own incestuous little world, even for a little while. In truth, Johnny thought maybe he had been the only one who really knew. The others knew something. Knew they had made a little piece of magic here. But Johnny didn't think any of them knew just how powerful a piece of magic it might turn out to be. As far as they were concerned they had delivered a record that would get their option picked up, get some radio play, a few tours. Maybe the money and future interest generated would be enough to guarantee they never had to work for a living.

But Johnny had seen more. Johnny had seen how big this thing could really go. All it would take was a bit of luck. Maybe it was because he had most to lose. After all, he was the singer/guitarist here. It was his name that was on the record contract. The rest of the band at least had the chance of re-emerging in other outfits. Singer/songwriters couldn't do that. Not if they had a strong visual identity (read good-looking), they couldn't. The public didn't accept them. Once a career crashed, it didn't matter how pretty you were—you were history.

There you go again, the well voice said. That word—crashed. Christ, you think you're something, don't you? Johnny told it to shut the fuck up. He was the one who had sold four million albums, played to more than a million people so far this year, if he wanted to compose his own elegy he had every fucking right to do so.

The helicopter lurched and dipped around him and Johnny realised they were in the air now. He stared out of the side-window and could see the ground fifteen feet below him.

'Are you a good flier?' the pilot said to him.

Johnny looked across at the man and grinned cheesily. 'Do I look queasy?'

The pilot pushed his lower lip out meditatively. 'Nope—you look fine, Johnny Dane. Just fine.'

Still grinning, Johnny frowned. Yep, this guy had taken his fair share of kickings that was for sure. Then why did he find himself grinning?

'Yeah, I'm a good flier,' he said through his grin.

'Then, it's okay if I step outside for five minutes?' The pilot's expression was deadpan.

Johnny looked into his eyes and laughed. Maybe the guy was okay, after all. At least he hadn't followed his witticism with a ba-doom-chi and some-thing pat like 'just a little pilot humour'. The older he got the more he was coming to see that the guys with the grins were really the interesting ones. The faces you had ignored or rubbed into the floor at school were the ones who, later on, you discovered had something to say about life. The ones who had been cool soon became too fucking cool to be in the slightest bit interest-ing. Cool had a way of becoming cynicism. And cynicism was dull and wearing and just too fucking easy.

'Could you wait until we get a little higher? At least give me a fighting chance to figure out the controls.'

The pilot tapped the clipboard again. 'Johnny Dane. You're all right, Johnny Dane.'

High praise, indeed.

'I thought you guys wore shades all the time,' Johnny said.

The pilot shook his head. 'Nah, that's you guys. We only go for that when we already know where we're going.'

You guys. So the guy did know who he was.

'Heard your record,' the pilot said in confirmation. 'I thought it stank.'

Johnny laughed again. 'Thanks for your honesty. I'll be sure to mention your appraisal when we reach the radio show.' Christ, how was he supposed to take this guy?

The pilot pushed a strand of hair behind his ear. 'It sounded like it was recorded in a fortnight.'

Johnny couldn't take the amused frown off his face. Whether the guy was just a wind-up merchant or not, it made an interesting change from the usual sycophancy or mute awe.

Awe, Johnny? The voice inside his head said wryly. Yes, awe. Now shut the fuck up like I said, Johnny told it. He looked out through the domed surface of the glass in front of him and felt a familiar pit in his stomach. The back seat wasn't so bad, but there was something dizzying about sitting up front like this, looking out over emptiness. Nothing except a twinkling city a quarter of a mile or one-eighth of a mile or however high they were beneath them. Night flying always reminded him off what it might be like to be in a deep-sea exploration capsule. There was no telling what might swim (fly?) past you at any given moment, a whole world of random and unexplained wonder waiting for you out there. When you had been flying for a certain amount of time, you even stopped hearing the noise of the blades. It was silent—silent as that deep-sea capsule drifting ever downwards.

Of course, if you had some kind of mechanical failure in a diving bell you didn't plummet from the sky. No, sir—you were apt to just drift on down through the darkness until you felt an unsettling bump and shift as you hit bottom and stayed there forever.

He wondered which would be worse. Underwater had a certain poetry to it, but the helicopter was definitely a little more rock and roll. Were there any statistics for helicopter deaths? And if there were, was there a subsection marked 'Famous Musicians'? He didn't suppose the figures were actually any higher for those in the entertainment business. It was just that they got reported. It was the same with drink and drugs. Millions of people had killed themselves by slow poisoning or a few too many bad pills one night, It just stuck in the mind and sold more papers if that person was someone everyone knew. Throw in rock 'n' roll (because we never did get over that fifties' thing about Little Richard and the Devil—did we, people?) and you practically had a bestseller.

'Guess you get to fuck a lot of girls in your line of work.' The pilot was looking at Johnny. The smirk was gone now. His face was all fake serious-ness.

Johnny nodded. 'Yeah, a lot. What about you?'

The pilot pulled back with his left hand and the chopper climbed a little higher. 'Nah, not me—I never fuck girls.'

Maybe that blowjob was on its way after all.

Another voice spoke in Johnny's head then. It wasn't the well voice. This one was the well voice's paranoid half-cousin. It asked Johnny if he had ever considered the possibility of journalists. Unscrupulous journalists. Couldn't some prick from a tabloid or music paper with a blank cheque in their pocket convince our friend the pilot here to tape a conversation with whatever superstar happened to be booked in on Air-So-Do-You-Fuck-A-Lot-Of-Girls? this season? Johnny could see the headline now: **I Get To Fuck A Lot Of Girls In My Line Of Work—Says Chart Superstar.** It wasn't the kind of thing you wanted your mother to glance at when she was out shopping for groceries.

He looked down at the pilot's pockets, but couldn't see any obvious bulge. Not that pocket tape-recorders were big enough to make a bulge these days. Relax, Johnny told himself. It wasn't all that likely really, was it? About as likely as . . . as dying in a helicopter crash? Whoops.

The pilot was speaking again. 'Statistics say you're safer in a helicopter than you are crossing the street.'

Johnny wanted to ask him if he'd read his mind. Instead, he said: 'Don't they also say right next door to a nuclear power plant is the least dangerous place to live?'

Two more headlines right there. **I Don't Trust Nuclear Industry Says Rock Star. I'm Terrified Of Flying Admits No. 1 Recording Artist.** Perhaps not so bad as that I get to fuck a lot of girls line, but no-one really wanted to be up there with Oprah on the front of the *National Enquirer*. No one with any sense, that was.

Anyway, it wasn't as if he was a novice, here. He had fielded enough questions about drugs and sex and left-wing politics and whether he was re-pressing any memories about being abused as a child to know when to keep shtum. He had even walked out on a couple of interviews. There was a pre-arranged signal with his manager, who would interrupt proceedings with a well-timed line about band business or sound problems. Couldn't walk out here, though. He decided to try a different approach. Get the pilot talking about himself. Here goes.

'You must meet a lot of big names in your job.'

The pilot brushed the same piece of hair away from his face again. 'In my job? Oh yeah, I've met them all. Buddy Holly. Ritchie Valens. The Big Bopper. Stevie Ray Vaughan was a personal friend o' mine. Course, they're all dead now.'

Johnny relaxed a little. That settled it. The guy didn't have a tape-recorder on him. He wasn't fishing for any spurious exclusive; he was just the world's biggest wind-up merchant. He shook his head and exhaled a short, clipped laugh.

The pilot turned his head sharply. The smirk looked like a scowl now. 'You think there's something funny about a guy's job? Huh? Is that what you think, Johnny Dane? You ought to pay a little more respect to the guy at the controls when you're a thousand feet in the air.'

Johnny held his hands up. 'Whoa, easy! I thought we were joking here.'

The scowl twisted into a snarl. 'Do you think Randy Rhoads was joking when we came out of that final loop? Jesus, you do your best to take a guy out properly—the best way you know how—and he laughs in your face.'

Alarm-bells started to ring inside Johnny's head. Wind-up merchant erased itself and became dangerous psycho. Next time, he was definitely taking the courtesy car. It didn't matter if the driver brought along his wife and family to suck Johnny's dick, from now on helicopters were out. Helicopters—or helicopter pilots—were far too freaky.

'I'll let you in on a little secret,' the pilot said. 'Glenn Miller—there was no freak storm. He is in the English Channel, but it wasn't the weather.' He flicked an invisible cap with his index finger. 'Yours truly, Johnny. Yours truly.'

Johnny found he was clutching his bag like some terrified old woman. Undoubtedly, it was all bullshit. If he had flown any of those people except Stevie Ray Vaughan and Randy Rhoads, the pilot would have to be at least sixty (forget Glenn Miller, that would place him somewhere in his mid-seventies). Unless, of course, Buddy and his pals had climbed inside a light aircraft with a five-year-old boy. Not likely.

Still, you had to fear for your safety when some guy who told you he thought your record sucked the big one was listing dead musicians for your benefit. He knew the pilot was just trying to spook him. Thing was, the pilot was succeeding.

The pilot leaned back in his seat. He lifted his feet and crossed them on the instrument panel. His hands let go of everything and locked themselves together behind his head. The helicopter's flight continued on as smooth as silk.

It's just autopilot, Johnny told himself. He flicked a switch you didn't see him flick. Don't panic. Go with the flow, here. Hang on in there until we're on the ground. Then, you can cave the guy's face in and drag him in front of an FAA tribunal.

'You should count yourself lucky,' the pilot said. 'They don't all go out this great. Hell, you know that. Some slip through the net, but I do the best I can. Take the King, for instance. I couldn't get that fucker in a helicopter for love or money. Oh, he flew—but with all those fucking people around him, I couldn't get a look in. And what happens? The fucker dies fat and on the toilet. I think there's a lesson for us all there, don't you? The guy who started the ball rolling, and I let him end up in Vegas wearing a sequined cape. Some patron saint I am, huh?'

'Some what?' Johnny croaked.

'Patron saint,' the pilot repeated, looking at Johnny levelly. 'The patron saint of rock and roll deaths. I'd shake your hand, but you're not allowed to touch me.'

Johnny licked his lips. 'Jesus Christ!'

The patron saint moved his legs so the left foot was resting on top of the right. 'No, he comes later in the chain. I'm just the guy who makes sure you don't get old or end up on Hollywood Squares. Cars, swimming pools, mysterious deaths in Paris hotels—I'm your man. Sometimes it's drugs or inhaling your own vomit—not pretty, but that's the way things are, I'm afraid. It's the legacy that counts.'

'No way,' Johnny heard himself say, but as Wayne or Garth had been wont to over-enunciate: Way. This was happening.

'It's the way it has to be.'

Johnny's knees had begun to tremble. His bowels felt like water. 'This isn't funny any more.'

The patron saint leaned forward and slammed his fist into the helicopter's windscreen. 'Christ—take it like a man, can't you? What do I have to do here to prove it? Do you want me to stop us dead up here in the middle of the sky? A triple-fucking-somersault? I can do that, you know.'

'Shit,' Johnny said.

'Not really,' the saint said. 'Aside from a few sick jokes it will all be pretty glorious. You'll be my biggest in a long while, Johnny. It should be really special. We aren't just going down, we're going down on the radio station. How about that for feedback?'

Johnny realised he could no longer hear the sound of the rotors. He looked up and the evidence was there. The blades were perfectly still above them, one pointing the way forward, one back, left, and right. But they weren't going either of those ways.

The patron saint smiled at him and nodded.

Johnny felt tears spill down his face. 'Will I feel anything?'

The patron saint sighed. 'Christ, Johnny—what do you want me to say to that? Gee, just the applause of a hundred thousand hands, Johnny—I'm not sadistic? Of course you'll feel something, it's a fucking helicopter crash.'

'All of them?' Johnny asked.

The pilot nodded. 'Eddie Cochran. Otis Redding. Janis Joplin. Bon Scott. I even did James Dean as a special favour.'

Something began to bother Johnny. Something he couldn't put his finger on. A niggle. One of those questions that scratches incessantly at the surface of the brain. If he was about to die, he didn't want to go out with something bugging him like that. Wasn't there some old actor who had been killed in a helicopter filming a movie? Or was it just another modern legend? It was strange what the brain could concern itself with in extremis.

'Vic Morrow,' the patron saint said. 'In The Twilight Zone. What an administrative fuck-up, that was. The powers that be were not best pleased.'

'Thanks,' Johnny said, but he wasn't talking simply about the answer to his question. A quiet acceptance had stolen over him.

'That's all I need,' the patron saint nodded. He reached forward, grabbed air and yanked back as if pulling a trapdoor lever.

Nothing happened.

The patron saint grinned. The instrument panel lit up and his face suddenly looked red in the glow from the lights and dials. 'Going down?'

And then they were falling. Like a bird that has been shot from the sky. Like an angel falling from heaven. Like Icarus heading for the sea. There was wind inside the cockpit. It pushed at Johnny's face and rushed around his head. It's like standing on stage, Johnny thought. Standing on stage and staring out into the darkness, waiting for the stage lights to come up. There was even that electric hum inside his body. The noise of the air was like the rumble of fifteen thousand expectant voices.

He looked at the patron saint and the patron saint was pushing that loose strand of hair off his face again. His cheeks and brow still looked red in the glow from the instrument panel, more like a devil than a saint.

'Personal demon, patron saint—what's the difference?' the saint laughed.

And, suddenly, Johnny's quiet acceptance dissolved. He was scared. More than scared. He wanted to open his mouth and beg for a deal, some way out of this. But that was impossible; the wind was stealing his breath away.

The saint-demon grinned. 'You'll be a legend, Johnny. You're Elvis Presley. You're Jimi Hendrix. You're Kurt fucking Cobain—with wings!'

It's a mistake, Johnny tried to say. My third album flopped. I never made it, you've got the wrong guy. But that wasn't true.

The lights. That was what was true. The lights were no longer silver stars down there below them. The lights were transforming themselves into recognisable shapes. Buildings and cars and streetlamps. There was even a large piece of neon. It was a station logo, Johnny was sure of that. Down there people were waiting for him, none of them knowing they were about to witness the biggest entrance of his career. Briefly.

The pilot leaned forward and his face was red now. This was no patron saint. Patron saints were pale and solemn and their faces were painted with wisdom and serenity. They didn't grin at you like that. Johnny watched as the saint-devil's hand went to its pocket. It pulled out a cassette tape and slotted it into the deck.

Helicopters don't have cassette decks.

Wrong.

Music began to fill the cockpit. Johnny looked below him. Concrete and steel and that splash of neon were rushing towards him. Soon they would be his world.

He glanced across and the saint-devil-pilot thing disappeared like the world's best magic trick. It was just Johnny now. Johnny and that country and western tape.

He tried to reach across and hit the eject button, but it was too late. Way too late. The devil did, indeed, have all the best tunes. They were all right on the beat and sung by good ol' boys and good ol' gals in fringed shirts and pointy boots.

Amen to that.

JUST ANOTHER CARNIVAL STORY
Jeremy C Shipp

Smiles and Frowns

The clowns' phosphorescent tears slowly reversed their paint-on smiles into grotesque frowns.

It was Billy's funeral. Almost. Woeful sobs and hysterical laughter, jumbled together in some sick way, pierced at Margaret's ears. These clowns—her family—all dressed in black, still managed to subsist as a mosaic of color with neon lights spewing down from holes in the ceiling. The air stank of too much sugar, like cotton candy shoved up her nose.

Though engulfed in glitzy chaos, she focused on the casket, and the urge to see her son overpowered the yearning to run away. Every step was a struggle; her clown shoes weighed a ton.

'Step right up, folks! See the boy in the casket!' The man in front of the casket held out his hand. 'Ticket please, ma'am.'

Margaret searched her oversized pockets. 'I don't have one.'

'I'm sorry, ma'am. You can't look inside without a ticket.'

'But he's my son!'

Billy sat up in his casket and stared at her with a mish-mash freak-show face, his lips vertical.

'Are you smiling or frowning, Billy! Tell me! Please!'

The man guarding the casket pushed Billy back into the darkness.

Innocence

Joseph made his best puppy dog eyes. 'Can we go to the carnival? Pleeeeeease?'

Margaret's heart beat a little faster.

Neal paused from the devouring of his bacon. 'You okay, Margie?'

'Yes. I'm fine.'

'What was that look then?'

Margaret bit her lip. 'Joseph, will you go in the other room so mommy and daddy can talk mommy-and-daddy talk?'

Joseph dashed out to his video games.

Neal tried his best to look innocent; mommy-and-daddy talk usually meant he was in some sort of mommy-and-daddy trouble.

'Don't worry, I'm not going to yell at you.'

'Thank god for that.' He studied her face. 'So what's this about?'

'It's just . . . well, Billy used to love going to the carnival. It was something we always enjoyed doing together. Now that the thing's back in town, I've been having some strange dreams. It's not that I'm afraid to go, or even opposed to it. I just don't want to break down in front of Joseph. A carnival's no place for him to learn that he has a . . . had a . . . '

'You want just me and him to go?'

'No, no. I'll go. I'm sure I'll be fine.'

Triviality

Neal was always drawn to those stupid carnival games. He had a horrible gambling problem in their early years of marriage and this was about the last venue in the pleasures of chance Margaret allowed him to dabble with.

This time he was drawn to a game that involved flipping rubber frogs onto plastic lily pads floating in a tank. 'I'm going to hang around here for a while, if that's okay with you two.'

'We wouldn't dream of keeping daddy from his frogs, would we, Joseph?' Margaret looked down at her son.

Joseph, though, was mesmerized by everything around him and probably didn't hear a word she was saying.

'Joseph and I are going. Don't spend our life savings, Neal.'

He couldn't hear her either, focused on that one golden lily pad—smaller than all the rest—which would bestow upon the winner some giant teddy bear that would end up with all the other giant beasts, in the basement, rotten and forgotten.

Back and Forth

Margaret wanted to be a good mother. She wanted this time to be about Mommy and Joseph and think only Mommy-and-Joseph thoughts. But Billy crept in everywhere they went. She saw him in a shadow; in the face of a clown; in the mirror house—one reflection stretched Joseph out a little and for a moment Margaret could see Billy there stuck in the mirror world, and he was happy.

And then Joseph went onto the flying bus ride. It took about three seconds before Margaret realized her mistake. The monstrous vehicle swung back and forth, a pendulum building momentum, and in her mind she imagined hearing something snap. She saw the bus soar through the sky and land, spinning and killing; a bloody tumbleweed. Joseph would die on a bus just like Billy had. Billy died and burned. The remains of all the children blended together and Margaret wasn't even sure if the ashes she had on the mantelpiece included any of his or not.

Mommy, please don't make me go on the bus, Billy had pleaded.

You'll be fine, Billy, she had said.

Margaret wanted to scream at the teenager manning the ride to stop the bus, but she managed to calm down and get a hold of her rational self.

The flying bus didn't break down, of course. She knew deep down that it wouldn't, but she still hugged Joseph tight when he came off.

'Mommy, why are you so happy?'

'I'm just so—so proud of you, Billy. You're becoming a big boy, riding big boy rides.'

'I'm not Billy, mommy. I'm Joseph. Who's Billy? Mommy?'

'He's—he's just one of my students from school. Mommy just made a mistake, that's all. I know you're Joseph, Joseph.'

Joseph smiled and dragged her to the next ride.

Four

'Come on.' Margaret tapped the back of Neal's head. 'Break yourself free of that stupid game and come and be daddy for a while.'

Neal didn't turn his head. 'I can't go now. Now that I've finally gotten used to this thing. Just give me a few more minutes and I'll hit the golden lily and that'll be the end of it.'

'Neal, I really need you to be daddy right now. I'm feeling . . . sick.'

'I can't give up now. I'm so close to winning the giant panda. Joseph, you want daddy to win you a giant panda, don't you?'

'I guess so.' Joseph's voice was very small.

Margaret forcefully turned him around. He was drenched. 'Why are you sweating so much?'

'It's hot out here. What do you expect?'

'You'd better get something to drink soon or you'll get dehydrated.'

'I will. I will. Just a few more minutes and I promise you, we'll be a happy family of four.'

'What are you talking about?'

'Me, you, Joseph and the panda.' He turned back around and continued flipping frogs.

The Energy

The clown, like most—if not all—of the employees at the carnival, was a teenager. 'What's your favorite animal?'

Joseph thought for a moment. 'I like Tasmanian Devils.'

Margaret laughed. 'He can't make a Tasmanian Devil balloon animal, honey.'

'I can try.' The clown went to work. His fingers moved with that perceptible Carnival Energy that made her feel younger than she was. Everything here was loud and quick and bright—except, she noticed, for the clown's expression, and the expression of every other teenage worker. Their eyes lacked the Energy, the excitement. Distant. Perhaps the carnival was too ordinary to them now. Perhaps having experienced the clockwork of the place, there wasn't any magic anymore.

'Here you go. A Tasmanian Devil.'

It was pretty much a balloon dog, but Joseph took it and smiled.

'Here you go.' The clown gave Margaret a metallic ticket.

'What's this?'

'Every twentieth balloon, you get a free ticket to the haunted cart ride.'

'Is it scary?'

'Not really. It's more stupid than scary.'

'Thank you.'

'Whatever.'

Sounds of Death

The haunted cart ride was a melee of various (and quite stereotypical) horror monsters and motifs; dropping skeletons; giant spider webs; high-pitched screams and deep-throated laugher. There was even a point at the beginning where the track split off in two directions: one tunnel marked Life, the other Death.

Really the only good part of the whole thing was the music. Every once in a while Margaret found herself with her eyes closed, allowing the eerie tune to soak into her. She was a music teacher but she had never heard anything like this before. As she listened, she realized that the artificial screams and laughter were a crucial part of the melody. It flowed so well. With the music inside her, she could hardly feel Billy's shadow inside her heart. She could almost forget.

'Mom, the ride is stuck.'

'What?' She opened her eyes and realized they were no longer moving. Bats on strings zipped overhead and a vampire cackled to her side. 'It's going to be okay. These things break down all the time. Are you scared?'

'No. I like it.'

'Good.'

A teenager walked to their cart from behind. Dressed in all yellow, he really clashed with all the darkness. 'I don't think we're going to be able to fix this thing any time soon, so you're gonna have to walk out of here. Sorry.' He fiddled with something on the front of the cart and the bar lifted off of Margaret's lap. She stepped out of the cart and walked up to Joseph's half of the cart.

'Crap, his isn't coming up.' The teenager scratched his demi-beard. He attempted to pull up Joseph's bar manually.

Margaret joined in but they couldn't budge it. 'You're going to be okay, Joseph. We'll get you out of there.'

The teenager bit at his fingernails. 'I'm going to get some tools.' He walked off without another word.

Margaret continued to yank on the bar.

'Don't worry about me, mommy. I'm not scared.' He yawned.

'Are you tired?'

'Yeah.'

She glanced at her watch and her eyes widened. 'How did it get so late! Your dad must be looking everywhere for us.'

Joseph was already asleep.

Margaret sat and would have fallen asleep herself if the teenager hadn't returned, clanking his tools.

'How long do you think this is going to take?'

'I don't know. A couple minutes maybe.'

She imagined Neal running around looking for them, worrying. 'I need to go find my husband. If my son wakes up before I get back, tell him I'll be back with his daddy soon.'

'Alright. Go down that way. There'll be a door on your right.'

Make You

The carnival was falling asleep; the special Energy well nigh extinguished. She ran around looking for Neal. The bright lights of the rides splashed by her. She found him in the last place she looked—back at the frog flipping game.

He stood there, nude, sweating all over.

Margaret wanted to believe that she had fallen asleep in the ride, that this was a dream, but she knew it was real. The pain in her heart, the shadow of Billy, was too real for this to be imaginary.

'Neal, what are you doing!'

He flipped a frog.

The teenager in charge of the game stared at them with lazy eyes, expressionless.

Neal flipped another.

'Neal, what are you doing? Why are you naked? Neal? Neal!'

He turned and looked at her. His face was twitching. The tremors expanded to his entire body. There seemed to be an energy there; an anxiety he couldn't release. 'Margaret?'

'What are you doing?'

'Gotta play.' He turned back and continued playing.

'Neal! Talk to me!'

He spoke, focusing on the frogs. 'Gotta play. Gotta win.'

'We have to go, Neal. Let's get Billy and go. It's time to go home.'

He started weeping.

With her hands, she forced him to look at her. 'What's happened to you, Neal?'

'I gave it away.' He cried harder. 'They wanted more, I gave them more. I gave them more and more. I gave them everything. My money, my clothes.' He flipped another frog. 'They still wanted more. I couldn't stop. I gave it to them. I gave them everything.'

She wanted to put her arms around him, but was too afraid. 'Neal, what are you saying? What's happening?' She looked at the teenager. 'Tell me what's happening!'

The teenager just stared ahead.

Someone—something?—grabbed her shoulders from behind.

Margaret spun around. It was Bette Clover, her neighbor. Billy and her son used to be best friends.

Bette's face was whiter than usual. 'Do you have Joseph with you?'

'No. What's wrong with you, Bette?'

'Where is he? Where's Joseph?'

'He got stuck. In the haunted cart ride.'

Bette cried. 'Oh god. It's too late. They'll do it to you too.'

'Do what? Who?'

'They're going to make you. They'll make you. Unless you run away right now. You have to run away.'

Margaret felt cold. It was the same kind of cold she felt at Billy's funeral. 'I can't leave Joseph.'

'You have to. They want you, not Joseph. They want you. I don't think they'll hurt him. I don't know. I'm sorry, Margaret. I don't know.' Bette cried so hard she collapsed onto the ground.

Neal flipped another tear-covered frog.

Choices

The balloon-making clown who made Joseph a Devil blocked the door back into the haunted cart ride.

'Move out of my way.'

He didn't.

Margaret tried to push him but he grabbed both her wrists. She squirmed to escape but he was too strong.

'Let me go! Stop it!' She kneed him in the groin but he didn't respond; didn't even blink.

'Calm yourself, Margaret.' The clown's mouth wasn't moving, but the voice seemed to be coming from his direction. 'Shhh . . . calm down. There will be time for hysterics later.'

The voice massaged her mind, just like the music in the ride, and she felt suddenly horribly calm.

'I need to tell you something, Margaret, and you need to listen.'

Margaret desperately tried to hold onto her anxieties. She wanted—needed to worry about Joseph. 'Where's my son?'

'Your son is fine for the moment. Whether or not he stays fine is up to you.'

'What do you want?'

'I want you, Margaret. I want you to open up and let me inside.'

'I want to see my son first.'

'I'm afraid that's just not going to happen. Here's the deal. In a short while, your son is going to wake up with a terrible feeling of dread inside him. This dread is going to grow with every passing moment and he will know a fear most beings have never felt. The second you let me inside you is the second this horror will stop. If we're quiet enough maybe we can hear him. He's waking up now.'

Margaret stayed perfectly quiet.

She heard him yelling.

'Mommy! Mommy! Mommy!'

The yelling evolved into screaming.

'Do what you have to do!' Margaret wanted to collapse onto the ground and cry but the clown held her up. 'Just stop hurting him!'

'When you open yourself up to me, I'll stop it.'

'I am! Make it stop!'

'You aren't. You can't just say that you are. You really have to do it. You have to yearn for me. That's the only way.'

Margaret closed her eyes and listened to Joseph's screams. She wanted the talking thing inside her. She wanted Joseph to be okay and if the talking thing went inside her there was a chance that Joseph would be okay. She desired the talking thing.

A chill rippled throughout her body.

Joseph's screaming stopped.

'Good job, Margaret.' The voice echoed in her head now. 'And now, clown, take us to the others.'

Reflections of Time

The clown took Margaret into the mirror house and the voice told her to sit in the center of the chamber. There were already nine people sitting there, including Bette and her husband, and some other people that looked almost familiar. She had probably seen them around the town. And there was Neal.

Margaret wrapped her arms around him. He looked exhausted beyond words.

'Do you have one inside too?'

He nodded.

Margaret wanted to get up and run away. She wanted to find Joseph. But the fear was too much. She couldn't move.

Emotionless carnival employees surrounded the ten people in the center, and with all the mirrors, there appeared to be an army of them, some stretched out and mutated.

The Voice inside Margaret spoke up. 'We're not going to lie to you. You're here to die.'

Another Voice spoke. 'If there was any other way, we wouldn't make you die like this.'

And another. 'Speak for yourself. I'd do it like this even if there were another way. They're Pure Ones.'

The Voice inside Margaret spoke. 'I know there are some of us who are apprehensive about what we are about to do, but we must remember that this is not only about us. This is about all of the Impure. We were not born Impure, we were made it, and we are dubbed evil because it's easier to ignore us that way. But we will be ignored no longer.'

Margaret found her own voice. 'Please don't kill us. We have families.'

The Voices laughed.

'Yes, we know you have families. Loving, wonderful families. You're the kind of people who go to the afterlife and meet their dead family members, and then forget all about the rest of us.'

'Who are you?'

'We're the darkness of this world. We didn't have good parents like you. We were abused and raped and abandoned. Darkness was forced into us. We were made to eat the pain of the world. And now that we're dead, we aren't allowed with the Pure Ones. We aren't allowed in your perfect after-life where everyone is happy. You wouldn't want us to contaminate you with the pain of our existences. So we are left behind, ignored. But no more. The Pure Ones will ignore the truth of reality no longer. We will have a voice.' The Voice stayed silent for a moment. 'I'm afraid the only way for us to get into the afterlife is to ride your spiritual wake. And the only way we can do that is if you are spiritually weakened—spiritually obliterated at the point of death.'

A realization hit Margaret hard and she almost screamed. 'God, you're not going to kill our children, are you? God. God.' Her tears erupted, imagining Joseph's bloody face.

'No, your children will not die today. They will live. Our carnival friends will kill you and you alone.'

Margaret looked at the blank faces of the carnies. 'Don't do it. Please. We have children. Children who we love. You can't let them control you like this. You have to wake up.'

Margaret's inner Voice chuckled. 'These teenagers act on their own. We cannot control them or anyone. That's what makes this so difficult to orchestrate. But we found a way. Finally.' He sounded very proud. 'The carnival is about the flesh and its appetites, its fears. We have the power to elevate those feelings. So you see these teenagers help us because they want to help us. They are our family, our children. We have given them the love our parents should have given us. They would do anything for us now. Anything.' The Voice paused as if making its final decision. 'Kill them.'

The carnival people closed in.

The clown who made Joseph the Devil approached Margaret and Neal with a knife. He began stabbing Neal in the chest.

There was no screaming in the room.

Margaret closed her eyes and imagined Joseph growing up without parents. He would probably live his life in pain and become an Impure One just like the Voices.

She felt something touching her chest and she opened her eyes to see blood all over her. The clown was stabbing her but she couldn't feel it. The Voice inside was protecting her.

Her life faded slowly and in those last moments of life, the pieces began fitting together, and she finally realized that these ten dying people were some of the parents whose children were on that bus. And she understood what the Voice meant when it said spiritually obliterated. Because as she stared at the clown's smiling face, she knew Billy and the other children hadn't really died on the bus that day.

Wake

The clown took Margaret into the mirror house and the Voice told her to sit in the center of the chamber. There were already nine people sitting there, including Bette and her husband, and some other people that looked almost familiar. She had probably seen them around the town. And there was Neal.

Margaret wrapped her arms around him. He looked exhausted beyond words.

'Do you have one inside too?'

He nodded.

Margaret wanted to get up and run away. She wanted to find Joseph. But the fear was too much. She couldn't move.

Emotionless carnival employees surrounded the ten people in the center, and with all the mirrors, there appeared to be an army of them, some stretched out and mutated.

The Voice inside Margaret spoke up. 'We will ride your spiritual wakes into the afterlife. But first, your heart must be weakened. You must be spiritually crushed.' A realization hit Margaret hard and she almost screamed. 'God, you're not going to kill our children, are you? God. God.' Her tears erupted, imagining Joseph's bloody face.

'No, your children will not die today.'

Margaret looked at the blank faces of the carnies. 'Don't do it. Please. We have children. Children we love. You can't let them control you like this. You have to wake up.'

Margaret's inner Voice chuckled. 'These teenagers act on their own free will. We cannot control them or anyone. That's what makes this so difficult to orchestrate. But we found a way. Finally.' He sounded very proud. 'The carnival is about the flesh and its appetites; its fears. We have the power to elevate those feelings. So you see these teenagers help us because they want to help us. They are our family, our children. We have given them pleasures most have never imagined. They would do anything for us now. Anything.' The Voice paused. 'Like killing you.'

The carnival people closed in.

The clown who made Joseph the Devil approached Margaret and Neal with a knife. He began stabbing Neal in the chest.

In the funhouse mirrors, frowns were forced into smiles. Their pain appeared cartoonist. But nothing could contort the screaming that consumed the room.

Margaret closed her eyes and imagined Joseph growing up without parents.

When silence erupted in her ears, she opened her eyes to see blood all over.

The clown turned to her and smiled. He raised the knife.

In those last moments of life, the pieces began fitting together, and she realized that these ten bleeding people were some of the parents whose children were on that bus. And she understood what the Voice meant when it said spiritually crushed. Because as she stared at the clown's smiling face—a face she finally recognized—she knew the children hadn't really died on the bus that day.

Billy brought down the knife.

WHISKY ON THE GRAVE
Justin Stanchfield

A raw wind blew down the canyon, a damp wind, driving off mountains still white with winter ice. A line of vehicles inched down the rutted road, slipping in the April mud, toward the blacktop half a mile north. The fading drone of engines left the sagebrush flat feeling emptier still.

Five men, four shovels and a gaping hole remained, sentinels standing watch over the granite markers and rusted iron fences. The men waited until the last car had passed round the corner, their feet cold, wishing the task was finished. Coats and suit jackets lay draped over fenders or hung carefully from prickly juniper branches. Four men stared at each other, none wanting to be the first.

The fifth man stayed in the shadows, saying nothing.

'Well?' The first, a bald, ruddy-cheeked man, picked up one of the shovels propped against the pile of dirt. He turned it in his hand, testing the balance as if it was a javelin.

'Might as well,' said the second. He was tall, older than the rest, broad-shouldered and callused, his face etched by the wind and rain until it seemed a thing made of stone. He drove his own shovel into the pile, pushing hard until it brimmed with sticky red earth. He tossed it into the grave. Rocks clattered against the varnished box, loud as a kettledrum.

'Jesus, Mike,' said the third, closest to the grave and desperate not to stumble. He shuffled away, his once polished boots now crusted with mud, the slick soles leaving trails in his wake. 'Be careful. Last thing we need is to cave the lid in.'

Mike gathered up another shovelful. 'Doubt we'll hear many complaints if we do.'

They laughed, these five, glad for the relief. Laughed and sweated, driving off the gloom the only way they knew. And if they laughed too loud it didn't matter. Someday other friends would laugh over their graves. Debts paid on credit.

Bite by bite, shovel by shovel, the pile grew smaller. Iron grated against stone, rock against rock as they tumbled into the pit. High overhead a pair of ravens wheeled, black silhouettes against a lead gray sky. Sweating harder now, the men rested a moment, leaning on shovels, drinking in the chill air. The fourth man, out of place in slacks instead of jeans, stepped quietly toward the pick-up. He opened the door and reached across the seat. A paper sack rustled in his hand as he came back to the pile.

He peeled the sack down and drew out a pint bottle of Early Times. He broke the seal with a twist of his hand but left the cap on, holding the whisky at arm's length like a bible. The sun broke through the clouds for a moment and spilled across the muddy flat. The bottle caught the light and threw an amber shadow over the trampled ground. 'Don't know about anyone else, but I'm ready for one.'

The man called Mike nodded. 'Yep, me too.' He took the bottle, drew off a long swallow and passed it on. Around the pile it traveled, each taking sacrament in his turn. The fourth man was the last to drink, the pint already half gone. He drank, lips twitching at the liquor's bite. Self-consciously, he held the bottle above the hole and poured a shot. The drops spread in the wind, whisky mingling with the greasy scent of sagebrush and new-thawed earth.

'You know what he would have said about wasting good whisky, don't you?' The first man grinned.

'Well,' said the fourth. 'I doubt he'll hold it against us.'

'Doesn't seem right, does it?' The third threw another scoop in the hole, his thinning hair plastered down by sweat. 'Work hard all your life and what do you get? A hole in the ground.'

'No one ever said life was fair.'

They fell back to work, a jagged rhythm, scrape, toss, scrape. Time passed unmentioned, the talk less as the grave grew shallow. Again the bottle made it's rounds, coming home all but empty. They buried it, an offering, something for the trip. At last they finished, the grave mounded over, an ochre scar against the rusty earth.

'Guess that's it.' The first man wiped his dirty hands across his pants then shrugged into his coat. He tossed his shovel into the back of the truck. The other's followed suit, gathering up their own coats and shovels. Four men, four shovels, drove away, the bottle empty, the grave full.

The fifth man watched them drive off, silent now and a little lonely. A patch of sunlight washed over him, fell through him, warmed the ground around him. He would have liked to have gone with them, but things being what they were, figured it best if he stayed put a while. It was getting late and he was so damned tired, and hell if he had anyplace else to go.

Others stepped out now, silent and sad, watching him, wondering it seemed. A few turned away. Others simply sat down on headstones or rocks, looking out at the fading light, blending into the gathering dark. One, older than rest and braver, sauntered toward him and smiled. He glanced at the whiskey bottle in the fifth man's hand.

'Mind if I have a pull?'

'Help yourself.' The fifth man handed him the bottle, surprised to find it in his hand at all. 'I suppose you don't get much of that around here.'

The old man chuckled, drank a long swallow, then handed it back. 'Reckon not,' he said, fading away. The fifth man watched him vanish. He sighed, took a last nip, let the empty bottle fall, then followed him away.

UNREQUITED LOVE
Robert Swartwood

Shadows haunt the cavern like ghosts from a slaughter, almost hiding the large metal pot in a cloak of darkness. In the middle of the small cavern it sits by itself, an ancient cauldron. The water inside is black and calm.

Silence dominates the cavern. Not a sound is heard . . . except for an occasional plunk! as a drop of water falls from the ceiling to the ground.

Every so often, from inside the cauldron, something stirs and slowly rises from the black water. Peeks out, then sinks back.

Again, only silence.

Plunk!

It is cold in this place, almost a winter chill. But the temperature does nothing to hide the smell of death and decay, even a strange mixture of urine and flowers.

Right now the cavern is deserted. Almost.

Behind the shadows, a dark spirit waits.

Ever since James first saw Catherine he knew he was in love. Every time he saw her, a strange sensation of happiness filled his heart and soul. He loved her so much; would do anything for her. James would even die for her.

But Catherine didn't love him. She hardly knew who he was. Just some guy in her class, that's all he was to her.

Just some guy.

What a freak.

Now James stood in a grove of trees and watched the dull rays of the sun as they slowly faded away. Around him he could hear the sounds of the forest: birds chirping, the faint singing of leaves as a breeze carried through, insects calling out to each other.

He'd parked his car up by the road, and after ten minutes of walking he'd come here, to this place, the place the woman had told him to meet her. He didn't know who she was, but she knew him. She knew exactly who he was and what he wanted.

He glanced down at the small cloth bag in his hand, tried not to think of the eye inside. But his mind kept racing, and he thought about the previous night, he thought about the cat he'd killed. He thought about taking the cat's eye from its socket.

He thought about all the blood on his hands.

'Stop it,' he muttered, his eyes closed.

'Stop what?' said a voice behind him.

James started at the voice, spun himself around, and saw the woman standing there in the shadows cast by the trees. She looked like she had the first and last time he'd seen her, on that night he had finally gotten up the nerve to ask Catherine out. His entire body had been trembling with fear as he walks up to her after the high school football game. She is standing with her friends by the bleachers. The game is over. The visitors have destroyed their home team by fourteen points.

People are all around, heading out to their cars in the parking lot. Catherine stays where she is with her friends, talking. As he walks toward her he questions himself, asks himself if he's doing the right thing. He has never even spoken to her before, and yet now here he is about to ask her to go out with him.

She is wearing tight jeans and a green windbreaker. Her blond hair is pulled back in a ponytail. James knows she is the most beautiful girl in the world. Perfect body, perfect skin, perfect eyes. Everything about her is perfect.

And before he even realizes it he is standing beside her, listening in on what she and her friends are saying. He hears their words but doesn't think about them. He is too nervous with what he is about to do.

Then he notices that Catherine and her friends are no longer speaking. He stares at her, unseeing, and finally blinks. He looks around and sees that they are all looking at him.

'Can we help you?' one of Catherine's friends asks.

He opens his mouth to speak but nothing comes. He tries again, swallowing, but still nothing comes. He is literally speechless, standing there like a fool, his mouth hanging open with nothing to say.

Finally he does make a sound, but it is incoherent, almost a grunt. Catherine and her friends exchange glances, then after a moment they break out with laughter. James wants to run away, wants to be alone, but his body is frozen and all he can do is stand there with his mouth open.

Suddenly his paralysis breaks and he turns. He walks away quickly, not running, but making sure he gets out of their sight as soon as he can. People are all around, but no one notices him. No one ever does.

And behind him, in the cool night air, he hears Catherine's voice, Catherine's dear sweet voice, as she says 'What a freak.' And her friends all agree, as they again start laughing.

James continues walking out to the parking lot, past the people waiting around talking to each other, past the visiting team as they make fun at how much James's home team sucked. Tears fall down his face but he doesn't wipe them away. He knows there is no reason to.

Many times in the past he has contemplated suicide, and now he has finally made the decision, he has finally decided that he is going to do it tonight. He has no friends, his parents pay hardly any attention to him, and the only person James has ever really cared for is Catherine. But it is obvious Catherine will never love him back. What is the point of living?

Then he turns toward his car and sees her standing there. She is watching him. Maybe forty, fifty years old, she looked striking standing there in her black dress. Almost timeless. But James thought about her eyes, and he remembered seeing them for the first time. He remembered how old they had looked, as if they had seen centuries pass. How knowing they had been, how wise.

How dark.

'Here.' He quickly held out the bag. 'I did it.'

The woman stepped forward, and he could now see her face, her pale, small face. She smiled.

'Good,' she said.

Suddenly nervous, more nervous than the other night with Catherine and her friends, James glanced around the grove they were in, he glanced up at the dark trees, up at the cloudless sky. He suddenly realized that the sounds he'd heard before—the birds chirping, the leaves rustling—were no longer present. Not even a single calling insect. He thought about Catherine, about how much he loved her. He thought about this woman's promise to him.

'Well, here,' he said. 'Aren't you going to take it?'

The woman reached, took the bag from him. She said nothing. Only stared at him.

'Now what? When . . . when will it happen?'

'Soon.'

'Soon? What does that mean?'

She was silent.

James sighed. 'All right, thanks. Just . . . thank you. If this really works, thank you.'

The woman nodded, once.

'Look,' James said, glancing at the ground. 'I don't mean to be annoying. It's just—'

But when he looked up the woman was gone. He looked around, quickly, and realized suddenly that the forest sounds he'd heard before were back. He even heard the wooden, hollow tapping of a woodpecker in the distance. He waited a long time, then closed his eyes. For a moment he thought he was going to think about last night, see the dead cat, but instead he saw Catherine.

He saw her dead, her one eye missing.

He saw the blood on his hands.

Shadows haunt the cavern like ghosts from a slaughter, almost hiding the two figures standing around the cauldron in a cloak of darkness. The temperature is no longer a winter chill, but warmer. And the smell . . . any of the smells here before are now gone. The only scent here is jasmine.

Suddenly, a third figure appears from the shadows.

'Where have you been?' asks the one figure.

'Out killing swine?' asks the second with a laugh.

The third steps toward them, holding out a small cloth bag. 'Ingredients,' she says.

'From the boy?' asks the first.

The third nods. 'Indeed.'

The second shakes her head. 'Young love. What a pity.'

'He wanted what again?' asks the first.

'Love,' says the third. 'No more unrequited love.'

Silence then, except a faint plunk! from the shadows.

The first asks, 'What do you expect will happen?'

'The boy?' the third says. 'Oh, she will no doubt return his love. But she will love him too much. He will become angry. So very angry.'

'And then?'

'Then he will kill her.'

All three begin laughing then, a high-pitched laughter that seems to scare away the shadows around them. The third figure opens the bag and pulls out the eye, holds it. Stares at it.

She tries to remember when it began, so many years ago, so many centuries. When Hecate first took them all under her control. The first victim was in Scotland, a soulless, power-hungry general. She tries to think of his name, his face, his eyes. She can't remember.

'Shall we?' asks the first.

The third nods. For centuries now it has been the same. They can always sense when their power is needed. Just like with this boy. They are never refused. Never.

She drops the eye into the black water. Then the three, hands linked, step closer to the cauldron, and stare into the darkness as they begin to chant:

'Double, double toil and trouble.'

Something in the black water begins to glow.

'Fire burn and cauldron bubble!'

And somewhere close, Hecate smiles.

PLAYING THE ODDS
Stuart Young

Itchy palms meant you were going to be lucky, that's what Ron's mum always told him. You were going to win the pools or maybe the lottery. But sweaty palms meant you were being taken in to see your boss who was going to kneecap you for ripping him off.

The two gorillas that came looking for Ron hadn't touched him since they bundled him out their car. They didn't need to; he still hurt from where they'd first greeted him. A friendly pat on the shoulder had disguised a vicelike pinch on his trapezius, crushing the muscle. He'd squirmed in agony but not enough to attract witnesses. The gorillas knew what they were doing; they didn't want to disturb the punters in the boss's casino.

Ron rolled his shoulder slightly as the two heavies marched him along the shadowy corridor. The movement didn't ease the pain; just told him it had turned to a dull ache.

At the end of the corridor he was taken through into a room. It reminded him of being escorted into some of the backroom poker games he'd played in. Except most poker games he went to only had cards and money on the table, not guns.

He rubbed his fingers nervously into his palms, trying to scratch the itch. The sweat made his fingertips slick.

The revolver lay on the table, the harsh glare from the naked light bulb glistening on its dark metal frame. But the gun wasn't the problem. It was the man who sat behind it he had to worry about.

Frank Dawson. Appeared from nowhere to become one of the biggest crime bosses in London. He was a mystery man; no one knew anything about him. Except that he was totally ruthless.

Ron sized him up, wondering how to play the situation. Dawson stared back at him, his grey eyes sharp and hard. His closely cropped hair added an edge to his craggy face, making him look like an escaped murderer. His expensive suit softened the effect. A little, not much.

Dawson nodded to the chair opposite him. 'Sit down, Ron.'

He did so, wondering for the millionth time about the story of Dawson's attempted murder. Another firm had hired someone to slot him, a mercenary type with a thing for automatic weapons. The psycho hosed an entire restaurant with bullets, killing everyone in sight. Except Dawson. He walked away without a scratch. Rumour had it he hadn't even ducked for cover. Ron was willing to bet a grand that was bollocks, Dawson was hard but he couldn't deflect bullets.

Even so, his palms didn't stop sweating.

'All right, Boss?' he said, trying to brazen it out. 'You wanted to see me?'

Dawson's lazy smile couldn't hide the intensity of his gimlet eyes. 'You've been taking liberties.'

God, please don't let him do anything to Lorna and the kids. Dawson was a vindictive bastard; you never knew how far he'd go. 'Don't know what you mean.'

'I think you do.'

He calculated quickly, the odds stacking up in his head. Dawson knowing about the card counting—two to one. Dawson knowing about the scam he had going with the croupier on the roulette wheel at Dawson's casino—three to one. Dawson knowing about Ron shagging his wife that time he'd been ordered to drive her home after she got drunk—ten million to one. If Dawson knew about that Ron would already be minus his favourite piece of his anatomy.

'I've already spoken to your partner—'

Partner. That meant the roulette scam. The odds didn't always play out how you expected them to.

'—and he spilled his guts.'

He's talking metaphorically, thought Ron. Probably.

'So if you just come clean about it we can move on.'

Ron's gaze dropped to the revolver. Two to one said this was a ploy to get him to admit to more than just the roulette. Maybe his partner hadn't grassed him up, Dawson hadn't mentioned him by name.

Time to gamble.

'Sorry, Boss. It was just a test run to see if I could get the same trick to work over at Harry Sharpe's casino. He's been a bit cheeky lately so I thought this'd teach him some manners. But I couldn't tell the croupier that 'cos I needed an honest idea of how well it'd work. I've still got the cash I got from your place, I'll pay it back tonight if you want.'

Dawson leaned back in his seat, nodding thoughtfully as he absorbed this. 'So you don't think I can handle Harry Sharpe by myself?'

'I'm not saying that. I know you can handle him. I just thought—'

'You can't help lying can you? It's a compulsion. Like the gambling. You love playing games.'

Dawson picked up the revolver.

'Here's a game for you. Roulette.' He spun the revolver's chamber. Ron stared at the revolving metal, fascinated by the whirr of its well-oiled mechanism.

'If you win you pay back the money you stole from me and get off my patch—I don't want to ever see you again. And if you lose . . . well, that's pretty self-explanatory.'

Ron felt the adrenaline explode through his body, powering him for a headlong flight. He didn't move; the door was blocked by the two heavies who'd brought him in.

'I'll go first shall I?' said Dawson. Ron blinked in surprise. He'd expected this to be the solitaire version. Dawson held the gun to his head and pulled the trigger.

Click.

Ron sat shivering; waiting for Dawson to pass the pistol over, wondering if he would actually have the guts to put it to his head.

'That was pretty easy,' said Dawson. 'I think I'll have another go.'

He pulled the trigger again.

Click.

'Hmmph.' He pulled the trigger again, three times in quick succession.

Click, click, click.

Ron didn't know how but somehow Dawson had fixed it so that he was left with only one chamber to try his luck against. The one with the bullet in it. This time the gun would definitely be passed across.

Instead Dawson kept the gun jammed against his head and started to squeeze the trigger once more. As the hammer drew back he grinned at Ron. 'Goodbye cruel world.'

Ron flinched away, knowing he was about to get drenched in blood and bone and chunks of splattered brain.

Click.

He looked back to see Dawson gazing at the pistol in mild puzzlement. 'That's funny. I could've sworn I'd loaded it.'

Ron sagged. Mind games—Dawson was letting him know what he was in for. Seeing the gun against someone else's head, even someone threatening his own life, was practically unbearable; it would be a thousand times worse when he was the one on the wrong end of the barrel.

Dawson aimed the pistol at the far wall. Ron watched him dazedly, a weird sense of *déjà vu* forming the sound of the expected click before Dawson could even fire. He watched the hammer ease back ever so slowly and then drop with alarming suddenness.

In the confined space of the dingy little room the explosion of sound was like cannon fire. Flame streaked from the revolver's barrel, an orange spear stabbing across the room. Another five spears followed, each accompanied by more cannon fire.

Clouds of cordite choked Ron's breath as he looked out from where he had covered his head with his arms. Dawson was admiring the tightly grouped collection of holes he had shot in the wall. Then he turned to look at Ron, his face impassive. 'I must've remembered to load it after all.'

Ron gaped at him. Dawson had just risked his life six times in as many seconds. It was a trick, it had to be. But he knew it wasn't. The stories were true—Dawson was invincible, death changed all the rules for him. Ron glanced over at the two heavies but they still stood immobile in front of the door, totally unmoved by the gunplay.

Dawson snapped open the pistol and spilled the empty shells onto the ground. Ron watched as Dawson reached in his pocket and produced another handful of bullets. 'Your turn.'

His ears still ringing from the shots Ron couldn't believe this was happening.

'Tell you what,' said Dawson. 'Seeing as it's your first go I'll make it easy for you. Only one bullet.'

He loaded the solitary bullet, snapped the revolver shut, spun the chamber. Placing the revolver on the table he looked at Ron. 'When you're ready.'

Ron stared at the revolver. He couldn't do this. His hands were shaking like crazy; his breath was as ragged as an asthmatic's and he felt like he was about to spray-paint the room with his lunch.

Maybe . . . maybe he could snatch up the pistol and shoot his way out of the room. Yeah—with one bullet. Against two heavies and the bulletproof Dawson. Even if he somehow made it out alive he'd be on the run for the rest of his life. Lorna and the kids couldn't live like that. And if he left them behind Dawson would find them.

'You promise you'll let me go?'

Dawson nodded. 'Scout's honour.'

He licked his dry lips. There was no other option. This was the only way to keep his family safe.

Goodbye Lorna.

Slowly he picked up the pistol and pressed the barrel against his temple. The hard metal was cold against his skin.

But six chambers and only one bullet weren't bad odds. He'd beaten worse than that. Loads of times. And his palms were itchy. That meant he was lucky.

His finger jerked at the trigger.

Click.

He sighed in relief, his body deflating like a balloon as the air escaped his lips. That dry, ugly, heartless click was the most beautiful sound he had ever heard.

A euphoric light-headedness came over him, his usual joy at winning multiplied a thousandfold, and for one crazy second he wanted to do it again. Then he got a grip on himself. Dawson wouldn't like losing. He had to be humble here, push down his glee.

He kept the gun to his head. Lowering it before Dawson said so would be a big mistake.

'I-I won.' He tried not to smile when he said it but he couldn't help it. At least it was a genuine smile, not a smug, rub-your-nose-in-it smirk.

Dawson didn't answer.

His smile faded. Had he done something wrong? He swallowed; it felt like gulping down a boulder. 'I won.'

Dawson raised his eyebrows. 'Did you?'

He barely had time to frown before the bullet blew the expression off his face.

SUBTERRANEAN VOICES
Kevin L. Donihe

The headstone was ancient, pitted by both time and weather. Once slate gray, prolonged exposure to the elements had stained the marker black. Atop an inscription, the stone bore the image of a grinning skull. Dense cakes of moss grew within the lines, imparting a relief effect. Beneath the skull unfurled a terse epitaph, rendered in Latin.

Sum quod eris; fui quod es.

'I am what you will be; I was what you are,' Karen Hammonds whispered. She did not comprehend the language, but had frequented graveyards long enough to know what sentiment the etching conveyed.

Karen reread the line and acknowledged the ancient promise's accuracy. A coldness traced up her spine, but she shook away the unease. It was senseless to allow something so trivial to keep her from enjoying the late afternoon twilight. Fall was just arriving and the nights were very jocund—perfect and beautiful.

Karen withdrew a sheet of typing paper from the ream under her arm and placed it against the marker. She reached into her coat and withdrew a red crayon. Once the materials were in position, Karen bent down to transfer the image from stone to paper.

As the inscription took shape, she realized how this etching could quite possibly prove the highlight of her collection. Her hand continued eagerly until stopping just before the skull's empty eye sockets could be rendered.

She had heard something.

Karen craned her neck to see past the stones. She feared someone had seen her at work and called out. She didn't think it abnormal to make rubbings of curious and antiquated markers, yet she knew some might misunderstand her intentions and think her a ghoul. Karen saw, with some relief, that she was still alone.

She turned her attention back to rubbing.

Seconds later, the noise returned. It was considerably muffled and sounded as though someone was trying to speak from behind a too-thick wall.

She spun around and found the cemetery as empty as before.

No matter, probably just the wind whistling through graveyard flowers. Karen dismissed the sound and completed her rubbing. Placing the crayon back in her pocket, Karen removed her work from the stone and looked upon it with pride.

Morbid yet beautiful.

She smiled. It was the ideal centerpiece.

Karen heard the sound again and dropped the paper.

Louder now. And it wasn't coming from the flowers. She could even feel the ground vibrate softly, as though the noise was arising from somewhere underfoot.

But that was impossible.

Karen listed and, again, the sound returned—soft and garbled.

'—me.'

She tried to convince herself otherwise, but the last noise was, without question, a word.

Karen put down both the ream and the crayon and walked towards the adjoining grave. She bent over and put her ear to the ground. She felt like a superstitious fool, yet it seemed as though the voice had issued from that mound of dirt.

But of course it hadn't. It was probably just a distant echo from the road and nothing more. Karen smiled at her own absurdity.

She listened nevertheless.

And heard nothing.

What the hell had she expected? To hear a twelve piece orchestra?

Karen laughed at herself and hoped no one had been close enough to see her behave so erratically. They would not only think she had an unnatural fetish for the dead, but spoke to them through the dirt as well. Karen lifted her ear from the grave but forced it back into the soil when the voice returned.

'Help me.'

No! It didn't say that! Damn it! It couldn't say that!

Karen pushed her ear deeper into the dirt.

Some burrowing animal moving underground. Had to be. Her imagination merely lent the sound a human voice. Things in graves do not call out to those above.

'Help me,' the voice whimpered.

Karen recoiled, nearly striking her back on the face of an imposing headstone.

'Let me out!' It spoke so loudly Karen could hear the words without holding her ear to the dirt. While the voice seemed both feminine and frightened, goose pimples nevertheless wrapped around both arms. Karen wanted desperately to run but her feet felt cemented to the ground.

'It hurts,' it shrieked.

'No, no, no, no, no,' Karen muttered as if the mantra could ward off the source of the voice.

'Please!'

She could take no more. Her paralysis broke and she ran. Karen refused to stop until she reached her car.

* * *

Back home, Karen sat down in front of the T.V. and flicked it on. The flashing images did nothing but irritate her and Karen soon discovered she could not concentrate on them. The sit-com family was simply too buoyant to tolerate for more than a few minutes.

She turned the T.V. off and reached for the book sitting on the coffee table in front of her. Karen looked down at the cover and grimaced. An image of a hand reaching out of a grave. She usually relished such art—despite its schlock value. Now, however, it left a queasy feeling in the pit of her stomach. Karen opened the book and began reading where she had left off prior to her trip to the cemetery. She got past the first five pages of Chapter 4 and then could take no more. Depictions of grave dwellers set loose on the aboveground world. Living flesh being ground by green teeth. Too much.

Karen closed the book without bothering to mark to her new stopping point and placed it—cover down—on the coffee table. She leaned back in the chair, her head tilted upwards. Karen heard her stomach growl but couldn't quite convince herself to eat. She was afraid food would only sour her already churning stomach. Karen looked up at the ceiling instead. Some of the patterns there reminded her of impressionistic headstones. She quickly turned her gaze to another corner where the designs seemed a bit more random. Still, her mind spun.

Five minutes passed. Karen unleashed a sigh. There was nothing to be gained in staring up at the ceiling. She stood up from the couch. Her legs suddenly felt unsteady and her head light. Maybe it would be best to just forget about it all and retire early.

Karen didn't even bother with brushing her teeth on the way to the bedroom or changing her clothes once she was there. She just slipped into bed and, after thirty minutes of tossing and turning, was asleep.

* * *

That night she dreamt of the cemetery. Roles, however, had reversed. Now she lay underground, calling up to whoever stood above her grave.

Karen lifted her hands and was able to see the dense red welts that had risen in the struggle to break through the wood coffin.

'Please!' She heard herself scream. 'The lid!'

Karen experienced pain as she pounded the oak. Agony blossomed in her wrists and traveled down her arms in steady currents.

'I can't breathe,' she continued, shrieking though her lungs burned and throbbed.

Soon the coffin would be a vacuum.

* * *

Karen shot up from the covers and, within seconds of waking, realized what she must do.

Hours earlier, she had feared the source of the voice, but now her mind had cleared. It couldn't possibly have been a corpse speaking—but it couldn't have been her imagination, either. Someone had been mistaken for dead and buried in an underground prison. Karen could not allow the victim to die. To do so would be murder.

She jumped from the bed and pulled on her clothes. She made her way to the basement while still buttoning her shirt. There, she picked up a large shovel from a rack filled with gardening utensils and examined its dirt-clotted blade.

Karen had never needed to dig a six-foot deep hole before and her tool collection wasn't well suited for the task. The going would be hard—maybe even impossible—but the shovel would have to suffice. She had nothing else that could tackle something as large as a grave.

With the shovel draped across her left shoulder, Karen made her way upstairs into the kitchen. She picked up the phone but, instead of bringing it to her ear, placed the receiver back into its cradle without dialing a number.

She couldn't tell anyone. They would ask her why she was at the cemetery in the first place. They would uncover her secret.

And what if they didn't believer her? What if during the time she spent trying to convince her friends of her sanity the girl in the grave died?

Blood would cover her hands.

That was something she could never allow to happen. The shame alone would kill her, or else turn her into a recluse. She would have to go at it alone. The digging would take time, probably until dawn, but she felt as though she had no other option.

Karen left the house without bothering to slip into her coat. The air would be cold, but, in light of the activity she was planning, she doubted she would need any protection from the chill.

* * *

Fifteen minutes later, she found herself back at the cemetery she had fled so eagerly. Karen felt an initial impulse to turn around and forget why she had come, but she remembered the mournful voice and pressed on.

Karen picked up the shovel from the passenger's seat and opened the door. She drew in a deep breath, left the climate controlled car, and stepped into the bracing night.

* * *

Scaling the fence was treacherous.

Karen threw the shovel over the fence so she wouldn't be troubled with its bulk as she climbed. Still, the going proved difficult. Her feet slipped and she nearly impaled herself on the spear-points before she was able to jump to the other side.

Although she had made it across unharmed, Karen hit the ground hard. On impact, her ankle buckled so far under the pressure that, for a few seconds, she feared the bone had shattered. Karen gritted her teeth and rose from the ground. There was no time to mend the aches.

Karen continued up the path. She searched for the grave but met with little success. The night had turned the cemetery into a twisting labyrinth. Everything had been rendered identical by a heady cloak. She searched the sprawling cemetery for a half hour before deciding her quest was doomed. There were no lights and the night was far too black.

She turn in the direction of her car and, at that second, heard a sound—barely more than a whisper:

'Let me out.'

Karen listened in an attempt to locate the source.

'Please, it's so dark.'

The voice was issuing from a dense cluster of graves underneath a willow. Karen strained her eyes and discerned the ancient grave from which she had tried to take a rubbing. Beside the headstone she could see a small box-like object. She puzzled over the indistinct figure for a few seconds before she realized it was only the ream of paper she had left behind in her rush.

Using the old stone as her guide, Karen looked to her immediate left and caught sight of the grave for which she had been searching.

Karen picked up speed before stopping a few paces from the headstone. For the first time, she stopped to read the inscription rendered there:

LINDA MARIE STAFFORD
MARCH 15, 1951—DECEMBER 14, 2000

Karen shook her head. The dates had to be in error. No one could stay alive underground without food so long. The air supply could not possibly last more than a few days.

But someone was alive in the tomb. Somebody who needed to be set free before they died.

'Don't worry,' Karen shouted. 'I'm here to get you out!'

'Please, I can't see!' The voice continued as if its owner had not heard Karen's words.

'Don't worry. Just don't worry. Everything will be fine. Trust me.' She promptly removed the first shovel full of dirt and threw it from the grave.

* * *

Karen's heart felt like it might explode in her chest. Her temples throbbed and her brow felt alternately cold and hot. She continued digging. She could not allow the poor woman to die at a time she was so close to safety.

'Only a few more feet,' Karen panted, her breath exiting her mouth in ragged, foggy puffs.

'Please! Please, I can't breathe! Oh God, I can't breathe!'

The voice only encouraged Karen to dig faster.

* * *

An hour and a half later, Karen's muscles were so stiff and inflexible that she could no longer feel her arms below the elbows.

'Can't rest,' she panted between unloading shovel-loads of dirt. She knew if she stopped, even for a second, she would loose momentum and not be able to restart.

And the poor woman would die.

She kept on.

But oh God did it hurt.

* * *

A few minutes later, the blade hit the grave liner with a resounding clash. Finally.

Karen jumped down into the hole. She stood on a firm outcropping of soil a few feet above the liner and gripped the vault's ring. She heaved and the slab cement lid parted.

Now she could see the coffin. It sat covered in a thin, greasy film, but that simply could not be. For someone to be living within, the grave would have to be fresh.

Then why had the soil seemed so firm?

Karen shook the question from her mind. No time.

'Open it! For God's sake, open the lid!'

'I'm coming!' Karen shouted back and grabbed the lid. It did not budge.

Karen wanted to smack herself. Of course it would be latched.

'Wait! I'll have you out in a second!'

Karen picked herself up and reached out over the mouth of the grave. Her hands found only grass until, what seemed like minutes later, they finally brushed against the shovel's blade. Karen gripped the handle and brought it down into the hole.

'Just a few more moments; that's all!' She shouted and brought the rounded edge of the shovel down squarely on the latch.

It refused to give.

'Damn!' Karen muttered and struck the lock again. This time, both the latch and the dull wood around it splintered into a dozen fragments.

'I'll be inside any second now!' She shouted. 'You're going to be free!'

Karen gripped the lid and opened it wide.

The odor that erupted from the casket was overpowering. She wanted to vomit. Karen looked down and her breath failed her.

She stood over a decomposing corpse.

But how? She had heard the voice coming from this grave. Maybe it was coming from the tomb to the right. Maybe—

The questions abruptly disintegrated in her mind. That part of her brain failed her the second she saw the corpse's eyes open to reveal a milky grayness.

'You freed me.' No longer sounded feminine, its voice was grating, coarse, sexless. 'Thank you.'

Karen could not move. She could only wait as she felt her mental circuits fizzle out one by one.

'We've been listening to you, above our graves, admiring our stones. You're bound to us.'

Somehow, Karen managed to goad her frozen muscles into clambering from the grave. She forced her right leg over the gaping hole just before she felt something wet and yielding clutch her left.

'Can't you hear them? Everyone wants out. But they can't make it on their own. They need a helping hand—and yours is the first. For that you shall never be harmed.'

The second the thing stopped speaking, the once silent graveyard burst into a cacophony of sound. Karen could now hear a muffled chorus of shrieks and the grating sound of a thousand fingernails scrapping against the wood of a thousand lids.

'One by one!' The thing laughed. 'One by one until we're all free!'

Karen managed to pull her leg from its grasp and flee the open grave. As she ran, she could hear the thing cry out.

Karen clutched her ears and refused to hear anything.

* * *

One Year Later

'Kill me!' Karen screamed to the crowd. 'For God's sake, just kill me!'

They ignored her.

'Please! I want to die!'

Karen ran through the middle of the clogged and reeking street and held her arms out in invitation. She was spurned.

'Damn you!'

Suddenly, from the organic phalanx, emerged the corpse she had freed. She was never able to forget its face, even after the others began to arrive.

Karen ran to the corpse and fell into its decayed arms.

'Please kill me. Everybody's dead,' she sobbed.

Its lips turned up in a parody of a smile.

'You own this world now! I don't belong here! Kill me.'

The dead woman spoke in a voice so raspy it was nearly unintelligible. 'I can't. Without you none of this would be. No one will harm you. Ever.'

'Please!'

The corpse failed to respond.

'I watched my family die! I watched everyone die! Just let me do the same! For God's—'

The dead woman pushed her away before Karen could finish and continued down the street.

Karen regained her balance and turned to the masses surrounding her.

'Kill me.'

Most of those she accosted simply turned away; others spoke directly to her. No one, however, acknowledged her request. They knew who she was and realized what a great service she had done them all.

Karen relented and collapsed to the street. She closed her eyes and blocked out the world she had helped to destroy.

DAVY
William P. Simmons

'Davy?'

Paul waited by the door for an answer, squinting to see through darkness, which shifted. The steady low hum of the refrigerator filled the kitchen with soft electric breath, and he listened for anything—the creeping patter of feet, a soft, hissing breath—that would help identify where he was.

Davy.

His son.

Paul squeezed his eyes and tried to make out the dark corners of the kitchen, the bulging shadows in the hall. The light switch was out of reach from the door, which trembled slightly behind him, moved by a gust of Autumn air which snuck a pile of red and orange, crinkled leaves over the floor and filled the foyer with the sour-sweet of freshly cut pumpkin and crisp night. A second gust wrapped around his legs and lifted a sheath of paper off the desk that Mary had surprised him with last Christmas. After he'd made his first professional sale, before he'd woken to the sour stench of gasoline and everything had changed.

'Son?

Waiting.

'Are you there?'

Silence.

Somewhere down the street, a dog barked. A few wrinkled shafts of light bled across counter top and wall, folding the dark over on itself as a car swam past his house.

'Davy? I'm home!'

He swallowed, walked into the kitchen, and released the door. It shut with a dull thud behind him, shaking timber and windowpanes until the house sounded like a deep, hollow cavern

Eyes near the counter.

Something running across the floor, squatting in a corner obscured by shadow.

A shiver of cool air.

'C'mon, Davy, stop playing games!'

He waited a full minute, listening to the house settle. He imagined himself in the chest cavity of a low, crouching beast. The heater in the cellars kicked on with a whisper. Warm air blew through the kitchen and hall vents, bringing feeling back to his chilled hands.

Paul threw the switch and a cold, bright wave of electric light tore through the shadows. When he saw Davy wasn't waiting for him in the corner after all, he walked into the living room. It was in a shambles: the magazine rack was turned over, photographs of him and Mary were shredded, fragmented faces staring listlessly at nothing, and the crystal lamp his grandmother had left him stood broken in a dozen or more fragments that crunched beneath his feet.

Davy was having one of his moods.

* * *

'A bad spell,' Mary told him the last uneasy night of their unspoken truce. The night before Davy turned six. 'He'll outgrow it,' she said, soft pale chin and lips washed in lamp light.

It had been her idea to invite the Sweeney boy to the party. His family had just moved in down the street, and she thought it might be neighborly to involve them in the party she had been planning for a month now. Paul hadn't felt right about it from the beginning, but he didn't want them to start another fight. That was one thing he *definitely* didn't want. So when she decided to invite the new boy, Paul just nodded and hoped that this time things would be different.

Old friends had stopped dropping by.

Although some of them still talked to Paul when he ran into them on the street, it was hard to ignore the nervous tilt of their lips or the distracted speculation in eyes he'd thought he'd known. Fred Wilson, who he'd grown up with, hadn't even stopped for him on the street the day before, when Paul tried to flag him down. And his daughter, Tera, still woke screaming about the rats.

* * *

Last year, Fred and Thelma had brought their daughter to play with Davy; that's when Paul began to learn how very bad things had become.

As the adults had sat around eating Chinese take-out and drinking beers, Paul had just started to settle into the comfort of his chair, listening to Fred brag about his new summer home.

And then the screams had started.

From upstairs.

Davy's room.

Paul had been the first one there, and God, the first one to see. Davy held the dead rat up to his mouth and kissed it, laughing, before he lowered it again, tried to force it into the little girl's mouth.

The whispers started, then.

They became a scream after Davy's birthday party.

* * *

The few parents, who'd allowed their children to attend, found excuses to come along. Paul saw behind their *'oh, we just figured we'd help out,'* facades; saw beyond smiles and chitchat and nervous, pale faces because he shared their fear.

Everything went smoothly before the cake.

Davy was surrounded by a mountain of presents, and Paul felt a tingle of shame and sadness watching him rip them open. Like any other little boy, he thought. The Sweeney boy had wanted to blow out the candles. He pouted when his mother, a round, plump woman who sounded like a muffled foghorn told him to behave. Davy had waited patiently for the boy to quiet down. While everyone watched, he took a gulp of air and blew out the candles, clapping happily when they flickered and died. The parents pretended smiles and his mother clapped her hands. Paul released a tight breath he hadn't even realized he'd been holding . . .

And saw the glint of the serrated cake knife.

And found he couldn't move for the few seconds it took Davy to slash it across the Sweeney boy's wrist.

Paul had been on him in an instant, slapping the knife from his hand. Nor had he stopped there. He couldn't, for the doubt and fear and low seething rage had been building for years, and he felt as if a coil had finally been unwound.

He slapped Davy.

Again.

The Sweeney boy was still screaming when the other parents collected their children and left. Paul didn't know who they feared more, him or Davy, and even after he'd paid for the Sweeney boy's Emergency Room visit, he'd had to practically beg to keep them from pressing charges or suing. But that didn't matter—not that even the people at work treated him a leper, or the cold looks on the street, or even the slowly dawning realization that his wife and him were becoming ghosts who just shared a house and a mortgage and the same last name. All that mattered was, for the first time in his life, Paul was suddenly, completely, very afraid of his own son.

'If you ever touch Davy again,' Mary told him after that night, 'I'll leave.'

Paul had said nothing.

There had been nothing *left* to say.

* * *

Paul didn't want to think about it.

Thinking didn't help; thinking only made him look behind him and wish his stomach wouldn't knot up so damn easy. Thinking brought tears—for Mary, for himself, for a life he'd lost because of one minute in time. A minute he couldn't ever get back.

He looked up from the mess on the floor when he felt the eyes watching. A shadow scuffled past the hall.

'I'm not in the mood for this tonight!' Paul shouted.

Only the beating of his heart answered.

* * *

The night Paul found the cat in the garden behind the shed; he slipped it into a plastic bag, flinching because it was already cold and rubbery.

He buried it behind the house where the shadows of the forest surrounded their property. In Harper's Mill, you were hard pressed to look in any direction without seeing at least a hint of treetops and the darkness that branches held like secrets between them. Even in the college district, among the college bars and campus dormitories, evidence of the untamed frontier that Harper's Mill had once been demanded attention. That night, he felt small and lonely in the forest's shadow.

Tab-Cat's eyes had been removed. Something *(somebody!)* had pried them out.

Paul found the little garden spade hung neatly in the garage.

—*Tabby-Cat*—

He asked Davy about it during dinner. The look Mary gave him made him feel like a piece of shit—not like a real man at all. *A man*, his father would have told him, *took care of business.* Paul didn't even know where to begin.

* * *

At first, he'd convinced himself that the *accidents* were really just that, the coincidences his wife insisted: Petra Worth, the neighbor trapped in the abandoned shed, crying because Davy locked her in; the mutilated birds he'd stopped telling Mary about because all it did was upset her; the dolls in the basement from when Mary was a girl, shears shoved in their plastic stomachs, hair yanked off.

—*Tabby Cat, his eyes pried out and fur matted red*—

* * *

On the stairs, beneath the chair.

'Davy?'

Behind the sink, from the windows.

'How long are you going to keep this up?'

* * *

'Does he get to go to Heaven now?' Davy had asked, curled across Mary's lap on the sofa when Paul told them about the cat.

Paul caught the tightening of her muscles, the warning flashing in her eyes. 'Children and death don't go together,' she'd told him on one of those rare occasions they had stayed up together, a jazz record spinning horn and bass into the pleasantly falling shadows. 'I know you don't agree, but I don't think it's something Davy has to know about. Not yet.'

But Davy *was* interested, and whether it was because Paul liked finally being the focus of his son's admiration, or whether he'd done it just to piss her off, he was secretly glad when Davy asked:

'Does he chase dead mice, now?'

Paul forced a sick smile and nodded. 'He can chase all the mice he wants,' he said, 'and sleep on the bed and drink milk until his belly explodes.'

'But not our milk. Dead cat's milk.'

'Right. He's happy now. People, animals, whatever—everything is happy when they die. They go to a . . . better place.'

Davy had chewed that over, tilting his head, leaning over his mother's lap. 'I think it would be fun, then. I'd like to be dead, someday. I wish we could all be dead with Tab-Cat.'

Mary's face had drained.

She'd grabbed Davy up and raced past Paul, throwing him the hurt, furious look that had increased in intensity and frequency the older their son became and the more their marriage sickened. The look said, *'You're a lousy father, Paul. God knows I shouldn't expect you to be any better of a husband!'*

The worse thing, the most horrible thing of all, was that he knew she was right.

* * *

Paul eased himself in the shredded cushion of the recliner where he could see the stairwell rising into the gaping darkness across the second floor. Davy was playing. Paul wondered if he was smiling and shivered.

The smile had done it.

That, and what he'd found in his son's room.

Don't think about it!

But he had all the time in the world to think now that Mary had left. He'd never realized the length, the massive space of the house before he found himself fending for himself for the first time since college.

The television flashed prosaic pictures of plastic looking men and women in meaningless dances between elegant restaurants to parties to bedrooms.

—He'd opened the door to Davy's bedroom—

Paul dragged his feet to the kitchen, looked through the fridge: a bottle of Ketchup with the top still sealed shut, some Chinese takeout that reeked, and a squashed box of baking soda. The freezer was more promising, piled with Salisbury steak and mashed potato frozen dinners. He chose one, set the microwave dial, and leaned against the counter while it cooked.

A shadow slipping around the corner.

'Why?' He asked, not liking how the walls repeated his words through air grown cold. 'Why, Davy?'

Angry banging in the living room.

The same every night.

Mary wouldn't take his calls, and last week, when he'd woken in the middle of the night to the crying down the hall, his mother-in-law had threatened to get a restraining order if he kept harassing them.

Paul returned to the living room, and stopped.

Davy stood in the middle of a pile of photo albums. His small body quivered, the matted hair at the back of his head still wet. Pictures of Mary, Paul's father, and Mary's grandmother looked sad and faded in the dusty light. Glossy eyes frozen in time stared at the ceiling, condemning the empty history of his life.

Paul cut into a piece of sloppy meat. His hands shook. The gravy was already congealing, and it threatened to make him remember something he didn't want to think about.

'You're wrong.'

' I love you, Son.' Paul lied.

'No,' Davy said as he walked across the filthy rug to the stair well. *'You never did.'*

* * *

Later that night, after the dishes were washed and the late show was over, and Paul had taken out the garbage and straightened up the house, and anything else that would keep him from walking the dark stairs to the top floor where Davy waited, he breathed deeply and forced himself to mount the steps.

Davy waited at the top, in the hall.

Davy outside his room, following him to the bathroom, trying to slip his hand into his, pinching when it wasn't taken.

'Mom cries a lot,' Davy told Paul as he tried to brush his teeth.

'I told you to stay away from her.'

'Mommy loves me,' the boy said. 'She wants me with her. Should I go see her?'

Paul started to speak, let the words fall.

The shadow stared at back with hard, unblinking eyes.

* * *

Mary had woken him early that morning, while dark nestled over the houses on Depot Street like a stifling blanket.

Rain died to a slow trickle from the eaves when Paul rubbed his eyes, stretched, looked through the dark for his wife, whose voice sounded too far away.

'What . . .?'

Then he heard it too—someone moving through the house.

Just last month, the Harrelson's, a quaint old couple who had reminded him of his Grandparents, had surprised a burglar. Now they were dead and the burglar was out on parole.

Paul didn't want to be another statistic.

He belted the robe against his waist and slipped down the hall, holding his breath in the dark. 'Be careful, Paul,' Mary told him, but he barely heard. It took him a few seconds to identify the sharp odor that grew stronger as he walked. He winced every time the floor creaked.

Gasoline.

Whispering.

Oh my god from Davy's room my god, Davy . . . ?

And he'd opened the door.

And Davy had stood there smiling in the middle of the floor with his Smurf pajamas, smiling, not afraid, not doing anything but trying to create a dry, whispering flash in the dark.

Paul knocked the matches out of Davy's hands, grabbed him by the arm.

Davy stumbling backwards, tripping on a loose thread of carpet. Davy's smile cut off with a loud crunch, eyes bulging when the back of his head joined the edge of the little desk Paul had given the boy last Christmas. Davy screaming once, not really a scream at all, just a tiny chocking gurgle. Arms twitching as one, thin, insignificant line of blood falling like a secret just between them as it curled in a small wet blanket around his legs.

Davy's eyes locking on Paul.

Davy dying, but never really gone.

* * *

Paul couldn't sleep.

When he closed his eyes, memories rushed him in a dark, angry river.

Screams from the hall.

'Give your old man some rest, huh?'

Paul heard the hysteria below his voice and no longer cared.

The screams and the blood and Mary crying while they waited for the ambulance.

'I'm sorry. Oh, god, I'm so sorry,' he whispered, pinching his leg to keep back the screams.

He waited like that, in his bed, in the dark, until the cries stopped.

A shadow passed the night-light that he no longer even tried to sleep without.

A cold hand on his leg.

—They go to a better place, son—

'It's not like that, Dad.'

The shadow slid into bed.

Small arms held him firm.

'We stay here.'

TAKE IT OFF, TAKE IT ALL OFF
Mark R. Kehl

Anyone who thinks Indiana is all corn and white guys playing basketball ain't never been in the northwest corner, where they used to make steel and everybody had a job. They still make steel here, but now the place is more like that old Ford buried in the weeds behind my grandma's house—a pile of rust and decay, home to rats and worse, and sure as hell not going anywhere.

It was middle of summer, and me and T.J. were sitting in Popeye's Chicken, watching rain streak the lights of cars passing by. During the daytime, we had the beach to keep us busy. Lake Michigan was no Caribbean, but it had sand and water and girls showing skin, which was all that really counted. No complaints from me. But at night we had nothing to do. At T.J.'s house, his dad was probably drunk and looking for someone to clobber. At mine, we had no cable. Not even thirty miles from Chicago, and reception was for shit. I hated summer nights.

What made it worse was Anita, this girl I met on the beach a few weeks ago. I would have much rather been with her than T.J., but she had a job down at the mall in Merrillville where her daddy worked security. She took all the overtime she could, only got one day off a week. I'd have gone down to see her there, but the bus didn't run that far. Anita: just thinking about her, I wanted her so bad I felt like I could fly there. We'd had our first real date last Sunday, went to a movie and back to her place. I thought we were going to do it, I tried, but she wouldn't let me get her clothes off. She said she wasn't ready. I was a rage of hormones, ready enough for both of us, but I cooled down after she started to scream. I thought I had blown it, but things were still okay between us. I saw her on the beach Tuesday morning, talked to her on the phone a couple times. She said she understood. We were going to see each other again on Sunday, but she made it clear she wasn't ready to take The Big Step. That's what she called it. Me, I was ready, but whatever. My whole life had become about killing time until Sunday.

Neither me nor T.J. had spoken for a while, just watching the cars go past on Harrison, when he announced, 'I'm going to Jack's Shack. Want to come?'

'Sure,' I said.

There it was, the decision that ruined my life, and I gave it about as much thought as scratching my ass.

We refilled our small Cokes one more time and then cut out of Popeye's. T.J., he always had this thing about going places he wasn't supposed to, ever since we were little kids. He had been in every shutdown steel mill around, all the secret places no one else knew about. It's what he did. I used to go with him sometimes, but I didn't get the same thrill out of it he did. He considered himself an explorer. Everybody else thought he was just some freak liked to go where only the rats go. But he was my friend, and we were bored, and Jack's Shack, well, that was something different from an old plate mill or a sewer tunnel.

T.J.'s Uncle Vic used to tell us stories about Jack's. Uncle Vic used to work in the mills before he lost a hand sandwiched between two 30-ton slabs. He was on disability a few years before Aunt Flori got fed up with him being around all the time and went psycho on him with a butcher knife. Back six, seven years ago, he used to watch us some nights when our parents were working. Uncle Vic tended to drink too much beer and then he'd start to teach us what he called 'the ways of the world.' Mostly, that was him telling us about getting hookers or that story about how he and some guys gang-raped a pizza delivery girl. We were pretty sure he made that one up. The girl's appearance changed every time he told it.

But sometimes he'd talk about Jack's Shack and how that used to be a hot place to go. There was a bunch of strip places on Route 20 then, all competing with each other for fat steel mill paychecks, and Jack's was the best, you asked Uncle Vic. They had the hottest girls. He talked about Sally and Roxy and Desiree, how they all knew his name and how they'd do special things for him, sometimes for free, because they liked him. But after talking about the Shack for a while, he always started to drink more, and his mood turned dark, like T.J.'s dad when he was drinking. He never did tell us what happened to make Jack's Shack shut down. I just figured it was like most of the other places on Route 20, another victim of the mill closings.

I was following T.J. down the sidewalk on Harrison, sucking on my Pop-eye's Coke, letting him lead because he knew all the shortcuts and back ways, the quickest route to anywhere. Past a block of burned-out store-fronts, we started to cut through a vacant lot, following trash-strewn paths past rusted-out cars and thickets of weeds. There was a fire burning in a drum toward the back of the lot. A few figures, homeless people and drunks, rubbed their hands around it. A few more huddled under a lean-to made from a piece of corrugated tin.

As we passed, I noticed a shadow slip away from the lean-to and head our way. I tapped T.J. and nodded. We stopped to wait, a little separated, so if whoever it was attacked one of us the other would have a clear shot at his back.

I was thinking crackhead, desperate enough to hit up two kids in a vacant lot. But it was just Oscar. He was grinning, showing perfect teeth, the smile the girls couldn't deny. A knit hat on his head, hands in the pockets of his zip-up sweatshirt, all casual like we ran into him cruising Broadway or something.

'The hell you doing here?' T.J. said, pissed because he'd been scared.

Oscar shrugged, glanced back at the fire. 'Hanging.'

'With the lost souls?' I said, not buying. 'Shit.'

Oscar shrugged again. 'You seen Kenroy Washington around?'

I looked at T.J. He wasn't getting it either. Kenroy Washington was six feet eight inches of future NBA MVP. He and his pals won the city three-on-three championship three years running, all because of Kenroy. He could have been playing with me and T.J. on his side and we would have won. He was that good, a human highlight reel, like they said on TV. He was starting Purdue in the fall, full scholarship. Far as I knew, he didn't even know Oscar's name.

'No,' T.J. said for both of us. 'What you want to know for?'

Oscar was looking around as he talked, like Kenroy Washington might come dribbling by. 'He got that sister, Gilda.'

That was all we needed to hear. Girls couldn't help looking at Oscar. Oscar couldn't stop at just looking.

'She saying I put my hands on her in one of them photo booths at the mall,' he said.

'You saying you didn't?'

'I ain't saying anything 'cept I'm staying the hell away from Kenroy Washington. What the hell you doing out in the rain?'

I looked at T.J. This was his mission. His call.

'We going to Jack's Shack,' he said.

'That nudie place, all closed up on Route 20? What the hell for?'

T.J. shrugged. 'See what we can see.'

Oscar looked at me for a real explanation. I held up my hands. 'We're bored.'

Oscar hooted. 'So you gonna break into some sleazy shithole and see if you can still smell the pussy ten years gone? You boys is sad.'

I smiled because I knew he didn't mean nothing, but T.J. glared. I nudged him hard enough to get us on our way again.

'Can't all of us have girls throwing themselves on our dicks, man,' I called back to Oscar. 'You one lucky guy. We see Kenroy Washington, we be sure to tell him that.'

I expected him to fade back into the rainy night, but he didn't. He trailed after us.

'Where you going?' T.J. asked, stopping.

Oscar gave him the grin. 'Gonna see the great explorer in action, man. That okay with you?'

T.J. glared at him a second, but being called 'the great explorer' seemed to thaw him some. He shrugged.

'Whatever.'

So on we went, T.J. in the lead, me and Oscar following after, shoulders hunched against the rain, hands in our pockets.

That was the second point things went wrong for us that night. Yeah, going in the first place was T.J.'s dumb-ass idea, and I was the fool who went along without thinking about it, but if Oscar hadn't come, things never would have turned out the way they did. No way. If he had just stayed hiding in that goddamn vacant lot, he and T.J. both would have lived to see morning.

* * *

We made our way, three shadows, through a neighborhood of square houses, each not much bigger than a two-car garage. Anita lived in a little house like that, and I wished I was with her instead of T.J. and Oscar. We reached Rosco's Body Shop and cut around the locked-up tin building, past a few cars that would never see the road again, to the rusty chain-link fence that ran along the back. Through it, across a plain of darkness, shone the lights of Route 20, splintered and blurred by the rain. T.J. knew a place where the fence was down. We hopped it and made our way across a field of weeds toward the shadows behind the buildings that lined Route 20—bars, donut shops, muffler places. Half the buildings were closed permanently, the rest looking on the verge.

We had to cross a drainage ditch that ran behind the buildings, like a moat separating them from the field. It'd been raining all day, all week on and off, and the moat was running thick and heavy. Still, it wasn't much of a jump, and I wouldn't have had any problem if I hadn't snagged the toe of my shoe in a clump of weeds. It robbed me of just enough momentum so I landed square in the water. I just stood there a second to get my balance, afraid off falling down flat. The cold water seeped into my shoes, filled the space between my toes.

Oscar snorted, almost choked trying not to laugh then gave up and let it out.

'Shit, T.J.,' he said, 'now why the hell didn't we think of that? 'Stead of making that nice, simple jump my grandma could make without her walker, we coulda just hopped right into the fucking water like a goddamn frog.'

T.J. didn't go along at first, must have still been pissed at Oscar, but then he got over it and the two of them were snickering in the dark, trying not to make too much noise.

I hauled myself out of the ditch, about a gallon of water running out of my shoes. My toes felt all slimy, wrapped in the clinging sock

'Fuck both of you,' I muttered.

We sneaked up the rise to a small Dumpster back of the Athens Family Restaurant, one of the few places on Route 20 still doing decent business. Oscar and T.J. crouched down behind it, still snickering and snorting, despite the rancid stink that came from the Dumpster. Ignoring them, I popped my head up for a look around.

Behind the Athens it was still, and next door, the dry cleaner's was closed and dark. Past that, Jack's Shack looked more like a bunker than a shack, squatting there in the middle of a desolate no-man's land. Concrete barriers with fingers of rusted rebar sticking out blocked the parking lot entrances. In the rain and the lights of passing cars, the empty lot was a sparkling sea of broken glass and gravel. The metal pole in the parking lot was as bare as an oak in January. I remembered from when I was a little kid the sign that used to be at the top of that pole, lit up aqua blue, the silhouette of a woman posed with one leg kicked up in the air. The sign had said, 'Jack's Shack' and 'Live Nude Girls.' It hadn't been there for years.

Beyond Jack's was a Donutland, and that put me on edge. Donutland always had cars in the parking lot, and this time of night half of them were cops. I pointed that out to Oscar and T.J.

'Whatsa matter, Eddie?' Oscar said to me, all theatrical, like he's on some sitcom setting himself up for a laugh. 'You getting . . . cold feet?'

Then he and T.J. were falling all over each other laughing again.

'Fuck you,' I said. 'I ain't getting busted for this bullshit.'

T.J. sobered up fast when he thought I was backing out. 'Don't worry about it,' he said, keeping his voice low. 'You ever see them cops in there? 'Serving and protecting?' They make a pyramid of Styrofoam cups and bore the waitress with dumb-blonde jokes. We could go do naked push-ups on the hoods of their police cars, and they'd never see us.'

That set Oscar off snickering again. I started to grin myself, picturing the naked push-ups. I'd only been busted for little stuff, shoplifting, vandalism, but my mom said next time I got myself in jail she was gonna leave me there. The cops put me on edge, but I couldn't back out now. With Oscar here, that'd be worse than jumping in the ditch.

'All right,' I said. 'Let's go.'

T.J. was a model of stealth as he moved, not too quickly, from the Dumpster to the dry cleaner's. I followed in too much of a rush and almost ran him over. Oscar strutted along after us like he was in a parade.

'You all are funny,' he said, not bothering to whisper. 'All this Mission Impossible shit. Ain't no one around to see us.'

As he stepped grandly up to where T.J. and I were waiting behind the dry cleaner's, a car door slammed shut over in the restaurant parking lot. Oscar dropped and spun like it was gunfire.

We all froze for a moment. A car engine started, and then an old Cadillac lit up. It crunched its way out onto Route 20 and away into the rain. Oscar looked at us, managed a grin.

'Yeah, you cool,' I said.

T.J. was already at the far side of the dry cleaner's, eyeing the last thirty yards to Jack's.

'Bad news is, we're just gonna have to run it,' T.J. said, studying the terrain without looking at us. 'The good news, though, is the building'll shield us from Donutland. The door is on this side of the place, down some stairs. Once we make it to the stairs, we clear. No one'll see us down there. Ready?'

Maybe he was still afraid I was going to back out, because he didn't give me a chance to answer. He was moving again, like a ghost swooping through the night. I cleared my mind, trying not to think as I took long strides across the cracked asphalt, like not thinking made me invisible or something. I stepped over a curb where trash was drifted like snow and into Jack's parking lot. The glass in the gravel glittered like gems. It felt like walking on the beach. Then I was in the shadow of the building, against a wall of black cinder blocks. The only windows were higher than I could see in, little things covered by metal grilles that looked painted over. I followed the wall, my hand against the cool cinder blocks, until the stairwell opened before me. Only five steps down. T.J. was there at the bottom, waiting. I turned around, my eyes at ground level now, looking back the way we'd come, across the jeweled sea. A car in the restaurant parking lot had its lights on, but it was too far to make out anyone in the rain. Oscar piled into the stairwell behind us. We shifted around, making room, crunching dried leaves and trash underfoot.

'Get out my way,' T.J. whispered.

He pressed up close to the door, and a little spot of light appeared, his hand wrapped around the lens of one of those little penlights, so only a tiny amount of light escaped. I could make out a bunch of graffiti on the door, weird symbols painted in red. I thought I knew all of the gang tags, but I didn't recognize any of these. T.J. played the tiny spot of light over where a padlock hung in a heavy steel hasp screwed to the door and the frame.

'Amateurs,' T.J. muttered. The light disappeared for a few seconds, then reappeared as he fitted the screwdriver head of his multitool into one of the screw heads. 'S'posed to hang these so the screw heads're covered.'

'Come on,' Oscar said. 'There's people over in the Athens parking lot. I think they looking this way.'

T.J. got the hasp detached from the doorframe and let it hang, the padlock still closed and holding it together. He crouched down and started working on the keyhole.

'Relax,' I told Oscar. 'You don't think Kenroy Washington got better things to do than wander around out in the rain looking for your sorry ass?'

'Eightball Rodriquez said Kenroy put his knee through the window of a parked car when he found out Gilda's pregnant. Ain't no fucking rain gonna keep him off me.'

The little metal scratching noises from T.J. working on the lock stopped.

'Whoa,' I said, holding my hands up. 'You got Kenroy Washington's sister pregnant?'

He glanced at us, then turned back to keeping lookout. 'I told you that.'

'Fuck you did. You said you got friendly in a photo booth. Shit, you one dead motherfucker.'

T.J. snickered, getting back to work.

'Fuck you,' Oscar said. 'That bitch probably screwed more guys than any hooker on Ninth Avenue. She just saying I'm the daddy 'cause she obsessed with me. Want me to marry her and shit.'

I had to laugh, but it might have been true. Oscar had that effect on women.

'So why don't you just marry her then?' I asked. 'Gilda Washington is hot.'

'Won't be in a few months, when she's the size of a garbage truck. Fuck that. I'm only seventeen years old. I got plans. I'm going into the army next year. No screaming kid is messing that up.'

The door swung inward with a groan of resisting hinges. T.J. stood, replacing tools inside his jacket, the light off. A dry, musty smell like old magazines wafted out and mixed with the rain.

'Get inside,' T.J. said.

I didn't move.

Oscar said what I was thinking: 'It's pitch black in there, man. Turn the light on.'

'Not till we get in,' T.J. said. 'I don't want anyone seeing the light.'

We stood there a few more seconds, the light rain falling, wet tires humming by on Route 20. I couldn't hear anything inside the cinder-block building. Like a mausoleum, I thought, so still.

'Shit,' T.J. muttered, and he went in. No light shone at all inside, nothing reflecting through the open door.

I looked at Oscar. I guess what was inside couldn't be any scarier than Kenroy Washington, because after another second, he went in, careful, a little bit at a time, like he was easing into cold water. That was it then. I had to do it. I took it slow like Oscar.

A few steps in, I started to go to the side, feeling for a wall. My shoes squished, and my feet seemed colder in here, numb, like a couple of dead fish. A groan from behind made me spin around. The rectangle of shadow that showed against the rest of the blackness shrank and vanished as the door swung closed. The fresh, rainy air cut off like a switch had been thrown, and the dry, dusty smell clogged my nostrils. None of the sounds of Route 20 made it in here.

T.J.'s light sprang on. For a little thing, the light seemed harsh and made me squint. We were in a small room with paneling walls, like we got in the basement rec room, dusty cement floor. Only other way out was through a doorway covered with a black curtain. Some newspaper ads were taped up on the wall, the paper faded brown, advertising Jack's Shack. We pressed in close to check them out, T.J. hitting them with the penlight. They were just faces and names: Tiffany Pink, Cherie LaFemme, Lili White, the Silk Sisters. The photos cut off at their bare shoulders, but my imagination took in what skin it could see, the pursed lips and big hair and hooded eyes. It put me in mind of the rest, what I couldn't see. As I continued to study them, Oscar pulled away laughing.

'Big fucking deal. Old newspapers. You really want to get off, you come down to my grandma's basement. She got all the old newspapers you can handle.'

'Shut up,' T.J. said, pulling away—with the light, so I couldn't see any more either.

'You pathetic,' Oscar told him, making a jacking-off motion with his fist. 'You can see more skin than that on the beach any day.'

I didn't say anything, but I knew this was different. Eyeballing girls on the beach was one thing, but these women . . . . They had power and mysteries. You looked in their eyes and you knew, they would show you a lot more than you'd ever see on any damn beach. They had it and they were willing to show it, and they knew how that made me feel. They knew, and that made all the difference in the world.

T.J. headed for the black curtain, and I hurried after, eager to see what else we might find. He went through first, Oscar and me right behind him. The curtain looked heavy but it wasn't. Some kind of fake velvet, thick with dust. It stuck to my skin where it was still wet from the rain, and I had a moment of panic, like it wasn't going to let go, sticking to me all over, me breathing in the heavy dust. Then I pushed through, Oscar beside me. We watched as T.J. played the beam of the penlight around the place.

It was bigger than I expected, the stage only a foot or two high, with a runway that jutted out like a pier into the middle of the room. Tables pressed to walls, chairs stacked on top, leaving a big open space in the middle. It was so still, like time didn't pass in here. It made me think of something I'd seen on TV, guys entering a tomb in Egypt that had been sealed and forgotten for thousands of years. The three of us wandered, silent. I headed for the long bar on the far side of the room while T.J. checked out a couple doors at the back of the place. Oscar jumped up on stage, goofing around.

The little bit of light T.J. carried at the back of the room was enough for me to make out the bar, see there wasn't anything behind it, the shelves empty, the mirror so dusty it didn't even reflect the flashlight. I made my way out from behind it as T.J. was coming up.

'Anything?' he said.

I shook my head. 'You?'

'Just bathrooms.'

Low lights came on. Music started to play, techno, a lot of drums and heavy bass playing slow and lethal, jungle music. The lights were set in little pockets in the ceiling and aimed so that they made the stage and runway stand out while making the rest of the place seem darker. The black curtain that stretched across the back of the stage startled to ripple like it was alive. I felt a spike of panic in my chest and bolted for the exit. T.J., he was with me all the way. But as we reached the smaller black curtain that covered the way out, we slowed, looking back. Oscar was still standing on the runway, grinning, moving to the music. The curtain backing the stage still rippled, like maybe a fan was blowing on it.

'He did it,' I said. T.J. looked at me. 'He had to.' I took a couple of steps back toward the stage. 'Oscar,' I called, 'how'd you turn them lights on?'

He just shrugged and kept moving.

Then a woman slipped from behind the curtain, at the center of the stage. Short black dress, spike heels, hair black like it'd been rubbed with coal dust, twisted into one sleek braid draped over her shoulder. Her skin was white as eggshell and looked almost as fragile. She took two steps out on the stage and stopped, arms crossed. She watched Oscar dancing and smiled. He hadn't seen her yet.

T.J. backed for the exit again, but I didn't move, torn. Yeah, part of me was screaming *get the hell out, dumb-ass,* but the rest of me was watching the way her hips swayed with the music, the hem of that short black dress shifting up and back like the surf on the beach.

Oscar turned and finally noticed her. His face bloomed with delight. 'Hey, baby,' he called over the music. 'You liking what you see?'

Her lips moved, but I couldn't catch what she said over the music. I edged closer.

'What you doing in here?' Oscar asked, dancing up the runway toward her. 'We thought this place was closed down.'

'It is,' I heard her say. 'Has been a long time.'

She took a few steps down the runway, until Oscar was only five or six feet away from her. She was still moving with the music, but more watching him. Girls always liked to watch Oscar, I thought.

'So why you here,' Oscar asked, 'dressed so fine?'

'Going to a party,' she said. 'Work.'

Oscar nodded as he danced. 'That's cool. You a . . . exotic dancer?'

She nodded, the braid slithering along her shoulder. 'Very exotic.'

I know it didn't make any sense. If she was going to a party, what was she doing here, where nobody had been for years? But I bought it anyway. I mean, why else would she have been there?

'How about you show us? My friends ain't never seen anything like you before. I'm sure they be real grateful.'

Her smile broadened at the suggestion. 'You first,' she said.

'Ooh, you playful,' Oscar said. 'I like that.'

He grabbed the hem of his shirt and rolled it over his thumbs, pulling it up and up to his chin. Then he hooked it over the back of his head, did some moves. Oscar spent a lot of time on the beach and on the basketball court. His skin was sun-darkened over muscle that looked both smooth and hard. He finished peeling the shirt off and tossed it at my face. I batted it aside.

'So what's your name?' Oscar asked.

'Lili,' the woman said, still watching him, still smiling, arms still crossed.

'Well, Lili,' Oscar said. 'Looks like it's your turn.'

He bowed and backed down the runway, giving her room.

I thought, no way, not even Oscar could get her to . . . But then she gave me a smile and looked off toward where I guessed T.J. was still standing by the exit, and she gave a little laugh I couldn't hear, like she couldn't believe she was doing this. She uncrossed her arms and slid deeper into the music like she was slipping into a bath. She stepped and kicked in those spike heels and I stopped breathing. She didn't move fast, but with a sort of confidence that let you know she knew exactly what she was doing to you. She slinked and spun, her braid whipping behind her. Each move gave me a glimpse higher up her thigh or stretched the fabric of the dress tighter over her ass or jiggled her chest. She knew what she was doing, and she was getting off on it as much as I was, which only made it more sexy.

I missed how she unfastened the dress, but suddenly it was pooled around her spike heels. Without looking in my direction, she kicked it toward me. I caught it, held the silky material clutched in both hands. Its smell, her smell, sultry, sweaty, spicy, made me lightheaded, and I stared at her there in her bra and panties, her hands on her hips as she raised her eyebrows at Oscar, challenging him.

Oscar started to move. He danced for a while, I'm not sure doing exactly what, because I was mostly staring at her, memorizing every detail. She still moved gently, caught up in the tide of the music, and I watched the movement of her body as if hypnotized. Finally, I was distracted by Oscar thrashing around. He had to sit down on the runway to get his shoes off, and then his pants. He sprang back to his feet dressed only in red boxers and held his hands out toward Lili.

My attention snapped back to her, not wanting to miss an instant, aching to see what I wanted to see, which was everything. She strutted toward him, wasting no time, shedding her bra before she'd taken two steps. She stopped a few feet from Oscar and said, 'Take it off—take it *all* off.'

Oscar stared at her chest, his dancing reduced to a vague shifting of his shoulders. After a few seconds, she stepped closer and said, 'Here, let me help.'

She gripped his upper arm, her white fingers kneading the muscle by his shoulder, and his smile deepened, his eyes on the twin nipples bobbing in the air before him, almost touching him, and I was starting to wonder if they were actually going to have sex right up there on stage. I wondered if I would stay to watch and felt a burn of shame, because I knew the answer.

Then the hand squeezing his upper arm yanked downward. The skin came off like a loose sleeve, revealing the naked muscle beneath. She did it as slick as a magician performing a trick. It was impossible, and she made it look easy. Oscar stared at the exposed anatomy of his hand, gleaming red muscle and white tendons. She dropped the empty skin, which lay crumpled on the stage like a discarded glove. 'Take it all off,' she crooned. She repeated the gesture and this time sloughed off the muscle and tendons, like sweeping the last of the melting ice cream off a Popsicle stick. The meat smacked hollowly on the stage. The bare bones of Oscar's arm, still held together by glistening ligaments, dangled at his side.

There was no thinking, no letting it sink in, what I had just seen. My legs were carrying me out of there. My last sight of Oscar was him staring at Lili, his mouth open and not working, as her hands reached out for him again. Then I was turned around, the black curtain rushing over me like nightfall. A little light shone in the entryway as the steel exit door was swinging shut, which was all I needed. I was through the door and starting to take the half dozen steps all at once when I ran into something. For a second, it was like falling through space, tumbling through darkness, touching nothing. Then I hit at the bottom of the stairs, thrashing and scrabbling in the trash to get myself turned over on my hands and knees. As I stood, I saw what had stopped me.

It was T.J. standing there, halfway up the steps. The half dozen figures who blocked his way at the top towered above us like a ring of trees. I was breathing hard, glancing at the steel door, afraid it would open. I climbed up to the third step, against T.J.'s back, to get as far away from the door as I could. That's when I recognized them, Kenroy Washington and his friends.

'That him?' came a rumble of a voice from way up there.

'No,' somebody answered.

I saw who that second person was, Leon Carr. Leon and me grew up together, on the same street. Used to do everything together, till it was time to go to high school. His momma didn't want him going to Eastside, so they moved, over across town so he could go to Kennedy, where I heard he played basketball. I guess he played with Kenroy.

'Where's that piece of shit calls himself Oscar Muñez?' Kenroy rumbled.

'Inside,' I said.

I didn't worry about selling out Oscar. Kenroy couldn't do no worse to him than what Lili had done. I felt the first twinge of guilt for running like I did.

'Show me,' Kenroy said, and he dropped down onto the first step.

There was no way around him, no way to throw myself out of the stairwell without one of his boys grabbing me, and there was no way I was going back in there with Lili pulling the flesh off people's bones. But I had so much fear and panic going on in my head, I couldn't think of what to do, couldn't think of anything to say. I guess T.J. was the same, because he just stood there on the step above me.

Kenroy didn't have the patience for it. He shoved T.J. in the chest with both hands, strong enough to send both of us stumbling to the bottom of the stairs and against the far end of the stairwell. Kenroy came down the stairs, the others right behind him.

'Show me,' he repeated ominously as he stopped on the last stair. He towered over us, dark and massive. I couldn't make out his face, just the silhouette of his big, shaved head. He looked like he could pick us up like kittens.

T.J. and I pushed open the steel door. The music still came from the next room, pulsing through the black curtain like it wasn't there. I listened hard for Oscar, but I didn't hear anything except that music, the bass line thumping along with the pumping of my heart.

T.J. shone his penlight on the curtain, like once he was this close Kenroy would forget all about us and go charging through like a bull. But he shoved us on ahead. I felt bad, because T.J. was first and I was glad it wasn't me.

Back through the curtain, I was expecting to see pieces of Oscar laying around, peeled off and scattered like dirty laundry, maybe just a skeleton with Oscar's face still dancing around up there. But there was no Oscar and no Lili. Nobody but me and T.J., and Kenroy and his boys fanning out behind us and filling the room. I caught Leon's eye, but if he knew me, he didn't show it.

'So where is he?' Kenroy demanded, looking around.

The curtain rippled again, and everybody focused on it.

'Oscar Muñez!' Kenroy called. 'Might as well come out. Get it over with.'

Lili stepped through the part in the curtain, dressed in her bra and panties, slinking toward the end of the runway. It was only then I realized I was still holding her dress balled in my hands, a scrap of midnight scented like heaven. Her eyebrows arched in delicate surprise as she took in the size of the crowd. I started to back away. Something pricked on the back of my neck and I froze. A knife blade rested flat on my shoulder.

'Where's Oscar?' Kenroy asked her, almost politely.

'In back,' she said, poised at the end of the runway, her body moving slightly to the music. 'Recovering.'

'Yo,' Kenroy said, pointing to two of his guys. 'Go back there and make sure he ain't sneaking out.'

The two walked along the side of the runway and then hopped up on the stage. After a few seconds of groping, they found the part in the curtain and slipped back there. The knife blade on my shoulder did not move.

Lili ignored them, moving in the music as if it were a breeze coaxing her into motion.

Kenroy, despite the smoldering anger that had driven him here, was watching her with an interested smile. 'You got something to show us?' he asked.

'If you got something to show me,' she answered, and I felt a cold place in my chest as I remembered her up there with Oscar—*Take it off, take it* all *off*.

She held out a hand to him, but he shook his head. He glanced around, and his eyes landed on me. He nodded his head toward Lili.

'You look like you could use some relaxing,' he said. 'Go on.'

I was paralyzed. Lili smiled at me, and I felt the flesh on my arms crawl as I imagined it slipping off the bones. I didn't move, couldn't think what to do.

The knife blade left my shoulder, and I felt a prick on my neck again, making me step forward. Lili's smile blossomed, as if she was getting the bestest birthday present ever. I was trembling, but I took the next step on my own. I couldn't help staring at the sway of her body. I stepped up on the stage.

She reached for my hand. I jerked it away, and everybody laughed but T.J.

'He afraid of girls,' someone jeered.

Lili gave me a look like she was hurt. I glanced over my shoulder toward the exit. The guy with the knife was grinning at me, his tongue poking through a gap in his front teeth. Leon was behind him, stone-faced. Another guy had the collar of T.J.'s jacket in his fist but was watching me. And Lili.

I felt her touch on my arm, cool, warm, electric, and I spun around, backed up to the edge of the runway like it was a cliff. She fingered the dress I held clutched in both hands. I didn't move. My skin tingled where she had touched me.

'Souvenir?' she said, her voice low, only for me. 'How sweet.'

She continued to dance, slow and meaningful, and moved back, pulling me along by her dress, a connection between us. I couldn't help staring. The movement enthralled me, the play and pull of firm muscle under pale satin skin, the hints and mystery of the scraps covering her secret places. Her scent, breathed in, got in my bloodstream and pumped through me until it felt like I was swimming in the smell of her, raw and fresh and sexy, so sexy it hurt, and I wanted to touch her, to sink my fingers in her soft flesh.

'You can't be real,' I whispered.

'Oh, I'm real.' Her eyes were inches from mine. 'As real as the feelings coursing through you.'

I felt her breath on my cheek like fire and then the sanity-shattering brush of her thigh against my crotch. The music rose, someone spinning the volume knob like a roulette wheel, and I was dimly aware of motion behind Lili, the long black curtain rippling with life again, and more women coming forth, a platinum blonde in pink leather, a black girl in white fur, twins in wisps and scarves like harem girls.

There was something familiar about them: the newspaper ads. They were the girls from the faded clippings in the entryway.

I heard hoots from behind me as the girls danced around out of my sight, shedding skirts and scarves and revealing skin and jiggle.

'Ain't gonna work, Oscar,' Kenroy called, but his baritone had lost its menacing edge.

Lili turned away, smiling at me over her shoulder. One hand twisted behind her and with a quick gesture like she was snapping her fingers, the bra came undone. She bent forward at the waist, her hands moving to cover herself, the braid whipping over her head like the strike of a scorpion.

That's when it hit me, and I had no say in how I acted. The horror filling me went off the scale and the world seemed to go slow motion as I spun away, jumping off the runway and past the guy with the knife, who had his shirt off and the hands of one Silk Twin down his pants, around the murky crowd of writhing flesh and glistening skin, back through the curtain and the steel door and up the stairs into the slap of the rainy night air. I sprinted across the parking lot, my sneaks throwing up glistening handfuls of wet glass and sand, hopped a concrete barricade and shot past the dry cleaner's. I ran full out until I reached the Dumpster behind the Athens Family Restaurant and slid in behind it like it was home base and lay there on the wet asphalt with the decaying trash, gasping, trembling with out-of-control emotions, terror and arousal and what all even I couldn't tell.

What scared me most, what finally made me turn and run, no matter if it got me cut or capped, wasn't how much I was afraid Lili would touch me and unwrap the flesh from my bones like the wrapper off a candy bar. It was how much I *wanted* her to touch me, to feel her fingers digging into my flesh, no matter what the cost or outcome.

Lying there in the rain, my sweat turning icy, the rough asphalt leaving its imprint in my skin, I thought I could still hear the music pounding from

Jack's Shack, feel the brush of Lili's thigh on my crotch, smell the deep, overpowering scent of her in my nostrils. Then I realized I still had her dress in my hand. I *really could* smell her scent, and I froze as if I had found myself holding a venomous snake. The impulse was the same, an urge to throw it the hell away from me, the fear that it was already too late. I rubbed the fabric between my fingers, drank in the smell. I thought, I should drop it in the Dumpster, never think about it again.

Then a figure emerged from the shadows around Jack's. T.J., I hoped, but whoever it was looked too tall. He ran without looking around, bolted across the front of the dry cleaner's and out of my sight. I caught a glimpse of him again when he reached the parking lot of the Athens—Leon. I heard an engine start up a few seconds later and then the scream of tires peeling out of the parking lot. The sound of the engine faded fast.

I lay there clutching the dress for what must have been an hour, until I was sure no one else was coming out. Finally, soaked, I pushed myself to my feet and staggered back into the weeds, back the way we had come. This time I walked right through the dark water rushing through the ditch. This time no one laughed.

* * *

Nobody missed T.J. in the days that followed, but the disappearance of Kenroy Washington and his friends had everyone talking. It got around that he had been looking for Oscar, who had also disappeared, and a lot of wild stories grew out of it. Oscar killed them all and fled, or Kenroy killed Oscar and his buddies took him away to avoid the law, or the bunch of them ran into some high-powered drug deal and all got sunk in Lake Michigan. The police never asked me, and I wasn't talking about it. They may have asked Leon, but I don't know. By the time I saw him again, we had other things on our minds. Didn't come up.

I tried to live and act like nothing was different, hung at the beach during the day, stayed home and watched staticky TV at night, tried not to think about anything.

Three days after that night at Jack's Shack, I had my next date with Anita. I spent a couple hours getting dressed and ready, the radio on, me dancing, watching myself in the mirror. I started to unbutton my shirt with the music, pulled it open, showing the skin underneath, not even thinking about what I was doing until I heard the primal bass beat of the music at Jack's, thought I caught a whiff of a familiar scent. I thought of the black dress, scrunched up under my pillow, felt an urge to go touch it, smell it, rub it on my bare skin.

Instead I turned the music off and hastily buttoned my shirt. Anita would be waiting.

Our date went about the same as last week's, at first—an afternoon movie, walking around Harrison Street, dinner at Burger King, and back to her place to watch TV, her parents out for the evening at their church, downstairs at the old firehouse.

The first I knew anything was different was when Anita came back from going to the bathroom wearing a robe. She stepped in front of the TV and opened the robe, let it drop. There she stood, nothing on, and said, 'I changed my mind. About The Big Step.'

Last week that was all I was thinking about. Now, all I could do was watch her, like I'd been watching the TV.

She didn't wait for an answer. She strutted up and slid herself on top of me, all hungry lips and groping hands. We kissed. She smelled like soap. Her skin was hot. I touched her lightly, just my fingertips. Her weight pushed me down into the cushions of the old couch. My scalp prickled with the heat. She writhed against me, but the pressure didn't feel sexy. It felt stifling. I struggled to breathe against her weight on my chest, her mouth on mine, my nostrils whistling and not getting enough air. Below my waist all I felt was the weight of her, crushing. The urgency of last week was gone, gone like Oscar and T.J. and the rest. All I could think of was Lili, the coolness of her touch, the promise in her eyes.

I couldn't take it any more. Anita was pawing at my clothes as I started to struggle to get out from under her. She moaned and gripped me tighter. I felt like I was being crushed and drowned, like an anaconda had me wrapped head to toe at the bottom of some murky pool, and I started to thrash with panicked strength, dumping Anita to the floor. She called my name once before I got out of the house, breathing deep breaths of welcome night air. I moved fast, deliberately, my stride steady in time with the bass line pounding in my head.

* * *

That night I slept naked with the dress spread out against me under the sheet.

The next day I started out like usual, headed for the beach in the morning. But I never made it there, just walking, walking. It wasn't just that I didn't want to see Anita. I didn't know what I *did* want. I wandered home around lunchtime and dropped on the old couch Mom kept on the porch in the summer. The afternoon passed. I thought about Anita, thought about T.J.

Thought about Lili.

As the sun was going down and the world turning gray, a long shadow stretched up the sidewalk. I watched it slither along the cooling cement until the figure casting it appeared on the sidewalk and stopped in front of the porch. I looked up at Leon standing there, hands in the pockets of his jacket, as stone-faced as he had been the other night. He looked around the old neighborhood, squinting a little into the growing shadows. Then he looked at me.

'I'm going to Jack's Shack,' he said. 'Want to come with?'

Without thinking about it, I said, 'Yeah.'

A LANDING FROM THE ROADSTEAD OF NEMOURS
Pierre Louys

MONSIEUR WALTER H—, whose name is too well known to-day to be written in full, was once my friend for twenty-four hours, on a day when both of us nearly died.

We had each embarked, without knowing one another, on an Atlantic coaster, the *Ville de Barcelone*, serving the ports which lie between the white city of Tangiers, Gibraltar, and Oran. There was storm everywhere. The Spanish papers we had bought at Malaga contained accounts of the loss of the finest cruiser of the fleet, the *Reina-Regente*, which had gone down in those latitudes at the base of a waterspout with four hundred and fifty-five officers and men. I can still see the newspapers with their funereal aspect and their immense lists of dead, filling the black-bordered front page, from the admiral in command down to the scourers of the ship's wells.

We sailed the same clay, in the midst of a false lull, which did not last half an hour. As soon as the vessel had cleared the dark green edge of the open sea, it leaped and plunged, leaped again, still higher, rolled on to its right side, and shuddered from end to end under the bursting of the hurricane like a little frightened bird.

A wave passed over the ship and broke with its whole weight upon the decks. Another washed the vessel from stem to stern, then came another, then a hundred others. All night we heard the crash of the heavy billows on the bridge, and the groaning of its planks. Sometimes we were tossed up on the crest of a sea like an eggshell in the spray of a fountain, and then the screw emerged and raced in the air with a harsh hissing sound like that of a siren in the midst of the gale. At moments, between two minutes of deafening uproar, we passed through silences so deep that we thought we had already foundered. Incomparable hours they were, of grandeur and of tragic beauty.

The next morning, when I went up on to the bridge at the end of the storm, a tall dark-skinned Moroccan, enveloped in a white burnous whose folds fluttered in the breeze, approached the captain.

'When we come Melilla?' said he.

'Melilla?' returned the master. 'Not for some time yet, my friend. In a fortnight. Next voyage.'

'What you say, a fortnight? I go Melilla to-day.'

'Yes. Well, you will have to go from Nemours. We made a straight run past Melilla. I should have sunk my ship if I had put in last night with the weather we had.'

The Arab gnashed his teeth in a fury. He growled out a 'Jekrab beitak,' in which all his anger snarled for expression: then he walked off along the bridge, gripping the nettings and gazing darkly at the coast of his native land, which shut in the eastern horizon.

* * *

The dining-saloon, when I opened the door, was empty, or nearly so. Two other passengers, out of the fifty on hoard, had been able to leave their cabins. The first was a lady and an intrepid traveller, the aged Marquise de S—, the mother of a French deputy whom Monsieur Jaures was already attacking. The second was Monsieur Walter H—. The latter addressed me with the cheerful good humour which follows bad nights at sea and resembles a smile of convalescence. 'I have just spent five years in Morocco,' he told me. 'And I am going to Persia by way of Marseille, Constantinople, and Batoum Tell me, do you like the Arabs?'

After this opening we were at once in sympathy.

Walter H— was at that time twenty-nine years old. His face was tanned by the African sun and closely shaved in the Oxford fashion, but it was French enough in outline and expression. He had been over all the roads in Morocco, and even some way into the Sahara. He spoke Arabic so perfectly that one day in the suburbs of Oran I saw him surrounded by natives, who took him for a Mussulman dressed as a European. 'Ah,' said he, 'you will only know the real Arabs when you get right down to the country between

Fez and Marrakech, below the Djebel Aiachin. (a mountain) Everywhere else the Arab, as a Turkish, French, or English subject, has already lost, with his independence, the nobility of his character. The most important sections of the race, merchants of Tripoli, Tunisians grown tame and clothed in their bluish silks, officials or respectable property owners of Algiers, they are all slaves under the yoke of Europe; and around them there swarms the poverty-stricken and cowed populace which would no doubt revolt if an opportunity arose, but meanwhile is content to beg.'

'While in Morocco itself—'

'O there! There you have an ancient race which has never been enslaved since the beginning of the world. I believe that is unique in the history of mankind. Eight millions of free men still survive there, sons of the great conquerors who once galloped in a single raid from the Indian seas to the basin of the Loire and established themselves almost in the very positions where they halted. They are the ancient Saracens! You must go and see them; they are superb!'

Meanwhile the vessel had cast anchor in a roadstead whose lines composed a harmonious pattern: the village of Nemours lay along the Mediterranean seaboard; Nemours, the only spot in Moroccan territory under the French flag, the only valley which Marshal Bugeaud could get the Sultan to cede, after the victory of Isly.

We stepped down into a boat, which was to put us ashore. The discontented Moroccan whom I had caught sight of on the bridge followed us and seated himself on the central thwart.

I looked him over; he had let the white cowl of his burnous fall back, and his fine head, supported upon an admirable neck, was erect. His features comprised every detail which is consid ered necessary for nobility of expression. A conscious majesty radiated from his brows and cast its shadow upon his black eyes. His thin lips and the formation of his nostrils bore witness to the purity of his lineage.

Walter H— got him to talk. His name was Ed Hadji Omar ben Abd-el-Nebi, caid of Sidi-Mallouk. On former occasions, returning from Tangiers, he had reached the home of his tribe by way of the port of Melilla, the foot paths of the Riff, and the banks of the river; but being prevented from following his usual route, he was now in some anxiety about the road from Nemours to Lalla-Marnia, for the powerful tribe of Oudjda was unfriendly to his own people.

I pointed to a pair of pistols which stuck out of his yellow sash, and observed: 'You are armed.'

He made a disdainful grimace and shrugged his shoulders.

'Crackers,' he muttered.

At that moment we reached the shore.

Then, when we were all three on solid ground and walking through the flowery valley ascending from the village, El Hadji Omar undid a fold on his white mantle, grasped with caution, almost with respect, the cutlass lying concealed along his thigh, and held it out horizontally.

'There is a weapon for you,' said he.

The cutlass was two-thirds of the length of a man's arm. The hilt was short but substantial, and gave a good grip; the guard was simply a strip of copper over the butt. The colour of the blade appeared a very dark blue laced with the gold ornaments of its delicate damascening, and quite plain at its cutting edge.

El Hadji Omar tested it with his thumb and first finger. His hand ran down as far as the keen point and rounded it with a swift skimming movement as if passing over a flame.

'With this,' he added, 'my brother killed a man and a woman with a single blow. With a single blow of the hand. It's a good bit of steel.'

A man and a woman? We wanted to hear the story. The Moroccan hesitated. At last he allowed himself to be persuaded.

We sat down on a green sloping bank in a corner of the valley, where the earth was covered with flowers. Vegetation of prodigious luxuriance invaded it from the sides of the mountain: of myrtle, mastic, and tree-briar surrounded jujube-trees covered with spring foliage. Tamarisk and hare's-ear mingled on the bank of a rapid streamlet where oleanders swayed to and fro.

And this was the tale we heard in that valley paradise.

* * *

El Hadji Omar had had a brother, Mahmoud ben Adb-el. Nebi, who had preceded hire as caid of Sidi-Mallouk.

Mahmoud had already married three wives, and he had long dismissed any idea of further nuptial unions when he met a strolling waif of a girl, and all of a sudden fell madly in love with her.

Her name was Djouhera. Djouhera is a word which means 'the Pearl.' She came from the plains of Tunisia, and wore the costume of her native village: a simple tunic of red, slit open on the right side, and exposing the breast where the drapery falls away. She was a shepherd's daughter, that is if her mother's story were true, for nothing definite was known about either of them, except that they had the appearance of two unbelieving gipsies. But nothing on earth or in dreams was lovelier than Djouhera.

Accordingly Mahmoud was not mad the day he found this girl by the roadside, but rather cursed with ill-luck; for she was walking with uncovered face so that every one could see her mouth, and was that not enough to bring a man ill-luck? It was quite natural that Mahmoud should carry her off in the first place so as to get possession of her, and should then marry her so as to make her love him, if God willed. But God did not will.

Djouhera gave nothing to Mahmoud but her small unconcerned person. In return she procured everything she wanted, even the divorce of his first wives and the consent of the cadi. She became absolute mistress of her husband and his household.

And when she had no more conquests to make she enlarged the sphere of her ambitions, desired to have other men as well.

Who were, then, her lovers? And who could count them? Never had the wife of a caid led so debauched a life. In the evenings she went up to the terraces, her face uncovered, her robe open, and if a man saw her she smiled instead of taking to flight. The young men of the tribe found one after the other that she always welcomed any one who happened to be on the spot. She used to take the first man she met to a place near a little door at the bottom of her garden under the low spreading branches of a rose-coloured almond-tree, and she was never detected, for she was so prompt to experience the pleasure of her sex that her tenderest assignations only lasted for the period of one embrace.

Now, one evening, in the midst of one of these fits of furtive excitement, Djouhera fell in love.

The shock of it came upon her like a stirring of puberty, all in a moment, to her great astonishment. It was a certain Ahdallah, a lad as poor as she herself had formerly been, one who slept in summer on the ground and in winter in the mosque, who transported her from voluptuous sensation to veritable passion. She eloped with him on horseback.

For days and days Mahmoud searched for some trace of them, but without success, for the girl had set off dressed as a man, and rode as hard as a lion-hunter. Desperate as he was, Mahmoud had definitely decided to forgive her rather than lose her, however disgraced he might be by so doing, for his love had scattered to the void every particle of pride he possessed.

But he did not know that he was to see what he did see.

When, at the end of his pursuit, he entered, at last, the room at the inn where he had discovered that Djouhera was, the lovers were so intoxicated with each other that they did not hear his footsteps. Mahmoud cried out twice, 'Djouhera! Djouhera!' then, without knowing what he was doing, stabbed with a single thrust the young man, the woman beneath him, and the floor below.

The man expired instantly. Djouhera uttered a cry which, though faint, was yet long as a cry of ecstasy. She opened her dying eyes wide, turned her head, and murmured:

'O Mahmoud, God sendeth thee . . . I prayed God to let me die in the midst of happiness. 'Tis He who hath armed thy hand . . . O God, how lovely a night is this my last . . . Thos Mahmoud, thou shalt die in pain, in old age and sickness . . . And I, pass away in a swoon of bliss . . . Take thou my blessing, Mahmoud; my blessing, Mahmoud; my blessing . . . '

Again and again she repeated, right up to her last breath:

'Take my blessing, Mahmoud; my blessing, blessing . . . '

El Hadji Omar, having finished his story, drew the cutlass for the second time from its sheath. I imagined I saw, indistinctly, reflections of crimson light upon the blade. Then we continued our walk through the long flowered valley. At out feet an Arab urchin was teasing in the dry sand a little black scorpion, furious and convulsed.

HARRIS HOUSE
G. Durant Haire

The institution hunkered atop the hill like a blight upon the landscape, looming over the town of Harrisville like a sentinel of despair, a place of suffering and misery where no one had been treated and cured, only locked, shocked, and medicated into deeper psychosis or death. For over one hundred years the solemn structure absorbed the violence and suffering of those within, every brick, every tile, bloated with anguish, pregnant with agony, ready to give birth.

* * *

'It's perfect!' Heather said, as Luke wheeled the Taurus into the drive.

'It looks a little neglected.' Luke shut off the ignition and sat staring at the house: An old Colonial in desperate need of maintenance. The white paint hung loosely from the siding like the bark of the gnarled birch that centered the front lawn. The roof was in no better condition, its once black surface now gray with rot. The boxwoods were choked with weeds and the front walk, hardly discernable from the lawn.

Heather opened the door. 'Just cosmetics. The structure is sound, they built them better back then, you know that.'

Heather strolled around to the back while Luke stepped into the front yard to survey just how much work this [perfect] house would take.

As Luke pondered the intelligence of buying this house, the realtor drove up.

'Hi, I'm Tom Barnwell. You must be Luke.'

'Yes,' Luke said, extending his hand, 'Heather's around here some . . . '

'Hi Tom!' Heather beamed as she came around the corner of the house.

'I love it!' She said, as Luke shot her a look, the look one gives a misbehaving child.

'Great, shall we go inside?' Tom replied.

The house reeked of mothballs and dust. Luke found the smell stifling, and immediately his head began to throb. The odor reminded him of his grandparent's house. That stale, ancient smell that permeated everything, including his grandparents. The smell conjured nostalgia of the days he'd been left with his father's parents, deserted for weekends, and several weeks during the year, left to that smell and his grandfather's hacking cough. Already he didn't like this house.

Tom gave a tour, pointing out the finer points of the house, something he had to work to find. He suggested the potential of this room and that, and Heather gleefully agreed with him at every occasion. Luke tagged along trying to look interested and fighting back a burning headache. His condition worsening as they proceeded, each step adding to the cloud of dust.

The tour ended; grateful, Tom and Heather stood in the kitchen discussing remodeling, while Luke pushed through the screen door out onto the porch, desperate for fresh air. He drew his handkerchief and was about to try and clear his burning sinuses, when he noticed a large building squatting atop a hill directly behind the house.

'Luke, honey, you okay?' Heather said, as she stepped off the porch followed by Tom.

'I'm fine . . . Hey Tom, what is that?' Luke pointed to the top of the hill.

'That's Harris House. It was built around 1894 as a place for the state to hide their worst mental cases, but it's nothing now, just vacant. I think there's some plan to turn it into some kind of museum or something. State won't demolish it because of historical significance I believe. I know it's a bit unsightly, but you could plant several fast growing evergreens back here, and you'd never even see it.'

'That's not a problem, ' Heather chimed, 'it's not like it's right here in the back yard. I agree with Tom, a few evergreens and we'll never see it.'

Luke stared at the decrepit structure. Something didn't feel right about the place. It gave off bad vibes. He shrugged it off. 'Yeah, I guess you're right. We'd never see it.'

* * *

'Well, what do you think? It's got a lot of potential doesn't it?'

'I don't know, Heather,' Luke said sitting his glass of tea on the checked tablecloth. 'You're going to think I'm crazy when I say this, but something just doesn't feel right about the place.'

Heather frowned and cocked her head to the side. 'What are you talking about? I mean, sure, it needs lots of work, but that's why the price is right.'

'No, that's not what I'm talking about. I've just got a bad feeling about it. My gut is telling me it's not the thing to do.'

'Luke,' Heather said, left eyebrow arching high over her eye, 'you're getting cold feet aren't you. Look. You agreed to this move. We talked about this. You promised me you had no problem with it. I thought you wanted to get away, have less distraction so you could concentrate on your programming.'

'No, that's not it. I'm all for the move, it's . . . I don't know. I can't explain it. Maybe you're right. Maybe I am a little apprehensive.'

'I'm sure that's all it is. And I understand. This is a big step for both of us. But it's going to be great. Just give it a chance. I'm excited about my position at the school. And you'll be able to focus on your business, grow your business. I need to know that you're with me on this.'

Luke wiped his mouth and reached for his wallet. 'You know I'm with you honey, I just . . . It'll just take some time for me to adjust.'

Luke paid the bill and they left the diner. The sun shone brightly, reflecting off windshields and hoods. Dogwoods radiated white and pink, birds sang frantically and bees swarmed the holly bushes that lined the parking lot. He drew a deep breath of fresh air, and almost smiled, when he saw it again. It loomed on the hilltop and, it seemed, could be seen from anywhere in town. Harris House. Somehow the sun didn't shine there, even though there wasn't a cloud in the sky. The building seemed to devour the light, and he noticed now, cast an unwelcome shadow over their future home.

* * *

Closing on the house had gone smoothly and quickly to Luke's surprise and Heather's delight. A definite change from the last house they'd bought. They rented a large moving van and made the move in one trip. It was six hours from Greenville to Harrisville; although, Luke didn't look forward to unloading the van, he was thankful when they arrived, Heather had worn out his ear discussing her plans for their new home. They arrived around

2:00 p.m. and immediately began the thankless task of unloading the van. They worked diligently for three hours, managing to get their bed and all of the heavy items in the house. They both needed a break and Heather decided to go get dinner.

Luke carried a box inside and sat it on the overcrowded kitchen table. He grabbed a bottled water from the cooler and went out onto the back porch. He looked up at Harris House; tried to imagine what suffering and anguish the institution had absorbed, what stories floated, trapped within those sullen walls, collecting like dust. As he stared, the singular feeling of unease he'd initially had about the place crept back upon him. The house seemed to glower down at him and his imagination crept into motion. The windows were now eyes sutured with rusty bars to keep the light out. The front gate, a mouth cage, to prevent the malignancy from infecting others.

The thud of Heather closing the car door brought Luke out of his daydream. An unwelcome shiver spiked through his body. He'd grown cold in the shadow of Harris House.

* * *

Two nights later, Luke heard the voices. They came in his dreams, slithering down from the dead building, traveling in the pale shadow of the moon, settling in his mind, infecting his subconscious, awakening him to the darkness within his own mind.

He stood just inside the decrepit gates of Harris House, an icy wind howled around him, carrying the sounds of voices, beckoning Luke in. Then he found himself floating to the front door, trapped in smothering blackness, unable to move yet moving. Closer to the house he came. The house now shuddering, moving yet not collapsing. Becoming as rubber, its windows now mad eyes, the sallow light emanating like a sickness from within. The doors twisted from vertical to horizontal and flew open like the giant maw of some hideous beast. Luke felt himself drowning in the black tar of the dream but powerless to respond. Through the doors he floated, a hot foul wind bringing him closer to the muttering. The stench of urine and excrement invaded his nostrils and he proceeded down a throat-like hallway, stopping before a door at the hall's end. The voices had increased in volume and he could discern sobbing and wailing amid shouts of command. He then passed through the door like one passes through a waterfall into the unseen cave beyond. The next instant he was falling, and his sleeping body jerked helplessly as his subconscious plummeted through dream space.

Now he found himself in the depths of a nauseous dungeon. The stagnant air filled with screams and shouts, with the stench of urine and blood. Inmates were chained to the walls enduring all types of torture. Administering the brutality were hideous caricatures of white-coated doctors with electrodes and machetes, broad-chested guards wielding cattle prods and rattlesnakes, even a few nurses with foot long syringes mutated into huge plastic mosquitoes, their steely proboscises probing for blood. Luke continued on, taking in the terrors like a captive in a sickening carnival ride. Then he saw Heather. She lay writhing, face contorted, mouth gaped wide with screams, yet making no sound. A man worked over her, inserting small cocoons into her rectum and bouncing with glee as they reappeared, bursting through her flesh as razorblade butterflies. Enthralled in bloodlust the man spun and Luke gazed helplessly into his own eyes.

Luke exploded into consciousness like a bullet from a gun, nearly coming off the bed. His heart thundered and his head pulsed pain in flashes behind his eyes. He looked at Heather, peacefully, blissfully sleeping and nearly vomited. He looked at the lovely form of his wife and knew he was going to kill her.

* * *

The next few weeks were hard for Luke. He found it exceedingly difficult to concentrate on his work. He fell behind on his current programming job, and risked losing the company's business. Instead of writing code, he wound up on the back porch staring at Harris House. He had nightmares almost every night, and when he was awake he could hear the vile voices chattering away in his head, each day increasing in volume. Heather, the woman he loved, would come home to a sullen and reticent husband. Luke saw what he was doing, how it affected Heather, but couldn't stop. Heather grew more distraught by the day.

* * *

'Luke, honey, what's wrong? I'm worried about you. I need you to talk to me.'

Luke lay in the bed facing away from his wife, nearly in tears. He hadn't had a good night's sleep in weeks. Every night, what should be peaceful rest, was interrupted by nightmare voices, by images of that insidious building on the hill and the phantoms within, beckoning him toward insanity. Luke's head throbbed, his mind reeled, his feelings for Heather turning sour.

'Luke, please. I don't understand what's happened to you. A month ago you where the person I married, now, now . . . I just don't understand.' Heather dropped her head as tears streamed down her cheeks. 'What have I done to deserve this?'

'And I don't understand why you can't understand. I haven't been sleeping well; I haven't been able to concentrate on my work. I need some time and space. What I don't need is you acting like a damn child. I'm stressed out enough as it is. I need some time to get myself together, and you're not helping with your crying and moaning. What you need to do is leave me alone.'

'Leave you alone?' Heather felt stabbed, and she began to sob. 'I don't understand why you're doing this.'

Luke couldn't believe what he'd just said. He hadn't meant for it to come out that way. That's not what he wanted to say. And now he found himself growing tired of Heather's pathetic crying, he wished she would shut up. He would make her shut up. No! No! That's not what he felt, not what he thought. Luke heard the whispering of voices somewhere deep in his head. Like an insect he could hear but not find, the sound pushed him towards madness. He wanted to choke her, stop the damn sobbing, he thought the chef's knife in the kitchen would feel good in his hand, and better ripping through his wife, spilling her pathetic guts on the floor. Luke snapped back, dear God, what was happening to him. He had to stop it, to get out of the house and away from Heather.

Luke jumped from the bed and threw on his clothes. He grabbed the car keys from the dresser and looked at Heather. She sat against the headboard, knees drawn up, face down, sobbing terribly. He wanted to say something, but knew it would come out wrong. If he got through this he'd try and explain it to her. Right now, he had to get away. He was terrified of what he might do.

Luke ran outside and jumped into the car. He didn't know where he was going; he just had to get away. He flung the car out of the drive and fled down the highway. As he drove his mind clouded, he could hear the muttering, the voices of Harris House, infecting him. He pushed the throttle down, trying to accelerate away from this madness, fighting for his sanity. The trees thinned along the road and moonlight spilled into the car. He glanced out the window and saw it. Sitting atop that hill, like a profane god on its altar. Lightning flashed behind his eyes. Pain erupted in his head. Voices rattled in his mind.

He jerked the car left onto another road. It didn't matter what road—any would do as long as it led away from that abomination on the hill. He drove for what seemed like an hour, when he came to the stop sign; he couldn't remember any of it. The pain was almost unbearable now, the voices scream-ing through his mind, clouding his reasoning. When he looked up, there sat Harris House, grinning in the moonlight.

As he sat zombie-like in the car, the stored hatred from that awful place infecting his mind, he could see himself going home, into the kitchen where Heather sat nursing a cup of coffee, waiting on him, preparing for a tedious, sleepless night of confrontation. He walked right past her without saying a word and opened the drawer beside the sink. He turned, brandishing the chef's knife, a rictus of insanity curling on his face. Heather's eyes ballooned as he rushed across the kitchen and plunged the knife into her stomach. She doubled over, gasping in disbelief, as he retracted the knife and plunged it into her back, over and over, ten times, twenty times. Heather fell to the floor, rasping and gurgling, swimming on the cold tile floor, trying to pull herself away. Luke stepped over her, yanked her head up, and slit her throat. Hot blood rushed out of her nearly severed neck and washed over the floor. Her head made a dull splat as he dropped it into the blood.

Luke screamed himself back to reality, denying the horrible vision with his entire being. Without further consideration, fueled by his love for Heather, he stomped the accelerator, and somehow maintained control of the car until he found a suitable tree.

'I love you Heather, forgive me' he said, just before he hit the windshield and the front of the car wrapped around the huge poplar.

* * *

The Taurus sat hissing and spewing, the smell of gas and anti-freeze per-meating the car. Luke slowly regained consciousness. He felt the pain in his body and knew he wasn't dead. But he felt different. Aside from his bruised body, he felt good. His mind was clear for the first time in weeks. Luke forced the crumpled door open and stepped out a new man. The voices once senseless and disturbing were now a reassuring force of direction. He smiled as he wiped the blood from his forehead, soon there would be much more blood. So much blood. But not his. He turned and walked towards his house, the pale shadow of Harris House blanketing him in its welcome em-brace.

ALTERNATIVE NIGHT
Charlie Williams

I was sitting in the living room, remote control in hand, watching mind-numbingly local news on the TV. It was not what I wanted to be doing. I wanted to be upstairs, sitting at my desk, surrounded by books, scribbling intelligent notes, nodding sagely as my mind absorbed difficult ideas. Learning. I wanted to be a successful student: to get a first, think about doing a PhD, turn down several job offers, go on to great things. But it wasn't going to happen. Not with me being the way I was. I flicked to a nameless soap. Maybe a sitcom.

'Fancy driving tonight?' It was Simon. He was sitting on the other couch sharpening his ornamental bowie knife.

'Driving where?' I said.

He got up and walked to the kitchen. 'Bentley's. Half an hour. You wanna get a move on.'

I shouted back: 'I'm not coming.'

He came back into the living room with two cans of beer. He opened one, sending little droplets through the smoky air, and passed it to me. Condensation trickled down the cold sides onto my fingers. Simon sat down on the other couch and gulped noisily from his can. Gasping for breath, he said: 'Neck these and I'll get another couple. We'll get a cab.'

I looked at my can for a while, listening to Simon drinking and belching, thinking. The books upstairs were no longer an issue. They had ceased to exist as soon as I had heard the sharp hiss of a ring being pulled. It was a more delicate matter that was bothering me, something that had been putting a downer on things since the beginning of term. 'Who's coming?' I asked.

Simon raised his dense eyebrows, too lazy to shrug. 'Dunno. The lads,' he managed to say between belches.

'Richey? Jon? Roger?'

Simon watched the screen for a while, breathing loudly through his mouth. I drank steadily during this time. 'You're not still pissed off at Roger, are you?' he said finally.

I winced, hid my mouth behind the near-empty can. 'No, course not.'

Simon went back into the kitchen for more beer.

By half seven Richey and Jon had joined us. I was beginning to relax, the beer massaging those tense muscles, ironing out knots, doing its job. The taxi was due any minute. Perhaps going out wasn't such a bad idea, I was beginning to think. We were only a couple of weeks into the second year after all. I could still get that first class degree if I buckled down later. Tomorrow, maybe. More significantly, Simon's comment was making me reassess the Roger situation. There had been enough tension, enough display of indifference on my part, enough cautious friendliness on his. Maybe it was time to let it drop. And besides, he hadn't arrived, and the chances of him showing up were getting smaller by the minute.

I could guess what he would be doing instead. He would be holed up in her room, the rest of the world forgotten. No words. No thoughts. No time. Just the moment, and what sensations filled it.

Hatred surged in my belly. It wasn't good, I knew that. He used to be my best friend and . . . Well, the past is the past.

I turned my attention to the others in an attempt to calm down. They were arguing about Simon's knife. Richey suggested that it was named after David Bowie. Jon thought Simon was weird for having it. Simon just waggled his eyebrows. The blade flashed as he turned it, sucking in every source of light. It was a beautiful knife, I thought, watching it. But completely redundant. Simon was a soft city boy. A knife like that needed to be used.

A car beeped outside. We drank up and got up. Simon put the knife in his room. The other two went outside, still arguing. I shuffled along behind them. I knew I had forgotten something, but couldn't quite . . . My wallet. 'Wait for me!' I shouted, and ran upstairs.

After a haphazard search, which let me know just how drunk I was getting, I found it. It was on the windowsill in my room, where I had spent the previous night staring across the bay. I ran downstairs, feeling more in the mood with every thudding footfall. I couldn't wait to get out there and amongst them. I ran out of the door and slammed it, expecting to see my three friends sitting in the back of the cab, the front seat left vacant for me. But the taxi was gone. They were gone.

'Hey,' said Roger. 'You ready?' He spoke with the same uncertainty that had marked our every exchange since . . . since he and Carly . . .

Carly also said hello. I couldn't look at her. She was holding his hand limply, unconvincingly. They stood by the kerb and watched me.

I casually turned away. 'Guys,' I said, blushing, hating life. I had seen the two of them together a few times since term had begun. But only in crowded bars, where I could walk away and brood. I stood on the pavement and looked at my car, for want of something better to look at. There was a lot of rust on the body, the hood in particular. It seemed as though some great hand had sprinkled mysterious brown dust over it.

'The others went ahead,' Roger was saying behind me. 'Not enough room. Another cab's coming.'

'Right, OK.' I could smell her perfume. Was that the same stuff that I had bought her? How could she do that? 'Oh, I think I forgot something,' I said, and ran back inside. What else could I do? I waited in Simon's room at the front of the house, peering out at them from the shadows, seeing how they were together. The cab arrived. I composed myself and went back outside.

The driver gestured at the seat beside him. I climbed in, suppressing my unease. The other two got in behind me. The driver smelt of smoke, as if he had just walked out of a burning house. He looked familiar. The sort of familiar that you know you'll never put your finger on. But his head was swathed in shadow. Murmurs reached my ears from the back seat as we sped out of town. My back was stiff, hands grasping tense legs. I wanted the journey to be over.

I could feel their eyes on me, and the thoughts behind them. They were trying to think of something to say to me, something to break the tension. They were thinking what a miserable fuck I was, silent and motionless, my back rigid. Of course, it was mainly Roger who was thinking this. I looked out of the window. We were on the coastal road up to Mumbles. The tide was out. Wet sand glistened under a low moon.

She giggled. I knew what that meant. He would be tickling the inside of her thigh. And why not? Life was for living. Why worry about hurting the feelings of an obstacle like me? I had had my weeks of grace, my opportunities to move on with dignity. I had chosen, for whatever reason, not to exercise my right to have it out with him or her; to punch his face, to call her a whore. These things were just gestures, the protocol of messy break-ups. They achieved nothing. She giggled again. I caught a whispered 'Stop it.' I turned again to the window, if only to demonstrate that I was not a statue. The sunset was over already. I saw stars coming into bud, gaining strength as the sky blackened. I felt my mind blackening with it, colour and light seeping out until only dark thoughts remained. The smack of wet lips behind me, a little involuntary moan of passion. I imagined myself out there, beyond the lighthouse, on one of those quiet beaches on the Gower, spilling dark blood on pale sand.

We were coming into Mumbles, slowing down for the roundabout. I could see the White Rose up ahead, where the others would be.

I could walk away in a minute, be rid of them both.

'Just by the pub, mate,' I told the driver. In the rear-view I noticed Roger raise an eyebrow, while Carly's large, brown, worried eyes looked back at me.

The car stopped. I pulled the door lever and climbed out, noticing that Carly made no move to do the same. Typical. I hesitated, then went to open it for her. But the car pulled away as my fingertips touched metal. The driver leant over the passenger seat and pulled the door shut, all the while accelerating. There was no traffic in its way. The last image in my head was Roger, through the rear window, throwing his hands up in a big question mark.

I stood at the roadside. My legs were numb. Part of me suspected some sort of joke, a plan of Roger's to break the ice. That was the part of me that needed an explanation. The rest of me still wallowed in dark waters, and accepted what had just happened, had no need for comprehension.

I looked at the pub across the road. There was fun and laughter in there, and the oblivion I sought. I walked stiffly across the road. My legs felt unstable. The tarmac was soft underfoot. There were no cars to worry about. Traffic seemed to have dried up in the previous couple of minutes. The pub greeted me with the warm, noisy illusion of good times that I craved. I slipped into it.

Bentley's was strangely subdued tonight. I guessed the euphoria that accompanies a new academic year had worn off. A sign on the door when we had come in said that it was Alternative Night, but I had been to these things before, and I knew that they were as popular as any other theme evening, if a little stranger. We stood around near the main bar, drinking, smoking, quietly taking the piss out of black-clad strangers. I was trying my best to join in, but my heart was not in it. I kept misunderstanding punch lines and laughing at the wrong moment. To get with the flow, I increased my alcohol consumption.

My body was tired. It was one night too many. I was feeling tense, but I tried to blot that out. I wandered away from the others, just to get my limbs moving. I felt out of place, as if I had wandered into the club in my dressing gown and slippers. The toilets were up ahead so I headed for them, just for a break from the racket and flashing darkness that were beginning to bug me. As I pissed, I wished that I had stayed at home. Why couldn't I just say no? Was I really so weak? I walked back out into the main area, bracing myself against the sensory impact. It was not as bad as I had expected. I was getting used it, I remarked, stumbling against a table.

I carried on drinking, and some time later found myself on the dance-floor, a bottle of beer in my hand. Backs surrounded me on all sides. I seemed to be the only one dancing alone. I didn't care. No one paid me any attention, which was fine. I didn't feel like smiling anyway. I felt like I was bobbing up and down in an ocean, going under now and then, but confident that I could keep it going for some time. I was OK like that and, though not exactly enjoying myself, the night was at least bearable.

My eyes focussed vaguely on something across the floor, an object floating elegantly in the water, rhythmically going in and out of view as the waves powered over the surface. I fixed on it for a while, using it as a point of reference to help me stay upright. It was the smile that brought me out of my trance. She looked at me with unmistakable eyes. Recognition finally kicked in. I smiled back, embarrassed. I hadn't seen Rachel all term. I can't say I had wanted to; she was too tied up in my own painful story.

Embarrassment sobered me up slightly, as if some internal alcohol accountant had struck two pints off the books. My movements slowed. Still she looked at me, still she smiled. The tingle in my groin took me by surprise. I hadn't known that feeling in quite a while. I had never before considered her in this context, being used to seeing her as both my best friend's girl and my girl's best friend. I felt slightly guilty for feeling it, despite the emotional freedom that was now rightfully mine. Then I felt stupid for feeling guilty.

It took two minutes of staring before I noticed that she was dancing with someone. Of course, I thought, what did you expect?

The physical act of dancing suddenly felt futile. As I turned to leave the floor the bottle slipped from my hand. I didn't care, and was prepared to just leave the mess where it was. But the airborne bottle caught my eye. It fell to the floor in slow motion, bounced noiselessly, then came to rest on its base, not a drop spilt. I looked around, scratching my head and feeling stupid. No one else seemed to have noticed. I picked it up, shrugged, and downed the contents.

I managed to get another drink without attracting the attention of anyone I knew, and headed upstairs, planning to lean on the balcony and watch people for a while. It was surprisingly easy to walk around unnoticed. Usually I would know and be known by many of the faces dotted around a club. Everyone went to the same places and, eventually, you got to know who was who. But tonight was different. I guessed that this was just down to the fact that it was Alternative Night, which was not my usual territory.

I reached the balcony and picked my spot. There were tables and chairs behind me, with a few anonymous people occupying them. Their area was dark and awash with smoke, so much so that I couldn't see their eyes. I ignored them. I didn't care about anyone at that moment. I was fed up, and thinking about cutting my losses and heading for home. My friends wouldn't miss me. From my vantage point on the balcony I couldn't spot any of them, so I presumed they were spread out amongst the shady tables and seedy booths that lined the walls, making half-hearted attempts to pull. Yes, I would finish my drink, then quietly go. I had enough money in my pocket for a taxi. Or maybe I would splash out on a kebab and walk home.

'Hi,' she said in my left ear. I guess she had meant to creep up on me, but her fragrance had preceded her. She leant on the balcony next to me. 'I don't know about you, but this is all a bit much for me.'

'H-hi Rachel.' I stammered. Nerves were shaking me up inside. I tried to reason them away. She had come to me, after all. 'I know what you mean. I feel like I'm not really here.' The words just came out, bypassing my consciousness. That was how I felt, but I hadn't known it until I heard myself say it.

She looked at me. 'This is the first time I've been out since . . . since last year.' If her eyes had been flirtatious before, now they were full of bitterness.

I put my arm limply around her shoulders, no reply on my lips. She seemed fragile and insubstantial. 'We all deal with it in our own way,' I said finally, as if I was some kind of self-help guru. 'Ultimately you've just got to accept things and move on.'

We looked out over the club, standing close together. The people down below jerked and flickered under the strobe. I felt dizzy, weak. Single words and disjointed phrases reached me from the darkness behind me. I closed my eyes, seeking respite. But behind my lids was only deep red.

'Are you OK?' she said.

I nodded dismissively.

'Carly really loved you, you know,' she went on. 'I think Roger did too, or does. He was always talking about you. That's what makes it so hard. I feel like I've lost so much. Do you feel the same?' She pulled me close as I spoke. There was need in her fingers.

'It's gone now. We won't be getting it back. No way.' I spoke with a firmness that I didn't feel. The voices behind me were getting louder, harsher. Some kind of argument.

'You're right. I know.' Although my eyes were downstairs on the dance-floor, I knew her face was turned to mine. I felt her warm breath on my cheek, smelt the vodka on it. I should turn to her, I thought, but something was in the way. Old ties, old guilt. Would it always be like this? Her voice, close, low: 'We should help each other.'

I should turn to her. Everything suggested it, and she wanted it. But I couldn't do it. My eyes stayed on the dance-floor, picking out faces through the strobing lights.

Rachel stroked my cheek.

All the faces down there were the same.

A little pressure in her desperate fingers pulled my face towards her.

Every boy was Roger, every girl was Carly: but each danced alone.

Her lips brushed on my cheek, whispering.

The strobe slowed, illuminating only rapid frames between stretches of darkness.

She kissed my cheek, edging towards my mouth.

In those glimpses I saw that their movements were changing, becoming frantic, urgent.

She pressed her body against mine.

I saw their faces. Fear was there. And pain.

She put her arms around my neck, her lips on mine.

The flashes of light dimmed. Splashes of blood, screams.

Her tongue slithered across my lips.

'No!' I yelled. Rachel's eyes flashed blackness at me. I stepped back. Behind me the argument was becoming an act of violence. A female voice shrieked, a man cried out in pain. I ran downstairs, pushing through people, confusion. Everything was wrong. I couldn't trust my eyes or ears. I had to get out, to get to Carly and Roger, to save them.

What had I been thinking of?

They were in trouble, and it was my doing.

Strange faces watched me as I ran past the bar and into the corridor. A barman with no arms. A bouncer without a mouth. A headless coat lady. I ran past them all until I was on the street.

Outside the White Rose I stopped. The roads were deserted. The only sound was the distant lapping of the rising tide. I felt sober despite the beer, though my thoughts were hazy and turgid. I stepped into the road, rubbing my eyes. It seemed to give way beneath my feet, but when I looked down it was solid. I had to do something. But what?

A car turned quietly into the road. I jogged onto the curb and watched it approach. As it drew closer, slowing, I recognised the taxi from earlier. I knew this was part of what I had to do. Almost immobilised by dread, I lurched into the road and held out my hand.

I squinted through the windscreen, but the driver was ensconced in darkness. All I saw were his hands, positioned firmly on the wheel. I bent down at the passenger door. The window was down. 'Where to?' he said.

'Where are they?'

'Who?'

'You know who,' I said. 'Tell me.'

He was facing forward, as before. 'Away from here.'

'Where?'

I saw his fingers tighten on the wheel. He breathed deep. 'Get in.'

I hesitated, but couldn't think. I got in the car.

His face was stone. The profile was hard-edged and suggested resolve, power. We drove past a street light which briefly washed him in yellow. Now I knew who he reminded me of.

Myself.

I had to look away, intimidated by my own image. The car ate up the road that wound around the coast, past the pier, out of Mumbles. We drove steadily through lanes lined with bungalows and gardens and paddocks, onto a main road that led West, into the Gower. Soon I was drowsy, tranquillised by the quiet hum of the engine. Despite the awful knot in my gut, it felt like any other late night taxi ride, rather than a journey that could lead only to horror.

We drove in darkness down narrow, straight roads across treeless, bare land. The car picked up speed gradually, gaining momentum as if pulled by gravity. We sat in silence, watching the blackness unfold before us. The knot in my stomach gripped me tighter and tighter as we plunged through the dark. I couldn't bear to be in the car any longer. But I had to reach the end, to find Carly and Roger. I knew that things wouldn't be right until I had found them.

A huge dark void to my left had to be the sea. The car veered in that direction. The headlights had gone out some time before, so I couldn't tell if we were still on the road or careering across the moor.

The engine cut out. We coasted to a halt. I got out, feeling tarmac under my feet and sickness in my belly. An empty car park. A grassy ridge was on one side, topped with pale sand. The moon came from behind clouds, revealing a path that led down to the beach. The driver had got out, and was walking towards the path, beckoning.

Everything seemed more solid down here. I was beginning to trust my senses again, as I stepped onto the sand. The memory of Bentley's, and the taxi ride that had just ended, seemed like a daydream from which I had just woken. The beach glowed under the high moon. I walked towards the water. There was something down there, something breaking up the purity of the white sand. I padded towards it, my legs labouring against the softness underfoot. There were footprints in front of me, different sizes, pointing in different directions. Then deep lines in the sand, splashed and dyed with some dark substance. Hand marks clearly visible, fingers clutching at nothing. I followed the trail of soiled sand down to the water's edge.

They lay there, skin improbably white, blood drained into the sand. His throat was ruined, its vital contents violated and exposed cruelly to the air. She glistened from head to toe, stuck and bled.

I vomited explosively, then turned, looking for the driver, the killer. I could see him nowhere, though I had sensed his presence behind me all the way to the shore. The rising water lapped around their corpses, cleansing their stains. Her limp arms rippled mockingly as a new wave bore them up. I put my hands to my face, feeling a scream rising. Something hard struck my temple. I looked: my fist was caked with blood, and clutched a bowie knife. Whooping uncontrollably I tried to drop it. But my fingers were set around it, as if I had been clutching it for hours. The tide was rising fast. My feet splashed in the shallow water as I hopped up and down, shouting incoherently at the knife.

It was only when I got back to the car that I was able to pull myself together. I remained still for a few minutes, breathing deeply, leaning on the hood. The metal was cold. After a while I pushed myself upright, brushed the rust off my hands, and got the car keys out of my pocket.

HUNGER
Spencer Allen

It is sheer madness in the grocery store, packed with the late afternoon rush of people in a hurry to be anywhere else. If they could, everyone would avoid this mad bumper car mania of a grocery store just after five in the afternoon. They would avoid it like a leper colony if that recipe didn't call for a red pepper or if the milk carton hadn't been sitting empty on the counter this morning.

The customers hate it, but the employees hate it worse. The high school girl at the register moans under her breath when she sees the cart I have pushed into her lane, with groceries ready to spill over I've piled them so high. Then she nearly gags when I step from behind the cart exposing my T-shirt, which I haven't bothered to wash, and the sticky brown stain crusting over the front of it.

This high school girl, Jada according to her nametag, begins tossing the groceries across the scanner—cookies, oven pizzas, ice cream, snack cakes—and tries to pretend that I'm not there. Even when the lasers don't pick up one of the bar codes, she slides it to the bag boy anyway. She wants me out of her lane. Wants me out now.

And I don't blame her, I'd be disgusted me too.

My daughter Anika is standing halfway down aisle six, watching me.

She is frowning.

'Hurry up with that,' I tell the bag boy, who is taking his time to do it correctly—not too much in one bag. 'Just throw it in there. Cram it into the cart.

Whatever.'

Then, as soon as it leaves Jada's hand, I rip open a box of glazed dough-nuts and stuff one, nearly whole, into my mouth.

Anika was born without a smile.

Moebius syndrome. When the doctor first explained it, I thought it was some kind of joke I didn't get or some disease he was making up to explain a condition he didn't really understand. But I found it on the Internet later that week—face paralysis from undeveloped cranial nerves, just as the doc-tor had explained. According to what I read, this very rare syndrome is sometimes accompanied with clubbed feet, webbed fingers, crossed eyes, or face deformities. At least Anika had been spared all of that.

She had all her fingers and toes when the doctor lifted her wet, wriggling body. But, for God's sake, who would have thought to count her cranial nerves too?

Anika's throat and lips wouldn't cooperate with the bottles we offered her, much less her mother's breasts. She choked all the time, constantly putting the fear of death into us. She would always have trouble with swallowing and keeping the saliva inside her mouth, the doctor explained.

Okay, we could live with that.

But Anika would never be able to smile. Or frown or smirk at a smart-ass remark or arch her brows in disbelief. Her eyelids would never flutter play-fully when eating up a compliment, and she would never bite her lower lip like Ellen did when concentrating on a difficult task.

Maybe it's a selfish thought on my part, but I would have traded all her fingers and toes just to see her smile.

Anika was dead for almost a year—just after Ellen finally left—before she came back into my life. Sometimes weeks, even months would go by after a visit, and then I would see her again. She would be staring at me from the window of a neighbor's house or from the backseat of another car. Some-times, late at night, I woke and found Anika standing over my bed, watch-ing me sleep.

Now, as I drive away from the supermarket with my backseat and trunk full of grocery bags, I see her standing in the parking lot. She is wearing the green flowered dress that Ellen bought for her two Easters ago. This is also the dress we buried her in, and it is all she ever wears anymore.

While I'm reaching in the back to grope through the groceries, my little red Escort eases into the other lane and nearly sideswipes another car. The ice cream is handy, and I use one of my knees to steer so I can open the carton and begin scooping my fingers into the quart of cookies and cream, shoving it into my mouth.

By the time I am home, a good deal of it has melted on my fingers and dripped down my chin and arm, but the carton is empty.

And Anika is smiling as I walk past her, into the house.

When she was eleven and wise beyond her years, Anika read Bradbury's *The Martian Chronicles*. There is a chapter in which the second expedition of astronauts comes to Mars and finds a community of Martians that wear masks to express their emotions. These beautiful golden and silver masks have frowns and smiles, and the Martians change from one to the other as their moods fluctuate. Some of the masks have two or three smiles when one is simply not enough.

Using cardboard and markers, Anika made her own masks. At the dinner table, when Ellen placed the dreaded bowl of soup—every meal was soup for Anika—in front of her, on went the frowning mask. A clown's red lips were drawn around the slit though which she breathed, and she had given it sparkling blue tears using glitter and drops of Elmer's glue.

The happy mask had golden sunshine rays around each of her eyes and brilliant pink lips. This came out on birthdays, game nights, or when we bought her a puppy for Christmas that year. Eventually she started wearing it to church—Anika loved church, loved singing the hymns though she couldn't really form the words—and people pretended not to stare at this cardboard girl smiling from the middle pew.

She also made a mask with three frowns stacked one on top of the other, which she kept for moments of embarrassment, like when a mischievous bit of slobber would fall from her lips in front of company.

I asked her once why she didn't have a mask with three smiles, like some of the Martians in Bradbury's story.

'I oh ee at on,' her stubborn lips and poorly formed tongue told me.

I don't need that one.

There are photographs of my daughter scattered throughout the house, but especially in the kitchen, where I spend so much time now. If Ellen took any of them when she left, I don't know which ones, but I doubt if she did. She was funny about things then, which is why she left me, I guess. Yet, I haven't had much room in my thoughts these last several months to worry about Ellen.

Once I scanned a picture of Anika onto the computer. I searched the Internet until I found another girl that looked somewhat like her, cut the smile from that picture, and pasted it over Anika's expressionless mouth. It looked pitiful and crooked, and the edge of the smile hung slightly off my daughter's cheek.

I framed it anyway, and it sits in the center of the table as I eat more of the glazed doughnuts. According to the timer on the stove, my pizza will be ready in two minutes. I feel like my stomach is ready to split open from all that I've eaten, and my finger trembles as I bring the last of a doughnut to my lips, coaxing it down my throat, though there surely isn't any more room.

Only once did I punch a guy on Anika's behalf.

It was on a vacation the three of us took to San Antonio in the middle of summer one year. Anika had just turned seventeen. The middle of summer is the wrong time to visit San Antonio, I learned, especially when you have a daughter whose face is paralyzed, making it impossible for her to squint her eyes against the Texas sun.

My daughter and I went shopping together one day when Ellen was sick with exhaustion, maybe, or dehydration—something that kept her in bed most of the morning. Anika wore a pair of obnoxiously large pink sunglasses—a pretend movie star—and tucked her long blond under a wide rimmed hat. I remember this poem in a book from which we read to her as a child. I didn't remember the title, 'The Sun', or the author, John Drinkwater, for several years, until I looked them up again to complement my obsession with the last three lines.

> *. . . Wouldn't it be fun*
> *If, walking on the hill, I said*
> *'I'm happy' to the sun.*

Every time she dressed in her sunglasses and hat, I can't help but imagine she's hiding her eyes from the sun because she remembers that poem and is ashamed that she, too, can't say, 'I'm happy' to the sun.

Understandably, Anika refused to eat in her awkward way out in public, but we stopped at a small café to plan out the rest of our afternoon. The place was crowded enough that we invited a young couple to share our table, especially since I'd only ordered a tea and we would be gone in a few minutes. It was a mistake, I learned too late, because the husband, Vance, didn't let the three of us have a word in as he complained about silly things, like how small the Alamo had been or how slowly the waiter moved at the café. Though I, at least, tried to laugh at his vulgar jokes, Anika had learned long ago not to laugh in the company of strangers. Since her lips and eyes didn't work right, her laughter seemed like bored mockery to anyone who didn't know. Instead she sat there silently.

As much as I hated Vance and his jokes about the Mexicans and the size of things in Texas, I tolerated him as best I could. Then, when Anika excused herself to the restaurant, Vance grabbed me by the shoulder and asked, 'What's with your wife, Man? You fuck all the smiles outta her last night?'

I cut my knuckles on his teeth.

Later, as we drove back from San Antonio, I had a lot of quite time in the car to think about what had made me angry enough to punch the guy. All of us—Anika included—had grown callous to ignorant comments from people around us. He thought she was my wife, though. Of course, he would have made this mistake since her face had grown loose and aged as the unpracticed muscles withered away.

But Anika was just a seventeen-year-old girl.

My *daughter.*

She was just ashamed to show her unhappiness to the sun, and Vance had turned her suffering into something dirty in my mind.

Anika stands near the sink, now, and watches me traipse from the dinette table and into the bathroom down the hall. Digging my fingers deep into my throat—something I've become very practiced at lately—I brace against the wall behind the toilet and try not to vomit on my shirt, soiling it anymore than it already is. Still not used to the weight I've gained, I was a little sloppy with this part this morning, hence the disgusting stain over my shirt.

Propping against the sink, I stare at a face that only resembles mine. Blood-shot eyes from so little sleep. Uncombed, raggedy brown hair. A face that must have been stung by a dozen bees the way it has swelled.

Maybe it wasn't the shirt, after all, that had repulsed the cashier.

Still woozy from vomiting, I stagger back down the hall for another meal.

I said I'd only punched a guy once for Anika, but that doesn't mean there isn't anger and violence inside me for those who have wronged her. Most of it, though, I save for the man who raped and killed her, leaving her body in the tall, wild grass behind some mall in Illinois.

I never told Ellen this about Anika's appearance when I identified her at the morgue, but she was sort of frowning then, though mostly with one side of her face. My first instinct was to tell the coroner that, no, it wasn't my daughter they had found. Sorry, it just wasn't her because Anika couldn't frown anymore than she could smile.

Finally, though, I calmed enough to ask about it why her face was like that. The way her face had been pushed against the dirt, he explained, held it like that long enough for rigor mortis to set in.

They fixed it for the funeral, though. Just our dead, emotionless daughter lying in the casket.

Maybe Ellen blames me for Anika's death. Even when Anika graduated from high school and started looking for colleges, Ellen argued that Anika wouldn't be able to defend herself against the crude ways of strangers or find happiness away from us.

I had been the one to suggest looking at colleges far away, where she could learn to survive away from our obsession with protecting her.

Anika listened to my advice, and now she is dead.

My daughter is dead.

I sometimes imagine her rapist hitting her, yelling at her, and growing angrier each moment because he couldn't work terror into her face. Couldn't send a tremor into her lips or strike the blank, placid expression from her eyes. She should have had a Martian mask for that, and maybe she would have lived.

At first I believed that Anika blamed me for her death too, and that's why she came back a year after her grave had been filled. She came occasionally at first, watching me cry alone at nights or at my desk at work, trying to pretend she wasn't there.

It took me months to realize why she had returned.

I believe my doctor when he tells me that if I don't shed some of these recent pounds, I will probably die of a heart attack soon.

I understand the repulsion of family, friends, and teenaged cashiers when they see the thing I have become. Skin like pasty clay. Breath that stinks of vomit. Urine stains on my pants because I can't afford to go to the restroom except to make more room in my belly.

But mostly I understand Anika's smile—given to her by death or God or my own wishful thinking—when I bite into the tender meat of a chicken breast or a piece of homemade pie, these pleasures that her deformed cranial nerves denied.

She finally knows these things through me, enjoying each wonderful bite vicariously. Anika touches those delicate fingers to her lips as the taste melts over her tongue and to her neck as the warmth trails down her throat.

Now that I understand why she has returned, she is with me all the time. Waking me in the middle of the night, even, because her hunger is so strong. When she grows hungry again, her mouth twists into that crooked frown she wore at the morgue. It seems she grows hungry so quickly now, so I will eat myself into a heart attack to keep the smile on her face. I've waited far too long to see it there.

Now, with the bags of groceries piled on the table around me, Anika's smile starts to falter, and I tear into a package of pineapple-flavored cream cheese, eating it like a candy bar.

Minutes later, as I am emptying a container of potato salad, I vomit again without the help of my finger or a trip to the restroom, but I keep shoveling the food into my mouth. Sometimes I almost push it down my throat because noon is shining through the yellow curtains, and I want her to say 'I'm happy' to the sun.

In her best moments, like when I open another box of cookies and take them two at a time, Anika sings the church songs she loved so much, her voice pristine, every word clear, and her smile possibly eternal.

Peace is flowing like a river

The cups of pudding come in a pack of six, and I scrap each of them empty with my fingers, using my tongue to clean the sides.

Flowing out to you and me

There is a carton of strawberries and a bag of sandwiches from the deli. The oven is beeping because the lasagna is ready. I think Anika would have loved lasagna.

I will eat them all to keep Anika's smile.

Flowing out into the desert

Her smile is bliss.

THE TREE FARM
Kurt Newton

When the tractor stopped, Craig did not want to get off. December cold was bearing down. A chill wind blew and he had forgotten to wear a scarf. The hilltop tree farm could not have picked a colder, more desolate place, he thought.

His wife, Janey, and his two daughters, Jessica and Jillann, looked around excitedly with rosy cheeks and runny noses at the sea of Christmas trees that surrounded them.

'Okay, folks,' the tractor driver said cheerily. 'I'll swing back this way in a little while. Good luck.'

Several other brave souls occupied the trailer wagon, pruning saws in hand. They stood and stepped off one by one and dispersed into the rows of evergreens.

'Craig, c'mon,' Janey beckoned.

Jessica and Jillann, bundled with the care of an Arctic expedition, leaped off the trailer and ran off down the nearest row, their red wintery coats swishing in unison.

'Craig!'

'Sorry. I didn't hear you. My ears are frozen.'

'I told you to wear a hat.'

At last, Craig committed himself to this venture. He stepped off the trailer and gave the driver a wave. 'You are coming back, right?' he asked the driver.

The driver smiled and revved the John Deere's engine and pulled away in a puff of white exhaust.

With the tractor gone, Craig suddenly seemed alone on this hilltop. He squinted his eyes. The sun was half an hour from setting and shone from an almost perpendicular angle. It provided no warmth at all. The breeze gusted and he zipped up his coat collar. The zipper grated against his chin, but it kept his hot breath close to his face.

'Craig?'

Craig followed his wife's voice down between the stands of six-foot high spruce. The ground was spongy with trampled grass, it crackled beneath his feet.

'What?'

'Oh, there you are. I almost didn't see you with that coat of yours.'

'What's wrong with my coat?'

'It's green, silly.'

'And yours is red, so what?'

His wife just rolled her eyes in frustration. She turned her attention to the tree before them. 'Here—what do you think?' Janey asked him.

Craig stumbled over a freshly cut stump. 'God damn it!' Jillann giggled. 'Yeah, that one looks nice. Want me to cut it?'

'Wait, I don't like it,' said Janey. 'It's got a bare spot.'

'How about this one, Mommy?' called Jessica from two rows over.

'That one's ugly!' said Jillann.

'I see some good ones over there,' Janey pointed and the two girls disappeared through the boughs. 'Stay close!' she shouted.

'Janey, jeez, not so loud. I think they heard you two valleys over.'

'What?' she said, agitated. And for the first time Craig could see himself through his wife's eyes. Whatever he had to offer, it didn't help. He was useless.

'Never mind,' he said, and his wife headed off in the direction of the children.

'I thought this one was just fine,' Craig voiced to no one in particular.

Another gust of wind rose. It made Craig's eyes tear. The tree in front of him shook.

They couldn't just pick a tree up outside the grocery store or at one of those roadside pull-offs where pickups parked and sold a dozen trees or so for cheap. No, that would be too easy.

Craig looked up and saw that one of the other families had already found their tree. They dragged it to the center tractor road that divided the field in half and huddled close round it like a prized marlin pulled from the sea.

They stood in the sun and waited for the tractor to return.

Again, Craig heard his wife's voice calling him. This time he deliberately aimed himself in the opposite direction.

The sun dimmed as he walked deeper into the rows. The downhill slope provided a welcome blind from the intermittent wind gusts. It actually felt warmer down here, thought Craig. Either that or hypothermia was setting in. He examined each and every tree he came upon. But with each stop, his wife's voice echoed in his ear as if it were his own.

Too tall.

Too thin.

Too fat.

Too spindly.

Too yellow.

Too uneven.

Too ugly. And when he finally thought he had found perfection, invariably, someone else had tagged the tree for pick-up.

If only they had gotten an earlier start. But there was the outdoor decorating to do, the setting up of the nativity and the stringing of the lights around the house. The days were shorter now and the remaining weekends were growing scarce. Not to mention the shopping. Janey was always on the go, dragging him here and there. And the girls were Janeys-in-training. When was the last time they did something he wanted to do? And more importantly, when did he cease being the man of the house? He used to be the center of things, but now, with the children and the house and the bills and the responsibility, he was nothing more than a prop that provided appearances and a weekly paycheck.

'Craaaaig?'

The call made its way faintly through the trees and down the well of his coat collar into his ears. They were probably looking for him. Maybe they found a tree? Maybe they were ready to leave now?

He wasn't. He would make them wait, abide by his time schedule for once.

He wove deeper into the thicket.

The trees seemed to swallow him. He listened, as his footfalls became distant thumps beneath his legs. He covered his ears with his gloves and could hear his heartbeat pounding from some place deep inside his body. When he heard the rustling of footsteps he ducked between two trees, not wanting to be seen. I'll show them, he thought. I'll make them worry, make them miss me for once, see what it's like not to have Ol' Sad-Eyes Craig to drag around . . .

The trees held him firmly with their soft boughs. He closed his eyes as the footsteps neared then veered off in another direction. He was alone once again. But this self-imposed isolation only reminded him how invisible he had become. What he really wanted was to regain that position at the center, a position he once held back when he and Janey first started dating, back when she used to look at him as if was the only thing that mattered.

Just then, there came a soft humming like a children's lullaby. It sounded so close. Craig turned and stared into the depths of the boughs beside him.

He saw movement.

At first he thought it just an animal lodged in the branches, a raccoon or wolverine. But as it uncurled from its fetal position, he realized it was a child. His presence must have awakened it. But this child was unlike any Craig had ever seen, except in fairy tale books with stories about wood sprites and bugbears and other unseen creatures of the forest—creatures that grant nightmares instead of wishes. It had bark for skin and pine needles for hair, and it continued to sing—a hypnotic drone of a song—even as it wormed its way toward him. Its mouth yawned open and Craig saw that it had several rows of twig-like teeth. Craig was frozen, unable to call out or break free, as the creature's eyes lit up like two embers, pinning him in place as if he had grown roots. A strange mist enveloped him. And as the creature disappeared he realized that he had invaded its territory. Now it would invade his.

When footsteps returned to this part of the field they were all but lost by the time they reached his ears.

'Here's one!'

'Oh, it's perfect.'

The voices were familiar, yet something inside of him did not want to acknowledge it. All he could do was stand there invisible to their holiday blindness.

He heard cutting noises and felt a slight tingle down by his feet.

'Hurry, mom, it's cold.'

'A little bit more . . . There!'

Craig felt the world turn sideways. A whumph greeted his ears as his head hit the frozen ground. The next thing he knew he was being dragged. One minute he was looking up at cold, blue sky, the next minute the frozen ground was scraping against his cheek.

Finally, the dragging stopped.

'Oh, what a beautiful tree,' someone said.

'Thank you,' replied a voice, a voice Craig recalled belonging to a woman named Janey.

'Where's Daddy?' asked a smaller voice.

(Jillann?)

'I think I saw him walking back,' said another small voice.

(Jessica?)

'I'm sure he'll meet us at the car. Now, bundle up, here comes our ride.'

As he lay there, the rumble of the tractor shook the ground. The cold and the painlessness seeped into his bones, making him feel almost wooden. Craig was saddened by this strange turn of events. Tears welled from his eyes and hardened like pinesap on his wind-burned cheeks. But a part of him was also glad. For, even though he would be just another holiday prop, he would finally be the center of attention.

At least for a little while.

THE TONGUES OF MEN, THE VOICES OF ANGELS
Jason Brannon

'This is insane,' Trace whispered forcefully, trying not to draw any attention to himself.

'It is, isn't it?' Ellen agreed, helping herself to one of the cardboard fans that were placed in between the hymnbooks. 'I almost wish that we had never taken this assignment. Judging by the amount of data we've collected, it'll take us weeks to decipher this stuff. I'll just have to get used to it, I suppose.'

Trace wasn't the least bit bothered by the fact that he would have to spend a little extra time with Ellen, but he tried not to show his enthusiasm. It wasn't such a difficult thing to manage under the circumstances. Just listening to the heavyset woman in the sheer, polka-dotted dress shouting in unintelligible syllables and fluttering her eyelids as if she might go into convulsions at any moment temporarily made him forget all about his feelings for Ellen and shiver despite the heat.

'Bow your heads in prayer,' Brother Hawkins instructed the congregation in that booming, televangelist's voice. 'Pray for Sister Liza as she speaks the language of angels.'

Trace and Ellen both did as they were told, listening in fascination to the string of unintelligible consonants and vowels that were streaming out of the large woman's mouth like an aural flow of gentle water. They never heard Brother Hawkins approach until he was crouched there in front of them, one hand on the pew for support.

'Are you getting all of this?' he whispered uncertainly, sweat glistening on his forehead.

'Yeah, we're recording every word,' Trace said quietly.

'Do you think you'll be able to decipher it?'

'We'll do our best,' Ellen said. 'But we're not professionals. This is a post-grad study.'

'Well, I hope you make some progress,' Brother Hawkins said solemnly, listening to Liza's shrill voice. 'The Lord works in mysterious ways, but I'm fairly certain that this isn't one of them. Sister Liza isn't really a woman who's known for her virtue.'

Trace raised his eyebrows in surprise, but didn't say anything. Brother Hawkins nodded to show that he meant what he had said and crept quietly back toward the pulpit. For their part, most of the congregation had their heads bowed and their eyes closed. Some of them were weeping. Some of them had their hands raised. Others were calling the Lord's name. Others were shouting it. And yet it was Sister Liza that could be heard above all the rest, sometimes mumbling like an incoherent drunk and other times enunciating each curious syllable. Brother Hawkins kept a handkerchief to his damp forehead as he listened to the revelations.

'Do you really think that an angel is speaking to us through this woman?' Ellen said. 'Or could it be that Sister Liza is just putting on a show to make the congregation believe that she's a little bit closer to God than everybody else?'

'That's what we're trying to prove, isn't it?' Trace asked as Sister Liza's voice crescendoed in strange syllables and strings of what might have been words. 'We're here to establish whether or not this is an actual language. If it is, we are going to try and translate some of it. Blame Professor Engalls if you don't like the assignment.'

'It's not that,' Ellen persisted. 'It's just that this is the third night of revival and not once has there been an interpretation of what's been said.'

'That's why we're here.'

'Not according to the faith that these people keep. In most denominations that believe in speaking in tongues there is always an interpreter there to share with the congregation what sort of message God is trying to deliver. There hasn't been anyone here to give those kinds of explanations.'

Trace was just about to reply when Sister Liza got noticeably louder. A chorus of amen's drifted throughout the church and Ellen moved a little closer to Trace, like a girlfriend who gets scared at a drive-in movie. It was all Trace could do not to throw his arm around her and hug her tightly to his side.

'I don't know about you,' Ellen said. 'But this sort of reminds me of Jim Jones and the big Kool-Aid party.'

'Amen to that. We'll just have to be careful if the stuff in the communion cup has a faint cherry flavor to it.'

Many members of the congregation began raising their heads as Sister Liza's voice died out and the angel ran out of things to say. Sweating profusely after ten minutes of religious filibustering, Liza nearly collapsed onto the pew and would have had it not been for the valiant efforts of two deacons who caught her right before her legs gave way. One of the women, perhaps a deacon's wife, brought Liza a glass of water. She drank thirstily like an animal that has been driven beyond its limits.

The Next Day:

Ellen wasn't quite sure why listening to the tapes gave her a disquieting sense of unease, but they did. Sister Liza's voice sounded like the cry of a wounded child as she kept repeating the same syllables over and over again, and it was difficult to imagine that she wasn't in any kind of pain at all. Yet, miraculously, the beefy woman had seemingly suffered no ill effects from the heavenly possession, if you could call it that.

At the moment, Trace was supposed to be interviewing Sister Liza about her experiences with the church, and Ellen had foolishly volunteered to start entering the data and the reels of tape into the computer so that the software could begin the arduous task of translation. Now she wished that she had let Trace do it. He had wanted to anyway.

Ellen made it all the way through the first night of the revival service without touching the stop button on the recorder. However, she couldn't bear to listen to another full hour of babbling and rambling and fluttering of tongues. As it was, she had barely managed to remain in her seat during the actual service. She decided instead to give Brother Hawkins a call.

'What, in particular, did you want to ask?' Jeremiah Hawkins said gruffly from the other end of the line, hacking and choking the instant the words were out of his mouth. It sounded a lot like a cigarette cough to Ellen even though Brother Hawkins openly preached against such damaging behavior. She decided not to mention it.

'First, I want to know a little about the church history. When was it built? Why it was built where it was. Who was the first pastor? That sort of thing.'

Hawkins sighed as if unsure of how to begin. 'I suppose it goes without saying that the church has been around for quite a long time in one form or another. Brother Halford T. Lindsey started it in the 1800's. I'm not too sure what made Brother Lindsey decide to start a church, but apparently enough people came to keep the doors open.'

Ellen could hear the apprehension in the old man's voice and knew that he was beating around the bush. As it was, she wasn't going to give him the chance to evade the subject and sugarcoat the truth.

'You said the church has been around in one form or another for quite a while now. What do you mean by that?'

Hawkins went silent on the other end of the line.

'Brother Hawkins?'

'Yes, I'm still here. I was just trying to decide whether I wanted to tell you what I know or not. Is this being recorded?'

'No,' Ellen lied, hoping that the preacher couldn't hear the nearly imperceptible screech of tiny wheels spinning the reels of tape.

'Good. It wouldn't do for my congregation to get wind of what I'm about to say, and if you make any mention of this conversation, I will deny it.'

'Fine.'

'That said, I guess I should start by saying that the church has been a church for as long as it's been standing. The ground it's built on, however, hasn't always been consecrated to the Christian God. Somehow, I think that Brother Lindsey realized that and either chose to ignore what he suspected or built on the site because of what he knew. Either way, we have him to thank for the way things are. Had I been aware of the situation, I might not have come here in the first place. Then again, I was young and naive and would have probably charged in with my crucifix held out in front of me and the good book clutched tightly in my free hand, intending to rid the world of evil like a son of Van Helsing.'

'Of course, it's sort of a long standing tradition among the ministers who pass through here to warn their successor of what to expect, but in a town this small there are always enough whisperings and surreptitious half-glances to warn anybody with eyes that there is something going on. But as I said, I was naive about certain things and merely thought the town was just dismissing me because they didn't think anyone was capable of filling Brother Michael's enormous shoes. And since Brother Michael died before I took over the church, we never had a chance to talk.'

Realizing that she was privy to information most townspeople were oblivious to, Ellen looked over at the recorder to make sure it was working. The level meters were flashing up and down and the wheels were rolling and pulling the spools of tape. Ellen couldn't wait until Trace got a hold of this. She only wondered if he was having as much luck with Sister Liza.

* * *

'That's really not necessary,' Trace said, holding his hands out in front of him, steadily backing away from Sister Liza.

'Yes, it is,' the heavyset woman said lasciviously as she carefully removed her bra to reveal a mountainous bosom. 'I haven't touched somebody like you in quite a while.'

'And you're not going to start now,' Trace was quick to reply, wondering how the angels could use a woman like this for a mouthpiece. 'I just want to talk to you about what happened in church during the past three nights of the revival.'

The mere mention of the house of God was like a slap across Sister Liza's face. Her lower lip trembled as she realized what she had been about to do and quickly redressed herself.

'God forgive me,' she said looking first toward heaven and then toward Trace. 'And you too. I'm terribly sorry. I don't know what got into me. It's like I wasn't even in control of myself for a minute.'

'It's O.K.,' Trace said gently, seeing the tears brimming at the corners of Liza's eyes. 'Just answer my questions and we'll call it even. Assuming, of course, that you're able to talk. And willing.'

'It's the least I could do after I nearly assaulted you,' Liza replied. 'I'm still not sure what I was thinking. As soon as you came into the house, though, all I could think about was throwing you down on my bed. Sometimes I wonder if I'm schizophrenic. Or possessed.'

'Was it anything like the way you feel when you speak in tongues?' Trace asked, keeping a reasonable distance between him and Liza.

'Yes, it was a lot like that actually,' Liza, said, sitting down on the couch, holding a pillow to her chest as though afraid of unwittingly exposing herself again. 'Still, that doesn't keep me from being embarrassed about what I did. I guess I've just lived by myself for too long and need a little company. But that's what church socials are for, not interviews with a college boy. Please accept my apology. I meant no harm.'

'Don't worry about it,' Trace responded, noticing just how sad and solitary an existence Liza had. Unlike most homes he had been in before, there were no pictures on the walls of family or friends, no messages flashing on the answering machine, no crayon-drawn pictures on the refrigerator from loving children. Instead, there were only paintings and prints of cats. Calendars. Figurines. Wallpaper. Live tabbies making themselves home in nearly every room.

And, of course, those half-hidden bottles of liquor that Liza didn't think anyone had seen. Trace decided not to make mention of that.

'You can sit by me,' Sister Liza said quietly, not daring to make eye contact with Trace. 'I won't rape you or anything.'

'I know that,' Trace said, taking his seat. 'So let's just forget any of this ever happened. I came here to interview you and we're at the point now where I'm about to ask my first question. As far as I'm concerned, your shirt has stayed on throughout this meeting and you have been the perfect hostess. Now, should we begin.'

Liza smiled a little and nodded, still obviously ashamed of herself. Trace ignored her blushing and hit the record button on his tiny handheld tape recorder.

'As you're probably aware, Ellen and I are doing a research project for a linguistics professor on the language that the angels use during a speaking of tongues. We hope to be able to eventually make sense of the words and translate what is being said so that we might either prove to the scientific community that this isn't a hoax like many skeptics claim or disprove the phenomenon entirely. I, for one, am under the impression that this is real so we're proceeding based on the assumption that you weren't just babbling and making up sounds to appear one step closer to God than the rest.'

'It's strange,' Liza said, rubbing her hands together as if she were warming by an unseen fire. 'I don't know why God would even want to send a message through me. I'm hardly what you would call the devout Christian. There are people in the congregation who are far more religious than me. And yet none of them have spoken yet.'

'Tell me about what happens when someone speaks in tongues,' Trace prodded.

'First of all, there is always a translator in the church to tell the congregation what is being said. It's a little puzzling that no one has translated my speeches thus far. Then again, I suppose it's true that God works in mysterious ways.'

'What does it feel like when you start speaking in tongues?' he asked, holding the recorder a little more toward Liza in order to capture every word.

'Actually, it's not that pleasant an experience,' Liza confessed. 'It's almost like an unwelcome violation. One moment you're in complete control of yourself. The next, you can hear yourself shouting a bunch of unintelligible gobbledygook. You know that people are watching you and wondering what you are saying. You know that most of them wouldn't want that sort of thing happening to them, and yet I have no control of myself in order to resist. The spirit always takes me by force, and I have no other choice but to yield.'

* * *

'Although I've only been here a few months, it's always the dying ones who shed a little light on what I'm dealing with here,' Brother Hawkins said slowly. 'The little, withered women on their last breath who utter one last cryptic sentence. The frail, shrunken men who have nothing to lose by breaking the silence. They've murmured their secrets to me right before they went to be with the Lord, and I'll have to confess that on more than one occasion I've tried to chalk it up to senility or deathbed hallucinations. Still, somehow I've always suspected otherwise. I've heard stories about tunnels running underneath the church, catacombs where pagan rituals during the middle ages were performed, secret passageways leading to untold evil and the bodies of dead crusaders who were hell-bent on vanquishing whatever dark forces were lurking beneath the earth. Honestly that's the reason I wanted the two of you to try and decipher what's being said in the speakings. Although I'm not sure why, I can't help but believe that all of this is related, and I'd like to know what's going on as a measure of precaution. After all, I need to know what we're dealing with in order to protect myself and my parishioners.'

'You act as though this isn't the first or only strange occurrence,' Ellen said flatly, wondering if they had been told everything there was to know.

'It isn't. There are lots of mornings I have entered the sanctuary to find Christ weeping real tears from his ceramic cross. Since there is an air conditioning vent nearby, I always try to convince myself that it's just a little condensation dripping down the face of the Lord. But I know differently. Sometimes there are tiny teeth marks in the communion wafers. I reason that a mouse or some other form of vermin might have done them even though the teeth are too widely spaced for anything that small. About two weeks ago, I walked into my office to prepare the next week's sermon only to find that something was different about the painting of James and John and Peter that hung on my wall. Ordinarily, the men were ministering to a lame woman, laying their hands on her as a measure of healing. On that particular morning, the reason why the woman couldn't walk was apparent as every orifice was filled by the excited, erect apostles. Honestly, it was nothing but pure pornography, and I hauled the painting out to the dump. I went back later and found that the picture was as it had been originally, but I couldn't bear to look at the thing again after what had happened. I've probably got dozens more of these strange little occurrences that might convince you that I need to be institutionalized, but they're all true. And while they wouldn't come out and talk to you as candidly as I have, there are several churchgoers who have had similar dark experiences.'

'So what you're telling me is that you think someone besides God is possessing your church.'

'I'd be afraid to tell you what I think.'

'Fine. Now let's get back to this Brother Lindsey. Whatever happened to him?'

'No one knows.' Brother Hawkins replied gravely. 'One day he just disappeared into thin air. It was almost as though God had chosen to take him like he had done once before with Enoch.'

'Is that what you think happened to him?'

'No, I think whatever's living underneath this church got him.'

* * *

'Sister Liza, because this is research I have to be thorough and ask you if your family has ever had any history of mental illness.'

'None,' Liza replied as she stroked the twelve-pound tabby on her lap. Trace nodded as if that were the very answer he had expected.

'Fine. Have you ever gone to church drunk?'

This question seemed to hit home more than the first. Liza's face was flooded with the red of onrushing blood and had there been a cat nearby, she might have squeezed it to death with her meaty fists.

'What kind of question is that?' she insisted furiously.

'I'm sorry,' Trace said, having the only answer he needed. 'I'm just trying to rule out every possibility that this could be some sort of hoax.'

'Well, then, no. I haven't gone to church drunk.'

'Very good. Now, let's go step by step through events as they usually happen right before you start to speak. Is that O.K.?'

'Yes,' Liza said, leaning toward the tape recorder. 'First of all, I never know when the voice will take hold of me. Usually, though, it's while we're singing that I feel the greatest pull.'

'And then what?'

'And then I just usually lapse into that other language all of a sudden. But I do feel something in particular when I'm speaking even though I can't control myself.'

'Yes, go on.'

'It's strange and you'll probably think I'm making this up, but I always have the urge after the voice releases me to go down into the old catacombs below the church and speak with the dead. After the voice uses me, I feel like I'm capable of talking with those old bones.'

* * *

'Brother Hawkins is convinced that there's something evil living under the church,' Ellen said wryly, arching her eyebrows in a show of disbelief.

'Sister Liza says she feels like having a chat with the dead bodies in the catacombs,' Trace replied with a smile.

'And this is legitimate research?' Ellen said as she fed the last of the tapes into the analyzing computer.

'More like mental rehabilitation,' Trace laughed as he watched the computer's progress on the screen. Ellen smiled, and it was just about the most beautiful thing Trace had ever seen.

As the micro circuitry hummed and buzzed, Ellen went about her work, organizing their reports, making small notations in the margins, thinking about the problem at hand. Trace tried to do the same, but it was difficult with Ellen right there beside him. Although Trace knew he had a lot of work to get done, he wanted more than anything to grab Ellen and press his lips to hers. But he knew that sort of brutish approach would destroy any potential chance he might ever have with her. So he tried to focus on what he had written and breathed a sigh of relief when the computer had finally finished analyzing the data they had given it.

'Well,' Ellen said calmly. 'This could mean difference in pass or fail. Are you ready?'

'Let's see what we've got,' Trace replied nervously.

The software that had been used to break down the tapes into words, syllables, consonants, and vowels was of Professor Engalls' design. Ellen trained the mouse pointer on a particular passage from the first night of revival and clicked. Immediately, they heard Sister Liza's shrill voice cutting through the speakers. Then, Ellen hit the 'translate' button and waited for the computer to tell them the result.

'Trace wants to fuck Ellen,' the computerized voice replied. 'And he wants to fuck her hard.'

Trace's mouth fell open, and he could feel the weight of Ellen's stare.

'What in the hell is that all about?' he was quick to ask, hoping to divert the computer's revelation.

'You tell me,' Ellen said flatly, her cheeks flushed with anger and embarrassment. 'I'd like to know.'

'I don't have a clue,' Trace stammered. 'It must be a glitch in the software.'

'So?'

'So what?'

'Is it true?'

Trace turned his eyes away from Ellen and it was answer enough.

'I'm sorry,' he said softly. 'Yes, I feel that way, but I didn't make the computer say that. Honestly.'

'You know this changes everything,' Ellen said, turning her back to Trace. 'Our research. Our friendship. The way I look at you.'

'Yeah,' Trace said despondently. 'I know.'

'That isn't necessarily a bad thing,' Ellen replied coyly after a few moments of silence.

Trace's face glowed brightly at the possibility, and it looked like he had swallowed a light bulb.

'Of course, we have to figure all of this out first,' she added. 'Starting with this little mystery of your lust.'

'Go on.'

'Well, we've got two possibilities here. One, you let this little secret slip about how you felt for me, and somebody sabotaged the software for a joke. Or two, there really is something wrong with this church and whatever spoke through Sister Liza must have known what buttons to push to make us respond.'

'I haven't told anyone,' Trace said flatly.

'Well, then, it seems that we've only got one possibility.'

Trace nodded in agreement.

He had just resolved himself to the idea that what they were dealing with was actually supernatural when without warning Sister Liza's voice boomed through the speakers like a spew of curses. Ellen moved a little closer to Trace as the strange foreign language contaminated the room with its palpable sense of menace. Not wasting any time, the computer quickly followed up with the translation and Ellen clutched tightly to Trace for support.

'I'm tired of being trapped down here,' the mechanical voice said. 'Let me out. That's the only way you'll be rid of me.'

Trace and Ellen both looked at each other, not really knowing what to make of the occurrence since neither of them had touched the keyboard. They were scarcely given time to contemplate the event, however, when the computerized voice began to speak again.

'God loves you and will protect you. Take heart children. Trust only in the Master.'

'I think our computer has gone schizophrenic,' Ellen said quietly, unsure of what to make of it all. Trace was about to agree with her, but Sister Liza's ranting prevented him from saying anything. Looking curiously at the computer, Ellen read the screen and held up three fingers to indicate that this particular snippet of speech was from the third night of revival. The two of them waited patiently for the computer to translate. Ellen hugged Trace for comfort when the mechanical voice began to speak again. She didn't even seem to wince this time at the mention of her name.

'Trace wants to fuck Ellen. God loves you and will protect you. And he wants to fuck her hard. Let me out. Trace wants to fuck Ellen. That's the only way you'll ever be rid of me. And he wants to fuck her hard.'

Having heard enough, Trace wasted no time in cutting the volume off. Ellen was already on the phone to Brother Hawkins.

* * *

'I don't like this,' Brother Hawkins said in a strained voice as the three of them headed down the steps into the catacombs. 'This isn't a hallowed place.'

'Who is supposed to be buried down here?' Trace asked, holding a lantern in front of his face to light the way.

'Ministers, the wealthy, the influential, those who had enough pull in life to guarantee their place here away from the common folk. But it was only after Brother Lindsey died that they were buried. Before he died, no one was allowed down there.'

'So what's the point in having catacombs if you're not going to bury anybody?' Trace asked.

'I think this might answer a lot of questions,' Brother Hawkins said grimly, holding up a book in the lamplight.

'What's that?' Ellen asked.

'Lindsey's diary. I've been so busy getting acquainted with the church and moving into the parsonage and learning names and faces that I haven't had time to read it. I suppose this must be passed on from minister to minister and I inherited it by right of my title.'

'Well, crack it open,' Trace urged. 'If there's something inside that relates to what we're dealing with, I think we need to know.'

'I already have a bad feeling,' Brother Hawkins said as he read the first page.

Trace and Ellen looked at each other skeptically. 'What?' they said in unison.

'And there was war in heaven,' Brother Hawkins read. 'Michael and his angels fought against the dragon, and the dragon fought and his angels, and prevailed not; neither was their place found anymore in heaven. And the great dragon was cast out, that old serpent, called the Devil, and Satan, which deceiveth the whole world: he was cast out into earth and his angels were cast out with him.'

'What's that?' Trace asked.

'Revelations,' the old minister replied. 'The story of Lucifer getting thrown out of heaven.'

'Why's Lindsey got it in his diary?' Ellen wondered.

'I don't know,' Hawkins confessed. 'But by the look of these pages, that's all we'll be learning. The rest have faded to the point that I can't read them down here in the darkness. Of course, we could probably decipher them up in the church where there's plenty of light.'

'We're going to find out what's down here,' Ellen said forcefully. 'With or without you. If you want to go up and read, that's fine. But we're staying down here.'

'I'm not going to desert you,' Hawkins said, sounding more than a little unsure of himself. 'After all, this is my church.'

'Well, let's stop talking and get going.'

The catacombs were largely dirt walkways and thick clay walls. Warped support beams held up sections of the ceiling and braced the main corridor, but judging by the way clouds of dust kept settling with each step they took, the thin, gangly slats weren't much comfort. Because the catacombs were usually sealed, the air down there was musty, and the three of them had to breathe shallowly to keep from gagging or coughing on the stench of death and swirling dust motes. Most of the vaults were either so old that the name of the deceased had weathered away or in such need of repair that the identity had been lost somewhere amidst the chipped stone and rubble that had fallen away from the tomb. Trace couldn't help but ruminate on how little these poor people were benefiting from their money now that nobody knew who they were anymore. Maybe the possessing spirit was actually one of the nameless and faceless down here, refusing to die quietly. Yet, somehow, Trace doubted that it would be anything that simplistic.

'How many times have you actually been down here?' he asked Brother Hawkins as they descended another flight of steps, going deeper into the earth.

'Twice,' Brother Hawkins responded, propping the pickaxe on his shoulder. 'And that was twice too many times for me. You can just feel the sense of wrongness down here. It's like an offense to the senses, and yet, you can't really put your finger on what's wrong.'

'That being said,' Ellen butted in. 'Do you really think we should have come down here with digging tools? I mean if there's something buried down here that gives off that kind of vibe, the smartest thing wouldn't be to let it loose into the world. Obviously, whatever we're dealing with has been here for a while. And I would bet that it's no coincidence that a church is built here. Maybe Brother Lindsey knew something nobody else knew when he started this church.'

'Well, miss, it was your idea to come down here,' Hawkins maintained.

'Yes, but it wasn't my idea to dig up graves. That was all your doing.'

'The answer is down here, you know?' the aging minister wheezed. 'And it won't be lying on top of the ground, just waiting for us to stumble over. We'll have to delve for every glimpse into the truth, and even then, I suspect that we might not find out everything. I would imagine only Brother Lindsey is privy to that sort of knowledge.'

'Is he buried down here?' Trace asked. 'If he is, maybe we should just ask him what's going on.'

'He's the one who actually set the precedent,' Brother Hawkins said, shifting his pickaxe to the other shoulder, ignoring that last bit about interrogating the long-dead minister.

At the bottom of the steps was what seemed to be one long hallway leading to a door that was set deep into the earth. Tree roots hung down from the dirt ceiling like greedy fingers that might snatch the three of them up at any minute, and moss clung desperately to the walls.

'Judging from the direction we've been headed,' Brother Hawkins said a little uncertainly. 'I think that we might actually be running beneath the cemetery. We must be at least thirty feet below the ground.'

'Just as long as a dead body doesn't drop through that ceiling,' Ellen said. 'I'll be fine.'

'I wouldn't say that until we've found out what it is we're dealing with,' Trace reminded her. 'Then you can say you'll be fine.'

'Maybe we should start with Brother Lindsey's tomb since he seems to be the start of a lot of things around here,' Brother Hawkins suggested.

'Agreed,' Trace replied, adjusting his lamp.

It came as a surprise to no one when the door at the end of the dirt hallway turned out to be Brother Lindsey's crypt. Stepping forward with his lantern, Trace was in the process of copying down the inscriptions that were etched into every square inch of the door when he heard Brother Hawkins start to murmur unintelligibly. He turned around in time to see the minister's eyes roll back in his head to reveal only the bloodshot whites.

Stepping away from the door to the earthen vault, Trace moved toward Ellen. Her eyes were white with fright as she listened to Brother Hawkins mutter in the same indecipherable language that Sister Liza knew all too well.

'It's got him,' Ellen whimpered. 'And we're down here all alone with him.'

'It certainly doesn't help my feelings that he's holding that pick axe.'

But they didn't have to worry about Hawkins using the tool on them. Instead, he went right to work on the door, hammering hard against the hard surface with all he could muster, all the while mumbling sing-song to himself in that strange tongue.

'Let me out,' he muttered as he swung the axe. 'Let me out.'

Trace looked at Ellen uncertainly.

'Do you think that that crypt might be best left alone?' he asked.

'I think I've been saying that for quite a while.' Ellen said. 'But what can we do?'

'I'll hit him in the back of the head with that lantern,' Trace suggested.

'No,' Ellen was quick to say. 'You can't do that. You'll kill him. This is still Brother Hawkins we're talking about here. He can't help it that something's got hold of him.'

'Well, I don't know anything about performing an exorcism so I guess we're out of luck.'

'I don't really think that's going to be an issue now anyway,' Ellen said, pointing at the huge chunk in the masonry. 'Brother Hawkins is almost in.'

Although the hole in the vault was small, it was consequential enough that the screaming could get out. Magnified ten times over, it was the same voice that had spoken through Sister Liza and was still using Brother Hawkins.

'Stop!' Trace yelled over the din, not knowing what else to do. Temporarily caught off guard, Brother Hawkins paused in mid-swing and looked back at the two college students who were staring at him like a couple of wall-eyed trout. That split-second in time when the gap in the rock was cleared was more than enough for Trace and Ellen to see what Brother Hawkins was about to unwittingly unleash into the world.

At first, all Trace could see were hundreds of gold chains dangling from the ceiling, but then he saw the numerous replicas of the crucified Christ attached like good luck charms. Of course, the shock of such a spectacle was quickly replaced by the horror he felt upon seeing the monstrous, grotesque winged skeleton locked in a deadly, fighting embrace with the human skeleton that had been Brother Lindsey many, many years ago.

'Is that what I think it is?' Ellen said, her breath issuing in gunpowder clouds despite the fact that she was sweating.

'Well after that little inscription in the diary, I would say it's an angel. A fallen angel.'

'This must be where it landed when God tossed it out of heaven. Brother Lindsey must have found that out and has been holding it captive down here for years,' Trace screamed over the shrieking. 'We can't let Hawkins open that door.'

But Ellen was miles ahead of him. The lantern came down across the back of Hawkins' head with a muffled thud, and he fell across the opening of the vault like a zealot reveling in the Holy Spirit.

'Quick, let's move him,' Ellen said, wincing at what felt like an icy hand close around her wrist. She jerked away instinctively, pulling Brother Hawkins as far from the broken tomb as possible.

'We've got to shut this thing right now,' Trace said. 'If God doesn't want to hang around with this guy anymore, then I doubt we do either.'

Little more than a black coil of smoke, the essence of the fallen angel seeped through the hole in the vault like water into a ship's hull. Trace eyed the weak support beams that held the ceiling in place and backed cautiously away from the quicksilver darkness.

'Ellen, wake Brother Hawkins up,' he shouted above the din of screaming and shrieking.

Ellen wasted no time slapping the old cleric in the face until his eyelids fluttered like the wings of tiny hummingbirds and he realized where he was.

'Let's go,' she said, pulling him to his feet. 'We don't have time to hang around.'

Brother Hawkins swallowed hard and nodded, grabbing the pickaxe he had dropped earlier.

'Come on, Trace,' Ellen hollered.

With a sharp kick, Trace took out the beam that held the ceiling in place and scurried backward as thousands of pounds of dirt collapsed on top of the dark miasma that had once been a servant of the light. Yet, as he looked over his shoulder, Trace noticed with equal parts awe and horror that the black, inky presence was squeezing through every available crevice in the cave-in.

'Go,' he shouted, breaking two more beams and running as the earth paradoxically fell from the sky. But the fallen kept its course, snaking through rubble and oozing between tight spaces.

'We're not going to make it,' Trace said as he reached the head of the stairs where Ellen and Brother Hawkins had stopped to watch the action.

'Yes, we are,' the preacher said, as he swung the pickaxe, bringing down what was left of the ceiling. Several decayed limbs could be seen protruding from the dirt pile as the dirt was settling, and although it was of little consequence, it seemed that Brother Hawkins had been right about the catacombs running beneath the cemetery.

Of course, the first sight of the black amorphism chased away all disgust of the disturbed corpses.

'We can't stop it,' Ellen shouted.

'Only God can deliver us from this evil,' Hawkins said reverentially, bowing his head for one last prayer. The darkness rushed at them like a locomotive juggernaut. And then the other shape shot out of the rubble like a flash of light in a shadow-filled room. Trace pulled Ellen up to higher ground as the remained of the floor gave way, however, Brother Hawkins fell as the earth slid beneath him.

'Hold on,' Trace said urgently. 'We'll get you out.'

But there was something in the old minister's eyes that disagreed with the notion of ever getting out of there alive. And what was more, Brother Hawkins seemed to be OK with it.

'The rest of the ceiling's going to go at any minute,' Ellen shouted. 'Maybe the floor beneath you too. We've got to work quickly and get some help.'

'No, that won't be necessary,' Brother Hawkins, said with a firm resolve as the earth rumbled and threatened to shift. 'The way I see it, Brother Lindsey could use a hand after all these years at the yoke.'

'We can't leave you here,' Trace said, looking back over his shoulder as the dirt came down in filthy cascades.

'We don't have a choice,' Ellen screamed.

'Go, both of you,' Brother Hawkins cried. 'Go.'

Trace and Ellen watched for a split second as the old minister wrestled with the decayed remains of a fallen angel, their eyes growing wide as the phosphorescent outline of another man lent his hand to the battle, subduing the traitor while Hawkins kicked the last of the braces away from the tenuous ceiling.

'Lindsey,' they both said as they emerged from the catacombs into the sunken-in sanctuary where the rescue teams were already on stand-by. It was obvious from the turnout of paramedics, firemen, and police officers that the destruction had been felt for miles throughout town. Immediately, two female EMTs rushed over and began attending to the two while workers rushed to begin clearing the rubble away from the entrance to the catacombs.

'Is anyone else down there who might be alive?' the fire chief asked them excitedly.

'Just Brother Hawkins,' Trace replied with a strain of fatigue in his voice. 'But I doubt he made it.'

'We have to try anyway,' the burly man in the yellow slicker said as he directed his crew toward the mess.

Too weary to go anywhere and curious to see whether or not Brother Hawkins might have survived, Trace and Ellen waited for three solid hours while the volunteers and firemen dug deep into what was left of the vault. Eventually one of the men shouted that he had found something and the rest of the crew hurried over.

'Is this Brother Hawkins?' the fire chief asked them with a tinge of potential concern.

'Well,' Ellen said with a smile. 'That looks like what he was wearing. And that face resembles his.'

'Yeah,' Trace agreed. 'But I would have to say that those wings most definitely belong to him.'

THOSE WHO SCHEME THROUGHOUT THE NIGHT
Michael Kaufmann and Mark McLaughlin

The watchful warmth of the big yellow eye flowed over the horizon, and Hell's tiniest agents were sent crawling away from the form on the bench next to the park's arboretum. Cameron threw off his bedcovers—Thursday's edition of the *Bi-State Times*—and greeted the dawn with a forced smile. He hated having to sleep out on the battlefield, but that was what soldiers did, right? But he was alive, the sun was out and so he was safe for another day from Those Who Scheme.

He looked around—no joggers or dog walkers. The park, as usual, was free of Norms at this early hour. He stretched his sore limbs and checked his bag. The knots were still in place, and he then wondered how many agents—the day walking, two-legged Schemers—he would encounter today. He looked toward the arboretum. He could see plenty of bright, velvety petals, everything from orchids to flowering cacti, through the glass walls. The Schemers loved pretty blossoms. But really, it wasn't all that surprising . . . They were no doubt attracted to the novelty of a vibrant, blooming spectrum. They didn't get to see colors like that, back in their realm.

Shouldering the bag, Cameron adjusted the collar of his coat. This one was lasting longer than his previous one. It was well worth the five bucks he'd paid for it at Good Will. He headed toward the food trailer at the north end of the park. Boy, he sure could go for a—

Behind you! Someone's following you! He wheeled around, searching the hedges for movement. *Nothing. Ah, but they're tricky. There'll be no rest for the weary today.* He cast one more look around him, and continued walking toward the trailer.

'Mornin', Cameron.' The heavyset, fortyish man in the bright orange food trailer scarcely looked up, busy at his griddle making a breakfast sandwich for himself before the morning rush.

'Good morning, Tony.' Cameron stood at the trailer's counter, looking around him every few seconds to make sure nothing was creeping up on him.

'Sleep well last night?' The cook poured himself some orange juice.

'Sure,' Cameron said, distracted. 'The night holds no terrors for me. An armed man with the right knowledge has no cause for fear.'

'Armed! You packin' a piece?'

Cameron ignored the question. He looked hungrily at the cook's meal. 'There'll be no rest for the weary today.'

Tony picked up the sandwich and took a bite out of it. 'I thought you said you slept well,' he said around a mouthful of bacon and bread.

Cameron looked at him out of the corner of his eye. 'You know what I mean.' He swung his head in a half-circle to the rear. Then he leaned close. 'Those Who Scheme,' he whispered.

Tony smiled, like he did every time. 'That again. Nobody's out to get you, Cameron. What are they scheming to do? Take that crummy coat of yours? I've got one with more padding in it at home—nice and warm. I'll bring it tomorrow. It doesn't fit me around the middle any more. I'm eatin' too much of my own cooking.'

Cameron's jaw set in a scowl. He did a quick scan of the park, then turned to stare suspiciously into Tony's eyes. 'Padding, eh? Padding can hide all sorts of funny business.' Then his eyes dropped down a bit. 'Strange how I've never seen your shoulders. You sure go to a lot of trouble to cover them up.'

'I put on a shirt in the morning. That's a lot of trouble? Don't worry about the coat—it's just got cotton in it, that's all. Or whatever cheap poly-fiber crap they're using for cotton these days.'

Cameron's eyes narrowed. 'You seem awfully helpful today, Tony,' he said. 'A little too helpful. You haven't been compromised, have you? You know what happens to double-agents.' He drew a finger across his throat as he looked around again. His eyes finally came to rest on the sandwich Tony had nearly finished.

'Double-agent? I don't even have time to be a single agent. This place is gonna be crowded with joggers in about five minutes. You look hungry. How 'bout a Bacon, Egg and Cheese Special?'

Cameron licked his lips and swallowed, but his face remained impassive.

'C'mon, it's on me,' Tony urged.

He's on their side. Or maybe he's actually one of them, one of Those Who Scheme Throughout The Night. 'You and your demon potions can be used on someone else,' Cameron cried. 'And don't think I didn't see you with that Schemer yesterday.' With that, he turned on his heel and stalked away. 'I'm onto you, Tony!' he yelled back over his shoulder. 'I'm onto you!'

* * *

Tony shook his head. 'Poor guy,' he said to no one. He wondered, as he often did, just how old Cameron was. The bum was skinny, with white hair and lots of wrinkles around the eyes, but he had a very young face, and his teeth looked good, too. Bums with good teeth were about as rare as hens with any teeth at all.

He started making a Bacon, Egg and Cheese Special to put in a sack that he would set by the back-right leg of the trailer. Cameron would be back eventually, and he would take it and eat it, and the whole morning's episode would be forgotten. The free food was Tony's contribution to the needy. It helped him to sit at ease whenever the priest talked about giving of oneself.

About a week ago, Cameron had told him all about Those Who Scheme Throughout The Night. Some imaginary bunch of weirdos from Hell who never slept, but they looked like real people when they were out during the day. They was something freaky about them, but he couldn't remember what it was . . . *Something to do with shoulders.* Yeah, and today Cameron had been going on about shoulders some more. Shoulders and demon potions! What a combination!

He made himself a note and taped it next to the exit of the trailer so he'd see it on the way out. **COAT FOR C.**, it read.

* * *

At two, Cameron came back to the front of the trailer.

Earlier, Operation Control had left a nutrition packet for him near the back of the food trailer, like they did every day. Delicious—exactly what he'd wanted, too. The packets had to be from Operation Control. Who else knew about his mission?

That morning, he'd spotted at least two-dozen Schemers in the park.

Who did they think they were fooling, with their squared-off padded shoulders? Of course, a long time ago, the Schemers had entered the fashion industry and now a lot of clothes for Norms had big shoulders. Part of their efforts to blend in. That made Cameron's job a lot harder. The Schemers had also invented make-up, way back when. They looked fakey, so they wanted everyone else to look fakey, too.

Tony had big shoulders . . . Yes, why hadn't he noticed that before? Maybe because the cook didn't wear a suit, like so many of the other Schemers, and he didn't walk around carrying a little styrofoam cup full of steaming demon potion. The Schemers called their brew by a lot of different names—coffee, latte, cappuccino—but Cameron knew that those were all just code words for Liquid Damnation.

Why, Tony brewed coffee for his customers—he even drank it! Further proof! Maybe some of the coffee in the world was okay, but not the sort brewed by the Schemers. The Schemers loved drinking Liquid Damnation. They practically lived off of it. The Schemers also made a variety of other brain-control beverages, too. All part of their plot to enslave the world.

With a look around, Cameron tossed his bag on the counter and leaned over it. Nearly all his fingers were poking out of his old gloves, but he didn't mind. Tony gave him a friendly nod.

'Yeah, I showed 'em, didn't I?' Tony declared smugly, as if in answer to a question.

'How's that?' the cook asked without looking up from his ledger. 'These figures just aren't balancing right. Elaine—that's the missus—she gets mad when the books are screwed up.'

'That Schemer with the little moustache,' Cameron said with a smirk. 'He'll scheme no more, I promise you.'

'Is that right?' Tony nodded. 'Hey, wait, I forgot. The price of bacon went up.'

'But what about you? Yes, what about Tony?' Cameron leaned closer and lowered his voice. 'The next time you're talking to your potion-swilling Overlord, let him know that I've been watching your kind follow me in this sector for almost two months now. I know you all want my files.' He patted his faded and fraying red duffel bag. 'The documents are safe!' He paused dramatically. 'But the Schemers are not.' A sly grin stretched across his face.

'Izzat so?' Tony closed his ledger. 'I'd forgotten all about the bacon. I can't believe prices these days. I mean, it's just pig meat. Not like they sliced it off some endangered animal. Farms have pigs all over the place.'

Cameron nodded. 'I'm sure your friends in the FBI have all the answers. Why don't you ask them? They're after me now—but of course, you know that already, don't you? Seems they were in cahoots with the Schemers—were working through them to get the documents from me. Seems they thought I'd be no match for a FBI-trained Schemer with a little moustache. Seems they thought wrong!'

Tony cocked his head to one side. 'What's all this? The FBI? A guy with a little moustache? You're not talking about that old Nazi guy, are you?'

'So!' Cameron raised an eyebrow. 'The Overlord is in fact Adolf Hitler. He's not dead after all. I should have guessed. You've slipped up, Tony. Now all the pieces are falling into place. Yes, it all makes perfect sense. This calls for a celebration!' He opened a cooler on the counter, pulled out a can of lemon-lime pop, and quickly checked it for puncture holes. He then read the ingredients. 'This delightful citrus beverage is sealed up tight and is completely free of your foul Schemer potions. Therefore, I shall purchase it.'

'What? You're actually going to buy something?' the cook said. 'Geez, a surprise development like that could give a guy a heart attack.'

'There are very few products free of evil,' Cameron stated. 'The Schemers have their grubby claws wrapped around everything these days.' He held up the can. 'But this I can trust, for it has no cola beans in it—and cola grows in South America—and the Nazis fled to Brazil because that's where the jungles are. And the Schemers love hot, steamy, shadowy places, Tony. As well you know!'

The cook laughed out loud. 'My God, Cameron, you should be writing for Hollywood! This goofy mumbo-jumbo you're spoutin' is better than half them Arnold What's-His-Ass action movies.'

'Arnold What's-His-Ass. I'll remember that name. Another of your conspirators, no doubt.' Cameron pulled out his wallet and took out a sheaf of bills.

Tens. Twenties. Hundred-dollar bills.

He flipped a ten onto the counter and walked off.

* * *

Tony stared at the ten-dollar bill.

'Jesus Christ,' he whispered. He picked up the money. *I've been leaving food out for that freeloader! He thought. He could have paid for all those sandwiches this whole time. Why, I've probably spent over five hundred bucks on him!*

'You know,' Cameron shouted from about twenty feet away, 'with the Feds breathing down my neck now, I think I'll move on. Maybe to South America.'

Tony shook his head. *So now you're just gonna 'move on,' are you? You're no crazy guy. You're some kind of goddamn con artist. You figure you've milked me enough? Gonna go find some other patsy now? I wish the Feds really were after you, you lying—*

'Tell Hitler to say his prayers,' Cameron was saying. 'Keep the change, Tony.'

Still playing the loony. The audacity of that bum!

He watched Cameron walk off in the direction of the arboretum.

He seemed to always hanging around there. That must be where he camped out.

Tony closed and locked up the food trailer. He then walked over to the arboretum. He couldn't see Cameron outside of the building. Maybe he was inside somewhere. He didn't know what he was going to say to the man—but whatever he said, he knew it wasn't going to be pretty.

Inside, he walked past displays of roses, carnivorous plants, blooming vines—he was surprised to see flowers on a cactus, since he didn't realize they ever sprouted petals and stuff. He'd never been in the arboretum before. It was actually kind of interesting. There was nobody inside, which made sense, because—

Well, the place stank.

He walked past rows of pots and displays, past a little fake creek running through a plastic canal. There seemed to be a lot of flies in the air. *What's that smell? Fertilizer?* No, it wasn't a poopy odor . . . He'd been in the food business long enough to recognize that particular stench.

Rotten meat.

Why hadn't anyone reported this? Who was supposed to be looking after this building? He tried to remember. He'd met the guy, some rich do-gooder who did volunteer work—Carl Something-Or-Other. He hadn't seen Carl in some time. If a worker quits, people know right away. But if a volunteer quits, or something happens to him . . . Well, it's not like he was punching a clock. And if the place began to stink, well, maybe people would just stay out. They wouldn't give it much thought. They'd just assume some fresh fertilizer had been added.

He went up to one of the displays—a flowery bush with plenty of flies hovering around—and pushed aside the leaves. The dirt looked like it had been dug up recently. He poked his hand into the earth and rummaged around. And soon enough, his hand grasped what felt like—

Another hand. But not moving, like his.

Dead.

His heart was pounding so hard It felt like it was going to burst out of his chest. He pulled, and a woman's hand and slender arm came sliding out, bringing with it a stench that made him vomit.

A teen-aged girl wandered into the room, saw what was happening and began to scream.

Soon more people were entering the arboretum, drawn by the screams, all sniffing and talking in loud, shocked voices.

Tony stared in disbelief at the arm. *The crazy bastard. He really was a loony, killing people and chopping them up. Hiding the bits here in the arboretum. Probably stealing their money, too. No wonder he had that big wad on him.*

Then he noticed something weird about the end of the arm. The part where it was supposed to meet the shoulder. People were staring at him, screaming, calling the police on cellphones, but he didn't care. The only thing that mattered in all the world, at that moment, was the end of that freaky arm.

Something to do with shoulders . . .

It didn't end in a bony, bloody stump. No. Instead it had a little chamber there, filled with wires and knobs and handles. He twisted one of the tiny knobs. At the other end of the arm, the hand clenched into a fist.

He dropped the artificial limb, grabbed the flowery bush near the base, and pulled out the plant by the roots.

'What do you think you're doing?' an old woman shouted. 'You should wait for the police!'

He knelt by the display and scooped away more dirt from the area unearthed by the uprooted bush. There was something under there. A body. A dead woman in a silky yellow blouse. Under the fabric of a sleeve, he saw the outline of the corpse's real arm, but it was too short, way too short. It would have needed some kind of—extension. Like a fake arm.

The ripe, sickly-sweet stench of the body was making his eyes water. *Oh my God, there's the dead lady's face.* But the face was loose and sloped at an angle from the rest of the head, like a thin rubber Halloween mask that was beginning to slip off.

He grabbed the tip of the nose and pulled.

The fake skin pulled away with a wet sucking sound, to reveal—another face. The contours were human, but the skin was slimy and as pale as the moon. Like the big nightcrawlers his dad would impale on hooks back when they used to go fishing.

He grabbed the collar of the blouse and pulled it to the side, to take a look at that tiny arm.

It looked like a gnarled pink chicken claw with too many digits. The horrible thing was streaked with bright purple veins.

'What the Hell is that?' shouted a man standing behind him.

Tony looked up, ready to turn and say something the man, when he happened to glance through the glass wall of the arboretum.

People on the other side were looking in, shocked looks on their faces.

One of them was Cameron. And he didn't seem too shocked.

He was now wearing a light-gray business suit and a dark-gray hat, and instead of that duffel bag, he was carrying a briefcase. He tipped his hat to Tony, turned and walked off.

The cook tried to hurry out of the arboretum, but it took him some time to work his way through the crowd—some folks were trying to hold him back, saying he needed to stay and talk to the police.

He ran around the park, shouting for Cameron. Finally he saw the man in the light-gray suit by the sidewalk, opening the door of a cab.

He ran up to him. 'Hold on, Cameron! Stop!' the cook cried. 'You've got to tell me what's going on around here.'

'I've already told you everything I can say at this point about the Schemers.' Cameron smiled. 'I guess you're not one of them after all. Glad I didn't kill you.' He gestured toward the cab. 'You want to come and help fight them? I'm authorized by Operation Control to enlist assistants as necessary.'

Tony shook his head. 'Are you kiddin'? I just can't run off to battle demons. I have a wife and a couple kids to think about.'

Cameron looked at him out of the corner of his eye. 'That sounds more like a reason to join the fight—not avoid it.' He shrugged. 'And people think *I'm* crazy.' He slipped into the vehicle and slammed the door.

Then the cab drove off.

A PLACE THAT THE NIGHT CAN'T TOUCH
Paul Edwards

I. Together, Alone

Choice excerpts from the diary of Louise Naughton, Graveshaw, East Sussex:

Oct 2nd

Marvin has ripped chunks out of my favourite dress. I suppose it's my fault really; I shouldn't have left it hanging around, though I make a point of not speaking to him for the rest of the day.

Oct 3rd

Spent all day running around the house, making sure that the slats are still nice and firm across the windows and doors. I knocked back in a few loose nails and replaced a rotted piece of wood that had screened the bathroom window.

Just noticed that there's a dead dog out on the lawn; one of the Creeps must have left it there. Its bright coils of innards look like pink, wet snakes in the sunlight, and there's a real disgusting smell to the air. It makes me feel sick every time I go outside.

Oct 5th

While in town, ransacking the grocery stores, Marvin went into my room and found my beautiful, leather-bound Hans Christian Anderson book of fairy-tales, which my grandmother bought me for my tenth birthday. He's ripped the book to shreds and eaten most of the pages.

I feel angry and depressed. I can't seem to stop crying. Marvin doesn't seem to understand my distress in any way and I'm seriously thinking about muzzling him again.

Oct 6th

I've come to the conclusion that muzzling Marvin wouldn't do any good at all—it would be an enormous step back from everything that I've achieved with him. I've got to condition him not to do these things. In the way I conditioned him not to eat me.

This afternoon, when I was rooting through the kitchen drawers, I found a pad of bright red circular stickers inside a tiny Japanese ornate tin. I have no idea what they are supposed to be for, but I am sure I can put them to use...

Oct 16th

Last night I forgot to put my earplugs in before falling asleep, and in the early hours of the morning the sound of the Creeps, scratching at the slats and doors with their black, filth-caked nails, woke me.

I sat bolt upright in bed. My whole body was trembling.

I could hear their thwarted groans above the screeching wind. The scratching intensified. Something bashed against the front door. I lit the blood-red candle next to my bed and the walls glowed a dark, dark crimson.

'You'll never get in,' I whispered, over and over to myself until it became a mantra. Then I reached across and snatched up my plugs, and as I squeezed them into my ears, the candle hissed and spat and went out and I embraced the silent darkness.

Here is a place where nothing can find me, I thought. A safe place. A place that the night can't touch.

Oct 29th

a.m. Training is complete—I hope! This afternoon I shall conduct a little experiment to see if my hard work has paid off.

p.m. I waited, patiently, in the kitchen. Everything was carefully prepared.

A little before six o'clock Marvin scuffled into the room looking for food. His enormous shadow enveloped the pale light on the dirty-magnolia walls.

Laid out upon the dining table were the remnants of last night's meal—slices of beef, cooked sausages wrapped in bacon, roast potatoes. He looked at it, and for a horrible moment I was sure that he was going to eat it.

But then he turned his head and stared at the opened tin of dog food on the side.

'Go on,' I hissed, and I indicated the tin with a slight movement of my head. Marvin looked at me.

'Go on, boy.'

Slowly, he turned around. Then he lurched towards the tin and gathered it up in his clumsy hands, grunting incomprehensively as he glared at the red sticker on its raised lid. I slunk back into the shadows, gnawing at my nails in apprehension. And as Marvin spooned his gnarled fingers into the tin and patted the processed meat into his mouth, I let out an in containable shriek of delight. 'Well done, Marvin!' I shrilled, clapping my hands. 'Good boy! Good boy!'

Nov 3rd

The stickers are working a treat; though somehow I managed to get one on a kitchen cabinet door, don't ask me how. I walked into the kitchen just a moment ago and found Marvin with his mouth clamped around the edge of the cabinet, trying to eat the thing! I couldn't help myself: I dissolved into tears of laughter.

But, suddenly, there was this tremendous snap, and the wood splintered and Marvin broke a few of his teeth. There was blood everywhere.

'Oh Marvin!' I sighed, grabbing the kitchen-roll on the side. 'Let's clean you up!'

Marvin's sitting quietly in the lounge now, feeling sorry for himself, bless his soul.

Nov 4th

The evenings are getting colder now. The prevailing wind rattles the loosening tiles on the roof.

Tonight I've retired to my room early, leaving Marvin in his chair in the lounge, his long hands in his lap, his hollow eyes fixed at nothing in particular on the wall.

The attic window is the only window in the house that isn't boarded up and from here I can see for miles. The moon stares back at me from a cavernous black sky like a sunken eyeball, silvering the wind chimes hanging from the windowsill and the cars in the driveway outside. The blue Escort doesn't start up anymore, and the yellow Citroen is almost out of fuel—soon I might not be able to make my weekly run into town for food.

Earlier on I saw Creeps, loitering by the woods at the end of the garden. They looked like grotesque scarecrows in the moonlight. Perhaps I was being paranoid, but I could have sworn that they were looking straight at me . . . Anyway, they're gone now. But they'll be back. They always come back.

Nov 7th

This afternoon, as I was reading an old Anne McCaffrey paperback in the lounge, I looked up at Marvin and tried to guess what his real name might be—I only call him Marvin because he kind of looks like a Marvin.

'You OK?' I asked him. He turned his head to look at me, and his ugly mouth cracked into a smile.

He may be stupid and slow, but he's nothing like those Creeps outside. Not now, anyway. And I feel so comfortable around him.

He's the closest thing I have to a friend, I suppose.

II. An Intrusion

a.m. Leaving Marvin to his own devices, I spent time watching the world through the window in the attic.

Under a deadpan sky, the Creeps gathered ominously by the hackneyed fencing that segregates the woods from the garden. I watched them stumble and fall into one another like drunkards. Moments later the rain came, and it streaked down the glass like tears.

Suddenly, there was a flurry of movement to the left of my vision: a young woman emerged from the woods, slipping in the mud and rain, bleeding from cuts across her arms and legs. She glanced around with wide, frightened eyes and saw the house.

I shrunk behind the curtain.

'My God,' I whispered. 'This can't be real.'

I twitched the curtain and looked again.

The woman scrambled over the fence, then ran the length of the garden and tried the doors to first the Escort, then the Citroen. When she found them locked, she charged towards the porch, her long dark hair whipping across her panic-stricken face, and pounded the front door with bunched fists. 'Please!' she screamed, 'let me in! Somebody let me in!'

I felt sick, confused.

Meanwhile the Creeps seemed to pour out of the woods; they staggered towards her in the grainy half-light, the rain pelting against their white faces.

'PLEASE! For God's sake, if there's anybody there, please LET ME IN!'

There wasn't time to think things through; suddenly I was downstairs, lifting the slats and releasing the catches of the front door. The young woman squeezed her way in. As I closed and locked the door up quickly behind her, I caught a glimpse of a ghostly white face through the gap that she left behind.

Silence.

She stood in the hall, her long, wet hair dangling in her face.

After a while she said: 'Thank you, thank you.'

I glanced at Marvin, sitting quietly in the long-shadows of the lounge, and before she could look I closed the door on him.

'You . . . OK?' I asked.

Suddenly the girl flung her skinny arms around me and started to cry—huge, choked sobs of relief. I felt her trembling body against mine and I was scared because I knew I'd done the wrong thing.

p.m. 'I'm so glad that I found you,' she said as we stood in the kitchen. Her eyes were black, bloodshot, as though she hadn't slept in days. 'My name is Gillian. I was living in town when . . .'

She looked away and folded her scratched arms across her chest.

I looked down at the floor. I didn't really know what to say.

'What is your name?' she asked, turning her head to look at me again.

'Louise.'

She smiled. 'I haven't seen anyone alive for weeks! I've been living in a cellar in the old tyre factory, you know, the one opposite Graveshaw Church.' She drew in a deep breath. 'One night those things broke in and almost caught me . . . but I escaped.'

For a while there was silence between us; there was just the sound of the rain streaming against the windows. Gillian fingered a silver St. Christopher around her slender neck. 'What do you think happened?' she said at last. 'I mean . . . is this some form of punishment, you know, from God? Or a science experiment that's gone wrong?'

I stared at my hands, as though I was looking for her answers in the creases and folds of my skin.

'My husband, Tom . . . he died suddenly six months ago. A heart defect. When I saw him that morning, standing there, in the porch . . . it was as if all my nightmares had suddenly turned real.' Her eyes welled with tears, but she blinked them away. 'He tried to kill me . . . He tried to eat me.'

I began moving around the room, peeling off my bright red stickers from the dog food cans, plates of raw meat and from the fruit in the fruit bowl. Gillian watched me. I saw disorientation in her eyes. 'Hey,' I said quickly. 'Why don't you rest a while? You look so tired. There's a spare bedroom upstairs, first door on the left.'

'Yes,' she said. 'Yes, thanks Louise, I think I will.'

She hesitated on her way out through the door. 'Is this your house?' she asked.

'No. I don't know who it belonged to.'

'Wasn't there anybody here?'

I thought of Marvin.

He was here.

I found him in the attic, after I'd boarded up the house.

'No,' I said. 'Nobody.'

Gillian smiled sadly. 'We're going to be OK here, aren't we? We can get through this . . . now that we've found each other.'

'Yes,' I replied, and returned the smile. But it was a false smile; it didn't reflect how utterly detached I was feeling from the world.

An hour later I crept upstairs, took my earplugs from off of the top of my bedside cabinet and slipped them into my pocket. Then I crossed the hall and tapped gently on the door to the spare bedroom. There was no reply, so I opened the door quietly. Gillian was sound asleep on the bed, her dark hair splashed across the pillow.

I moved to the foot of the bed and stared at her for a while.

The shadows in the room lengthened, as it grew dark outside.

'I'm sorry,' I said, and my words seemed to hang in the air. You have to understand, it's not that I didn't like Gillian. It's just that I liked my world the way it was; everything was simple, there were no complications. You see, the house, this place, it's all mine, it belongs to me. It is my own private, beautiful world. Nothing can touch it; not the night, not anyone.

Downstairs, I heard Marvin move from the lounge into the kitchen.

I leaned over Gillian. Her eyelashes fluttered. Tenderly, I touched her forehead. When I brought my fingers away, there was a single red sticker on her brow.

Marvin was clattering through the drawers looking for food when I came back downstairs. As I stood in the doorway to the kitchen, he turned his pallid face and looked at me with dead, dead eyes.

'Marvin,' I said, pointing to the ceiling. 'Try up there. Up there.' He stared blankly at me. He couldn't read guilt, or fear, in my face. That's what I love so much about him: he can't detect any weakness in me at all. 'Upstairs,' I said again.

Suddenly he nodded his head and moaned excitedly and I caught a glimmer of understanding inside those hollow eyes.

I stepped out of his way.

He lurched past me, and then ascended the stairs. And as I heard him enter the spare bedroom, I pressed the plugs into my ears so that I wouldn't hear a thing.

EYES OF HAZEL, KISS THE EARTH
Darren Speegle

It was supposed to have been a simple deal. I was there to get something from him. He was there to get something from me. It was the sort of transaction I had been involved in a dozen times before. The trouble was, he wanted more from me than was in our arrangement. He wanted not just the baby; he wanted me to deliver the seven-week-old package to a different spot, and on a different night. He had the money, which he gave to me, but he didn't have the means to see after the infant right now. Tomorrow night was better.

The means to see after it? What was that supposed to mean?

'Then why did I bring it along?' I asked, feeling uncomfortable beneath his discerning stare.

'It' was a boy. In this business you lose sight of such things . . . on purpose.

'I had to make sure it was healthy.'

I didn't care how discerning he was, how the hell was he going to know that by looking at the infant? That particular episode of that particular prime time TV series which shall remain particularly nameless had shown us all that. Business dropped like a balloon for three months because of that show.

I didn't bother avoiding such issues anymore; I showed them the papers, I charged them half of what I once did, the rest was their concern. Now, don't get me wrong, mine was a legitimate business—any of my clients would have told you that—it's just that you can't ever be too sure, can you? I did all I could do at my end, even had my own pediatrician, to whom I gave a generous cut. No, the reason I got out of the business had nothing to do with baggage. It had to do with this gentleman standing here in front of me, although I'd no idea then I was headed for the unemployment line.

I voiced the thought. 'How are you going to know if the baby's healthy by looking at it?'

'Oh, you know,' he said, '... whether it's plump, colored, that sort of thing.'

That should have been a dead giveaway. In fact I remember thinking—not for the first time in my dealings with this gentleman—that although he didn't have the *slick* of some of the lawyers with whom I'd crossed paths, there was still this hard-to-define, even askew something about him. Never mind that when he laid his judgmental eyes on me, he was accusing me less of unsavory practices than of being a lost soul. As far as I was concerned, righteousness itself had a funny smell to it. I asked myself a question I had asked myself more than once before. What did I know about the quality of the home into which the child was going? What about *their* health? Were they a plump couple? Were they colored? Were they *that sort of thing*? It's a beast, the living, no doubt about it. The questions abound, but the answers are scarce.

I eyed him, perhaps as openly as he eyed me. But in the end, one concern prevailed. What was I going to do with the baby for the next twenty-four hours?

I bade the gentleman goodnight and took my package home with me. I had nowhere else to take the little guy. The parents of the teenage girl, apparently of some status in the community, had told me quite plainly that they wanted to sever all contact now. I was to do as discussed with the money, and that was that. We did not know each other. We had never had any relations of any kind.

I phoned the doctor in my employ and asked him what I would need for the baby. I'm ashamed to say I was ignorant in that regard. I realize how unprofessional that must sound, considering the line of work I was in, but I was unmarried, an only child, and simply had never had to do the part before. The doctor told me not to be concerned; at that age the baby would be no trouble. He was kind enough to pick up the essentials and bring them to me, so I wouldn't have to drag the infant back out. I learned changing diapers, preparing formula, burping, a whole new discipline that evening. I had literally never had a baby in my possession for longer than thirty minutes.

My guest woke only once during the night. I held him for a while, singing what songs I could recall from my own weehood, telling him how I wished he had a name. His mother's parents had advised her against naming the baby. Which was understandable, I suppose, but it left me with this plump, pink baby with hazel eyes and no identity. I don't know, can a seven-week-old have an identity?

After spending the whole next day with him, I felt this little guy did. To the extent that when eight o'clock rolled around, I didn't want to take him to meet Mr. Doe. I had grown sort of used to him. He hardly ever cried, and spit up on me only a time or two. I was forced to remind myself that, although the service provided was a winner for all involved, the baby remained a product, and it was best not to lose sight of that fact.

We drove out to the designated spot; 'Little Guy' nestled over there in his seat, quiet as you please. The church was in a more well to do neighborhood, where you might, in fact, expect to find a couple with means enough to purchase a baby boy. When I wheeled around behind the structure, I found that Mr. Doe hadn't arrived yet. Shutting off the engine, I said to my passenger, 'Well, Little Guy, I guess we'll have to wait.' But I was uneasy.

As I remember it, far worse than the nervousness of waiting in the darkness behind a church in that neighborhood was the discomforting silence that had settled over the interior of the car. It had the flavor of that thing that follows a spat with your date. Cry, I wished at the baby. *Goo. Gurgle. Babble. Do something.* I would have preferred he had been asleep, then I wouldn't have had to face those knowing hazel eyes.

Gratefully, less than five minutes after our arrival, a knock came at the rear passenger window. Mr. Doe's face looked in. With his thumb he motioned I unlock the door.

'What are you doing?' I said as he got in.

'Drive,' he said. And pointed a handgun at my head.

Glancing over at the baby, I began, 'I don't know what y—'

'Drive.'

'Where?'

'I'll let you know.'

I turned the key, put it in gear and drove. We pulled left out of the church parking lot. A mile down we turned left again. In a few minutes he indicated a dirt road to the right. Though I took it slow, it was rough going, and Little Guy started crying.

'Yes, he does seem to be a healthy one,' Mr. Doe said from the back seat.

I silently wished him a *rot in hell* as we bounced around a bend and the road came to an abrupt end at the edge of a field.

There must have been a hundred of them in the field, many with torches, all cloaked. They were material in the flash of the headlights, shadows as I shut the beams off at Mr. Doe's command. The night was young but deep. We were in that strange territory between the suburbs and the country, just beyond the fringes of the artificial light but not so far out that the land was cast in the unfiltered radiation of the spangled heavens. We were in that sightless territory where babies had no names and adults draped in dark garments bartered for them like packaged meats.

He had given me two commands. Shut off the lights. Shut off the engine. I obeyed only one. The little guy, you know. It was the little guy's party, no question about that, but no one had bothered to ask if he could make it. As his temporary guardian, I said uh-uh, he could not make it. Whatever these people were up to—ritual sacrifice, cannibalism, God only knew—they would have to go somewhere else for their plump, colored infant.

I threw the shifter in reverse, floored the pedal. The car surged but a huge weight resisted its going anywhere, as though the most functional emergency brake ever made were engaged. I pushed the pedal so hard, it's a wonder the thing didn't go through the floor. Then it was over. I'd had only as much time as it took for Mr. Doe to recover from the initial lurch of the vehicle, and that was mere seconds. He now had the nose of his gun against the top of the baby's wailing head, right there where I knew Little Guy's soft spot to be.

'Shut the fucking engine off!' he yelled.

I did.

'The keys,' he ordered, gesturing with his free hand. As I handed him the ring, I saw faces staring in at me from all three of the back windows. The car fell. In my adrenaline storm, I hadn't even realized its rear wheels had been lifted off the ground. Needless to say, I have never owned another rear wheel drive.

'Out of the car!' Mr. Doe ordered.

I obeyed. They met me, torchlight flickering, distorted faces peering from deep within cowls. The *déjà vu* crawled over me like hairy spiders. I'd felt the first twinge when I saw their robes in the headlights, now was immersed in it. What in God's name were they going to do with the little fellow? I felt I should know, that I had drifted through some amorphous foretelling of this nightmare

. . .

The passenger door opened. Seconds passed as the straps were removed, then the bundle came up in the light for a moment before being gathered in to a chest. The crying weakened and died, like a torch spent, pitch drying on colored skin. As we moved across the field, I watched them pass the baby from one to another. I noticed how gingerly they handled it, how tenderly they touched those streaked cheeks—and not just the women but the men as well, as they passed their torches to their neighbors so they could experience the child personally.

I was pushed along in the tide of bodies, remaining unmolested otherwise. I wondered what would become of me but rather suspected I knew the answer. The how was what was in question. As we approached the middle of the field, I felt the current slowing. We formed a circle around a spot where I presumed they had taken the baby. Gently, and by many hands, I was ushered through the bodies and to the circle's center. Mr. Doe was there. So was the baby. He held the bundle up in his hands, up towards the heathen night sky. The baby was silent as he kissed it and brought it down to his chest again. He held out his hand to one of the figures nearby. I saw a glint of metal as the implement was placed in his hand. I rushed forward, unrestrained, unsure of what to do when I got there.

'But it's only a spade. See,' he said, holding it up in the torchlight.

'Wha—what are you going to do with it?' I stammered.

'No, my friend,' he laughed. 'What are you going to do with it?'

I took a step back, shaking my head, the *déjà vu* bristling in my flesh, the sweat starting to twitch from my pores. 'I won't. I won't.'

'Have no fear,' said Mr. Doe. 'It's an act, that's all.'

'An *act!*'

'Only an act. Here, take the baby. I'll show you where.'

Yes, the baby. Give me the baby. Let me touch it again before you do it.

He handed the bundle to me. I pulled back a bit of cloth, looked at its little—

'What have you done to it?' I cried.

Even as Little Guy gazed up at me, his eyes lost the last of their whites to the expanding, saturating pigment of their lenses. The orbs were now entirely hazel.

'It's not *I* who have done it,' said Mr. Doe. 'The child's body knows it has found its way home.'

'I don't want it!' I shrieked, holding the bundle out at arm's length. Towards him, the other one, anyone . . .

'Come. Come here to the spot.' He put his boot on what looked like a random point in the grass. With a motion of his wrist, he flung the spade into the ground.

'Right there,' he said. 'That's where.'

Although I saw the spot he had marked, although I had watched the blade pierce the earth, it was far from my focus. I continued to hold the baby out from my body, repulsed by it, terrified of it, and yet unable to drop it or to throw it at one of them for fear I would do it injury.

'I can help you,' came a calm masculine voice. 'Give me the baby.'

It was the one who had supplied the spade.

I gave it willingly. He would not hurt the baby. I sensed he would not hurt him.

His hood got in the way as he bent to the baby. He removed it. The baby issued a sound, a cooing, affectionate sound. The young man issued a sound of his own. I could see the side of his head but little more as he gazed at the baby. I demanded he turn and look at me.

He did, and what I thought I had seen by the fragmented light was now confirmed. His face was only barely recognizable as the face of a man. It was gray in the torchlight, its texture rough, creased, even *knotted*. His hair—which I had at first thought it to be a ritual wig, a prop of some kind—was not hair at all but a wild Gorgonian confusion of vine and earth and leaves.

I whirled, eyes darting around the circle, from figure to figure, hood to hood. Darkness stared back at me from within the cowls.

'Show yourselves,' I demanded. 'Drop the hoods. What in Christ's name *are you?*'

One by one they began to remove their hoods. But the faces that were revealed were as normal as my own, each and every one of them, none even vaguely resembling the grotesque features of the young man or the baby.

I turned back to him. As terrified as I was, I found it within me to form words.

'What is the baby to you?'

'He is my son.'

'But the girl . . . his mother?'

'When I am away from this hallowed place and walking among you, I am a handsome young man.'

'What *are* you?' It was a whisper.

As he smiled, dry cracks formed at the corners of his mouth, threatening to spider web across his gray bark-like skin.

'I am not a god. I am a liaison.'

'But . . . what do you want from me?'

He gestured. My eyes went there, but I didn't understand.

Mr. Doe retrieved the spade from the earth. 'We want you,' he said, 'to dig.'

I did not want to dig. Above all . . . *don't make me dig*. Sometimes, you see, on those rarest of occasions, you remember the *déjà vu* before the *déjà vu* remembers you. You recall the smell of the soil before you break it with the shovel. You glimpse, for the merest second, why it is you are here. And then it's gone, leaving only the knowledge that you are a baby merchant.

I accepted it from Mr. Doe in a hand that shook uncontrollably. I knelt down and began to dig.

'How deep?' As I threw the first scoop.

'Deep enough to plant a sapling,' said Mr. Doe.

That at least I could fix on. It had substance to it. I dug until I thought the hole of adequate depth for the potted tree I pictured in my mind.

'Now?' I said.

'Keep digging.'

I continued, rounding the hole out a certain way, A stroke here, a stroke there, another few inches in depth. That terrible knowledge I had glimpsed as he held the spade out to me still hovered, poised to descend on me. I paused, wiping my brow with the back of my hand. I was perspiring profusely, though it was only a spade. And a hole big enough to bury your cat in.

I glanced up at Mr. Doe. My lips quivered.

'A bit more,' he said.

I went at it again. Scoop after scoop, but still rounding, still measuring, as if baby trading were only my day job.

At last he said, 'That is sufficient.'

I rose slowly, spitting the dirt out of my mouth. As the circle moved closer, the torchlight dancing across the walls of the hole in the earth, I would look no place but there. They began to chant, the circle, and as their voice lifted, the knowledge descended, its talons like razors as they tore into my sweaty, dirty flesh.

Even when he offered it to me in his extended hands, my eyes remained in the pit I had made.

Mr. Doe put a hand on my shoulder, turned me around to face them.

'Why me?' I implored. 'Why *me?*'

'It didn't have to be you,' Mr. Doe said. 'In fact it was my full intention to take the child away last night and never see you again. Then I caught a glimpse of that empty place inside you and reconsidered. Since I was only going to take him home with me until the ceremony tonight, I decided I would let you experience him. As well as the ceremony itself.'

My eyes, stinging with tears, drifted to the bundle that was being presented to me. The one presenting it peered at me through his hazel eyes and said, 'No one could benefit more than you. Take him. Plant the sapling so that he may grow up to continue the cycle. Plant the sapling and let him take root in that desolate place in your soul. Go ahead. He is a liaison. Between man and the earth.'

I heard the sound again. Despite the chanting around me, I heard the voice of Little Guy. Cooing, affectionate.

'Please,' I choked. 'I—I can't.'

But I did. God help me, I did.

Though I've never managed to bring myself to return to that field to see what sort of boy he's growing up to be.

RAG DOLLS
Christian Westerlund

She never got tired of watching the stars. They fell now, like pebbles shimmering down a dark well, drowning in an endless sea of obscurity. Somehow they always brought tears to her eyes, whispering the way they did, about far and ancient memories, of worlds beyond ours.

She gazed quietly into space, letting her soul soar up there among the glimmering stars, each one of them a fluttering light, a story that needed to be told, to make people open their eyes and look, to watch as dreams were crumbled like sandcastles.

But the stars did not ask anyone to look. They just kept falling down the blazing night, waiting for that one special wish to be uttered in the darkness. The one of a lost and lonely rag doll, the one that would set them all free, bursting like angels up into the night air.

Her name was Amber and she lay flat out on her back, in a dirty old alley somewhere in the world, listening to a silent dripping somewhere far off in the night. There was something reeking there in the alley, an odour of things gone bad, rotting, thrown out into the darkness. Trash cans lay pushed over and scruffy dogs were sniffing among the heaps of garbage.

Amber sighed, quietly.

The stars always brought strange memories back to her. Memories she could not fully understand. She recalled similar nights, when she had been lying flat on her back, watching the stars. But there was also the feeling of wood around her, and a soft scent of mothballs and dirty old fabric. And, somehow, a big dog sniffing and drooling over her, chewing on her cloths—or maybe something else.

Those were the only memories she had, the rest was blank, only a vague feeling of kids pulling her arms and a soft smell of liquorish in the night air.

Suddenly, Amber felt someone poking her.

She lifted her gaze and saw tear-stained sunken eyes and a cob-draped little face. She pulled back at first, but calmed down when she realized it was just another homeless child, living among the boxes and the heaps of trash there in the alley.

The dirty little boy smiled, shyly.

'So pale,' he whispered, peering at her pale skin.

Amber looked down at her bone white hands, the black nail polish, and the white, fluorescent skin that covered the thin little body. She hid deep under the folds of a black leather jacket, afraid that someone might see her body and wonder what she was.

'Yeah . . . pale,' she said, looking at her skin.

Other children come out of the darkness, emerging from shadows and creeping out of boxes, peering at her with glowing eyes. All homeless, all of them with the same hollow expression.

The chubby little boy next to her poked his nose up into the air and smelled her carefully.

'You smell funny, like old attics,' he chuckled in a high, childish voice.

'I know,' said Amber.

He fumbled with her leather jacket.

'Who are you?' he asked.

Amber wanted to take him and hold him tightly, whispering, 'I don't know, I don't know. I have no memories, none that makes any sense. And I don't know why my skin is white like snow and feels like worn fabric.'

But she did not. She just leaned back against the wall and sighed.

'No one,' she said. 'I am no one.'

But the dirty little boy smiled at her, and somehow his eyes were just like the stars there in the darkness, whirling and glimmering with a soft promise of tomorrow.

Amber had always felt comfortable among children, she knew that. And the little boy made her feel a little bit of happiness there in the night, for the first time since she could remember.

He crawled up in her lap and laid his chubby little head against her shoulder, and she held him so tenderly as only a mother can, rocking him, whispering a sweet hush to him in the shimmering starlight.

'Who am I?' she asked, quietly.

And then she wept, silently, holding the scruffy little boy close to her.

The carnival waited.

The sky burnt in hazy ambers above the world, roasting stars over an open fire, to a fine, brown crisp. Carrousels slowed down to a lazy mechanical tinkle, and the horses, on their brass poles, were hidden under moth-eaten canvas. Ticket-booths were padlocked, the last confused costumers walked away from the mirror-maze, and the ancient old fortunes-tellers all closed and folded their wicked eyes. There was nothing more for them to see, no palms to be read, no fortunes to be told. Moth-like hands were laid over dried-out chests, as the witches all lay down to sleep.

Then the carnival stopped waiting.

Amber came walking across the green meadow, listening to the crickets' drowsy serenade. She gazed quietly at the carnival and something woke inside of her, a feeling of recognition. She looked at the brightly coloured tents, at the canvas that covered all the wonders, and all the wide-eyes children that had to be dragged home by their parents. And somewhere far inside of her, there was something that made her whisper a silent, 'Home'.

She stood for a moment, watching the freaks that stood close together in the night, whispering and hushing at each other. Their faces were melting, growing together, misshaped and unrecognisable, a ground of nightmares brought to life.

'I knew you'd come back,' someone whispered behind her.

Amber spun around and found herself looking right back into a broken mirror. An old gypsy witch stood there, smirking, chewing on mummified lips. She looked just like someone who has been pressed down and down in a dumpster, and then pulled and waded out again, like some sort of strange accordion. Her eyes disappeared somewhere among all the wrinkles and the warts. Her skin seemed to have belonged to a lizard once, now strapped and wadded down over a hollow skeleton.

'They always come back,' said the witch.

'What are you talking about?' asked Amber.

The witch smiled, silently, showing up a toothless old mouth that chewed wishes and secrets as other people might chew their dinner. Warts grew in her mouth too, like strange fungus.

'Look at you,' whispered the witch, 'So beautiful. Pale as death himself, all dressed in black. And your eyes too, why they almost look real. Hard to believe they were only buttons a couple of days ago, ripped from an old farmers shirt. Heck, girl, you almost look human.'

Amber stepped back.

'What are you talking about?' she repeated.

'You really don't remember, do you?'

The witch stepped forward.

'They must have been horrible for you, these last few days. Wandering around with no memories, with no life.'

Amber shivered.

'What am I?' she whispered, faintly.

The ancient gypsy woman chuckled in dry, hissing voice.

'Tell me, Amber, does you skin still feel like fabric when you touch it?' she asked.

And suddenly Amber saw the wooden sign outside the old tent, the blatant, crooked words that proclaimed:

RAG-DOLLS

And they lay in a big wooden box, staring off into the distance, torn and ripped rag-dolls, thrown upon each other in a big pile, close together. Some of them had been ripped open and had their stuffing pulled out, some were missing an eye, but they were all dead and silent, watching the stars—like they always did.

'No,' whispered Amber, and hot tears rolled down her cheeks.

'Yes,' said the old witch. 'You were always the most beautiful of them all, Amber, so perfect, black upon white in a never-ending dream. I remember when I sewed you together, your black little button eyes and the stuffing in your body. That was a fine night, Amber, when I ran that flashing needle in and out of your little fabric body.'

'It's not true,' wept Amber, sinking down on her knees.

'Of course it is. Do you have any memories? Do you remember your childhood, you parents, anything at all? Do you remember ever being loved?'

'No.'

Amber lay on the ground and the wind came to her, carrying the smell of liquorish and cotton candy, and she knew that this was where she belonged.

'Why?' she asked.

'Why?'

The witch leaned down over her and grabbed her arm, clenching it tightly with her bird-like fingers. 'Do you want a reason?' she whispered, and Amber felt her sour, rotten breath in the darkness.

'Does the world give a reason for turning everything sad in autumn, when it crumbles all the sandcastles and allows the wind to blow away all the footprints of June and July?'

Her grip around Ambers arm tightened.

'Does time give a reason for taking your beauty away from you?' she whispered, running her long fingers down her own face, as if she wondered where her youth had gone. 'No. It does not,' she snapped. 'There are no reasons here in this world.'

Amber lay weeping in the grass.

The witch sat down next to her.

'My sweet Amber. So beautiful and pale. I gave you the greatest gifts of all, I gave you life. And I will let you remember the echoes of this world, Amber, I'll let you keep these memories.'

The world sighed around them, and suddenly Amber felt very small, nothing more than a doll. She felt her pale skin cracking up, turning into soft fabric, and her eyes, slowly, turning into small buttons, ripped off a farmer's shirt.

The last thing she ever saw, before the world went dark, was the face of an ugly old gypsy.

The chubby little boy sat alone in the alley. Dark winds blew in his dirty little face, and he dug quietly in a big pile of trash, looking for something to eat.

He missed the pale girl. The one who had held him so tenderly, like no one else had done before. Tears rolled down his cheeks now, at the memory of her and her long, dark hair.

Suddenly, there were footsteps behind him. The little toddler spun around; frightened that someone might try to take his trash away from him.

There stood the ugliest woman he had ever seen, short and crooked against the pink florescent lights of the neon city. She pinched her warts for a moment, then she held out something to him, a strange little rag-doll, torn and ripped apart. It was made of white fabric, and then wrapped in a small leather jacket. One of its eyes had been chewed off.

'This is for you,' said the witch. 'That's what she would have wanted.'

And she gave the doll to the surprised little boy, then she strolled off into the night.

The boy held the rag doll silently, peering curiously at it, black upon white, and its strange little eye that was nothing at all.

But then he got bored of it, and threw it away back into the alley.

It lay there for a while, in the dirty gutter, until some stray dogs found it and began to tear it apart.

THE PROCESSION
Paul Kane

A t first he thought it was a fault with the camera. Light being let in through the back. It wasn't a major problem. Indeed, some of his most successful stills had been happy accidents (underexposures, film doubling back over itself inside the camera . . .). But there was something different about these shapes.

Bob Greenan held the glossy paper up to the light. What had once been simply black dots on the negative were now bleached splotches running diagonally along the length of his landscapes. Ill-defined and patchy, they stood in a row on those monochrome hills, which were the subject of his pictures.

The first nineteen images had been fine; perfect in fact. Just what Bob had been hoping for. The sun setting on Derbyshire's famous rolling hills, casting shadows over the puff pastry clouds and creating singularly natural chiaroscuro patterns. A photographer's dream.

But as the sun was dragged ever lower and lower, so imperfections had appeared on each shot. A sum of five in total. Bob didn't remember seeing any lights when he'd clicked the shutter those final few times, yet here they were with no explanation other than a possible crack in the camera casing itself.

The photographer examined his Praktica, though for the life of him he couldn't find anything wrong. And anyway, surely that wouldn't cause the light to line up in such a way; larger on the left hand side, and tailing off the closer to the sun they came. Almost like a queue.

Or a procession.

Puzzled, he pulled on his red bulb again and slipped another negative into the enlarger. The inverted image shone through a filter and, after focusing it, he exposed a new piece of photographic paper for a few seconds. Then he dropped it into the developer tray on his right.

Slowly the scene revealed itself. The same thing again, more white shapes traipsing over the gradient, disappearing into the distance.

Stop bath next, then fixative, and Bob had another enigma ready for inspection. He hung it on his drying line with a clip and scratched his head. Maybe the sun's rays had reflected off the lens somehow. Could that have caused such a pattern to emerge? He doubted it. For one thing the sun had been a dying one, incapable of squeezing that much light out (hence the need for 400 speed film), and for another, any reflections that may have been caught would've appeared randomly all over the place: in the sky, the bottom corners . . . Not in this orderly fashion.

Fresh out of ideas, he ambled over to the darkroom door and went back into the cottage proper. He was greeted by a russet blur bounding towards him. Sammy, Bob's energetic red setter, jumped up his legs in a desperate bid for attention.

'Hey boy.' He ruffled the dog's coat, avoiding the huge, slobbering tongue lolling out of the side of Sammy's mouth.

Bob sat himself down in front of the TV and flicked it on with the remote. Sammy jumped up onto the couch beside him. The picture wasn't brilliant, but he could see all he needed to. Some man in a jester's outfit was being bombarded with custard pies. He tried another channel: a current affairs programme. And another: a badly acted soap opera. With a sigh he snapped off the power.

It was still relatively early, despite the darkness outside telling him otherwise. He'd been in the cottage all of ten days now and had done nothing but work the whole time. Of course, that was one of the main reasons why he'd bought the property in the first place. So he could escape from the rat race whenever he wanted to and concentrate on his art. For a professional photographer there was nowhere on earth quite like it. Wildlife, picturesque views, rock formations. The lot. There was enough material here to stage several thousand exhibitions and fill a million hardback books.

But man cannot live on bread alone. Or in Bob's case, sandwiches hastily eaten while scouting for locations or printing up. It was time to get out a bit, meet some of the locals (what few there were), and, more importantly, sample the bitter.

He knew just the place.

A short fifteen-minute drive down the winding road from the cottage brought Bob to 'The Wanderer's Rest', a pub he'd passed several times before but hadn't visited yet. Until now it had been enough for him to know it was there if he needed it. If the loneliness ever got to him or he felt the desire to interact with something that didn't bark back. His headlights uncovered a flat square of concrete next to the inn. Hardly what you'd call a car park, but big enough for the amount of trade the place received.

Inside, it was just as he'd anticipated. Stone walls with wooden beams and tables, attractive watercolour paintings hanging over the fireplace, and a medium-sized—but adequately stocked—bar. One or two patrons were scattered about the room, quietly enjoying their drinks. Bob felt at home right away.

'What'll it be, sir?' the broad innkeeper said. His cheeks were almost entirely red, and those huge forearms were a testament to many years spent hefting beer barrels and crates around.

'Pint of bitter, please.' Bob sat on one of the round stools at the bar, waiting for his drink to be served.

'Not seen you around here before, sir. Just passing through?' asked the man as he placed the frothing liquid on the counter.

'Er, no. I've bought a little cottage up the road a way. The white one over—'

'Aye. I know the one you mean,' he interrupted, holding his hand out for Bob to shake. 'Why didn't you say so before? First drink's on the house. I'm Abe Fenton, by the way. Owner of The Wanderer's Rest.'

'Pleased to meet you. Bob Greenan.' Bob took a swig of the bitter. It was strong and had real bite, but went down the throat so smoothly it might have been pure honey itself. He let out a grunt of satisfaction.

Abe smiled. 'So Bob, what is it you do, then?'

'I'm a photographer, for my sins.'

'What, like for a newspaper or something?'

Bob laughed. 'No, more artistic than that. Well, I like to think so.'

'Well you've certainly come to the right place for it. Some gorgeous sights round here.'

Bob nodded. 'I'm working on a series of landscapes at the moment. Trying to capture one particular spot at different points in the day.'

'That right?'

'Only there seems to be a problem with my camera or something. Sounds good, doesn't it? A photographer with a broken camera.' Bob laughed again and supped some more of the bitter, the pleasant atmosphere relaxing him.

'What's up with it?'

'Not really sure. Some pictures I took up on the hills there came out with white marks on them, sort of going across the frame—'

'When was this, then?' The landlord's face had gone pale and his jaw was twitching.

'Yesterday.'

'No, no. I mean what *time* of day.' His voice had an impatient edge to it.

'Around sunset. *At sunset*, actually. I wanted to . . . ' Bob noticed the man was shaking his head. 'Why, what's the matter?'

Abe leaned over the bar and motioned for Bob to do the same. 'Didn't anyone tell you? I suppose not . . . You didn't ought to be hanging around up there so near to nightfall,' he whispered.

Bob was intrigued. 'Why?'

Abe tapped the side of his nose; Bob was surprised to see that old gesture still in use. 'Suffice to say that I don't think them marks on your photos are down to the camera.'

For a moment or two Bob wasn't sure what Abe meant. Then the realisation slowly dawned on him. 'You can't be serious,' Bob chuckled, though he could see the man was earnest enough.

'Think what you like. Only you haven't been here as long as I have. Heard the tales. Some funny things happen on them hills at night. All I'm saying is you should stick to takin' pictures in the daytime, Bob. I'd certainly sleep easier if you did.'

Bob felt like laughing again, except he didn't want to offend Abe or his beliefs. Not when he was the proprietor of the only pub for miles. Instead, he thanked him for the warning and promised to be careful in future. Abe seemed to settle for this and was soon back to his jovial, easy-going self. Bob joined in the conversation, said hello to some of the regulars when the landlord introduced them, and even took part in the round of joke telling that appeared to be a ritual pastime in the pub.

But at the back of his mind was the thought of those lights on the hills, and how he couldn't wait to get out there and take some more pictures.

On his return to the cottage, Bob went straight to the darkroom to get his prints.

In Bob's mind Abe was a guy who'd read too many 'Unexplained' books and listened to one old folktale more than he should have done. Nevertheless, his warning had fired Bob's imagination. There was an angle here he could use to his advantage (*exploit* was such a nasty word). If indeed something strange was occurring on those hills, and there was bound to be a logical explanation, then it was definitely worth investigating. Who knows, it could lead to his best collection yet. Some of his work might even end up abroad or garner interest in the States.

Excitement was replaced by bewilderment, though, when he plucked his photos off the drying line. Something had changed. He couldn't put his finger on it immediately, then as he looked more intently he saw that the blobs which had been so indistinct before were now slightly sharper in focus. He could see the outlines of figures, actual figures, roaming across the hills. They were still pallid and fuzzy around the edges, but there was no doubt whatsoever: these were human beings walking over the peaks.

Or at least they had been, once.

Quickly Bob hunted for the contact sheet he'd made earlier from his negatives; tiny replicas of the snapshots he'd taken. Reaching for his magnifying glass, he was astounded to find that those last five images had altered as well.

'This is insane,' Bob mumbled to himself. Once a print was developed it couldn't just mutate like that. Maybe he'd mixed the chemicals incorrectly in his hurry to get started earlier today, or had bought a dodgy batch of photographic paper with a hole in the lightproof box.

But these assumptions were torn apart soon enough. Even the negatives themselves now had black figures on their plastic surface, proving that it had nothing to do with either paper or chemicals.

Bob had never seen anything like it in all his years in the profession.

A glass of scotch helped calm him down, mixing with the bitter already in his system. Sammy danced around him, staring worriedly up at his master. 'You might well look like that, boy. I think I'm cracking up.' Perhaps Abe Fenton had been right about the hills. And if he was, then this could be bigger than Bob had first imagined.

All he could do now, however, was sit on the couch and inspect the pictures again, ignoring as best he could the circumstances surrounding their appearance.

The 'people' in his photos all had their backs to him, so he couldn't see any of their faces. They looked for all the world like refugees fleeing a war zone, the kind you see on news reports far too often nowadays. Poor, wretched individuals with only a handful of belongings, forced to move out of their homes, their towns, their cities.

The similarity wasn't lost on him. Was this group doing the same thing, running away from some terrible tragedy? And if so, what was it? And where were they running? Their destination was just out of sight, over the hill in the distance; or over the next one, or the next . . .

Bob couldn't help wondering what had caused the phenomenon. Could this be the site of some past disaster? A battle from the middle ages? A plane crash? He made a mental note to check the libraries in the nearest town as soon as possible.

Bob cast his eye over the forms again. Was he really looking at a reflection of some bygone age? A snapshot? If so, how come *his* camera picked it up?

These questions churned around in his mind for hours. Bob would stroll over to the window, peering out into the black night as if expecting to see the procession go hiking past. That way, he could simply ask them . . . if he had the nerve.

Eventually the alcohol he'd consumed took hold and Bob dropped off to sleep on the couch, the pictures clutched in his fist, and Sammy sprawled across his lap.

His dreams were preoccupied with one subject.

Bob stumbled across the darkening countryside, his feet made of cement. Ahead of him he could see a brilliance, gleaming sporadically. As he came near he realised it wasn't just one light, but rather a succession of incandescent outlines moving deliberately towards the setting sun—which itself boiled and bubbled into a swirling sky.

The photographer struggled to catch them up, absently wondering where his camera was. These scenes were incredible and he had no way of recording them for future inspection. Bob tried to call out after the string of oversized fireflies, but no sound would emerge. *I have to know,* he thought. *Why won't you tell me . . . ?*

More and more of the objects were emerging from behind a slit in the landscape. No, not a slit. Bob knew it was the edge of a photograph, its white border unmistakable. He was trapped on the paper with no means of escape. How was that possible? How was any of this possible? The only answers lay in front of him, and Bob urged his body onwards.

Closer, closer, until his fingertips were within inches of the nearest light, turning as it morphed into a recognisable contour.

Bob touched the thing's back. It was freezing. With both hands he tugged at its shoulder in an effort to spin it around. To see . . .

The shrill ring of the telephone shook Bob violently awake. His arms were outstretched, hands grabbing at nothing. He brought one palm back to shield his eyes from the sunlight invading the room.

Beside him on the coffee table, the phone persisted; its head-ache-inducing wail demanding that he answer. Clumsily, he shifted round and snatched up the receiver.

'Hello? Hello? Bob are you there?' The voice was distant.

'Yeah,' he answered, rubbing his eyes.

'Bob, it's Ian.' Bob didn't know why he was so surprised. His agent, Ian Swain, was the only person who had his number out here.

'Hi, Ian. What time is it?'

Ian paused, a little thrown by the question. 'Er . . . It's half eleven.'

Shit! I've overlaid. 'You're joking?' said Bob.

'I never joke about time, Bob. You know that. Time is money and—'

'Money is your god. Yeah, yeah, I remember. What do you want?'

'Just seeing how you're settling in. How the work's coming along.'

Bob leaned over and scooped up his pictures, which were now all over the floor. He looked at them for the hundredth time, as if trying to convince himself they were real. The figures were still there. If anything, they were more pronounced than the night before. Bob could even see hands and feet. And were there folds of clothing on the nearest one?

'It's funny you should ask that, Ian, because I'm holding something in my hand right now that'll blow you away.'

'Really? *That* good?'

'That good.'

Bob heard him whistle down the line. 'Well, don't keep me in suspense. What is it?'

'I'd rather you came out here and saw for yourself. I've only got a few at the moment, but I'm going to print up some more this afternoon and I'm off out to shoot again later.'

'All right, tomorrow it is then. I'll look forward to it. Anything you need from the civilised world while I'm coming?'

Bob grinned. 'That's okay, I think I can manage. See you when I see you.'

Bob replaced the handset. A quick shower, shave, feeding of the dog, and then he was back to work. He'd wasted enough time already. He didn't intend to waste any more.

He hadn't worked so enthusiastically on a project in ages. Between lunch and tea Bob produced in the region of twenty prints based on the five 'faulty' negatives. Close-ups, large scale blow-ups, details . . . By 5 o'clock he'd done all he could with that batch. It was now a case of going out and seeing if he could get lucky again. Same spot, same time of day. In theory it should work.

Bob loaded up his bag with film, checked his Praktica over twice again just to make sure (he didn't dare swap it), and even slipped an automatic into his coat pocket.

Sammy jumped up and down as he headed towards the door.

'Not this time, fella. It's too important. I'll take you for a walk tomorrow. I promise.' The dog cocked his head and whined, clearly wanting to go with Bob.

Or wanting him to stay.

And then he was off, making his way up the path to find those special hills. Before it was too late.

To his chagrin it took him longer than he thought it would to reach the place. Something was diverting him, holding him back. But he was determined, fuelled by a driving curiosity. He had to know. *Had to!*

By the time he arrived the sun was already quite low in the sky. Again he marvelled at the stunning cloud formations, the red streaks slicing them in halves, thirds and quarters. Nature's plan was wonderful to behold.

Bob raised his single lens reflex, took a light reading, adjusted the aperture, and clicked off a couple of shots. He couldn't see anything unusual, but then he hadn't seen anything the other night either. Best to make sure.

The sun was almost in position, the same height as it was on the photos (and he should know; he'd studied them hard enough). Bob lined up another shot and depressed the button. The shutter snapped across. Wind on, then again, wind on. As the shutter came back this time, Bob spotted a faint light through the glass. Now at last he had something to go on. If he could just get closer . . .

A kind of madness gripped him. Bob ran up the incline, camera still welded to his face. He could hear his own breathing in his head, fast and deep. A little bit further, a bit further-

Something caught his foot and sent him flying. He landed hard on the tough grass, rolling over to protect the camera. The bag dropped from his shoulder. There was a yelp.

Two eyes flashed, a panting noise: Sammy. Somehow he'd escaped from the cottage and followed on. Bob raised himself up.

'What are you doing here? Bad dog!' The canine growled, auburn fur erect on his back. Bob had never seen him like this before. Sammy was usually such a well-behaved pet.

He traced the dog's gaze, looking for something that could explain this abnormal behaviour. He soon found it.

There, walking across the hill, were the figures from his photos. Only now he saw them with the utmost clarity. Men, women, children, as white as milk. All trekking purposefully along. Bob still didn't know where they were going. Or what compelled them to proceed.

He was up and running again. In a replay of his dream Bob reached out to the nearest one.

'Who are you? Where are you going?' he shouted, grabbing at its wrist.

The figure turned.

Didn't anyone tell you?

Sammy was barking from somewhere behind him. A far off sound.

You didn't ought . . .

There was no pulse in that wrist. Only coldness; an icy cold.

. . . to be hanging around . . .

No blood was being pumped through this being.

. . . up there . . .

Bob was looking into the eyes of a dead man.

. . . so near to nightfall . . .

A dead man with his face.

And now Bob became that man. He was part of the procession, crammed between a pasty teenager with tattoos and a distraught woman holding a baby close to her chest, the teardrops streaming down her face. His fear became amazement as he gaped back along that line. It stretched out as far as he could see. There were thousands, no, millions of walkers, going on *ad infinitum*. And in front of him it was the same story. Bob could only guess, but it seemed to him that the cavalcade encircled the entire globe, invisible to all but a select few at select times, in select locations. The spirits of people who'd died during that day.

'I—I don't belong here. I have to go . . .' Yet even as he spoke the words, he knew how wrong he was.

Because at that precise moment he saw Sammy standing barking over his own limp body on the hill. Bob Greenan's neck was twisted, his black tongue protruding from his mouth; his precious camera still in his hands.

And he acknowledged the call the others followed. A summons. Something dragging him along the peak. Blinkered like a shire horse, he strode on, his resplendent soul glowing brightly.

Bob's head was emptying. *Purged.* He'd wanted to know where they were going and soon he would find out . . .

As the sun disappeared behind that hill, a shroud of darkness covered the land. And when, in the morning, the shroud was lifted, there was nothing left of those spirits who had marched along in the procession.

Ian Swain pulled up outside the cottage at ten am only to find Bob's dog Sammy scratching at the door. For a full five minutes Ian knocked and shouted for Bob, but no one answered. He assumed the photographer must have taken Sammy for a walk and the playful dog had sneaked away from him somehow. Thankfully one of the windows round the back was open and Ian managed to scramble inside.

The cottage was indeed empty; the bedroom, living room, the kitchen . . . not a sign of life anywhere. Tired of waiting, Ian entered the darkroom. He began looking round for the pictures Bob had raved about. Were they really as good as he made out?

But despite searching high and low, all he could find were a stack of prints on the desk, plus a few stills clipped to the drying line.

Ian inspected each piece in turn, pulling a face. Surely there had to be some kind of mistake. These were landscapes all right, Bob's speciality. But most were overexposed almost to the point of being black. And a couple, yes one or two at best, had big white splotches running across the middle where the camera had let in light at the back . . .

LORD OF HOSTS
David Robertson

I had never found it difficult to reaffirm the faith of others, all I had to do was demonstrate my own and it seemed to draw it, as though by osmosis, from them. And so it was with my peculiar parish as we motored easterly across France. The soldiers would come to my quarters at night, always alone and with the same mortal fears. To-a-man young, common and frightened, they would gaze at the crucifix upon my wall as I spoke, and a little of my life story, how I believed that God had brought ME, HERE, NOW for some unfathomable reason, would reassure them more than a youth filled with Sunday school ever could. They needed hope, not theology. But who to give hope to an inexperienced chaplain when the ground that his belief—no, his very life—is built upon, begins to shudder and shift?

For it seemed to me that we were again living the Last Days, racing towards the front-line, and Armageddon. My nights were spent in prayer; the same thoughts recircled my mind. Had Lucifer finally gained as much power as his former Master? Or was this a purging of an impure world? God remained without comment. Why was I, his humble, faithful, celibate servant being sent into the flames? I felt like Job, which gave me no comfort, only further contradictions.

But all such speculations ceased the moment we reached the Front, together with whatever scant traces of faith I had left. The God I had believed in was everywhere, and in everything; and there was no God in that battlefield. I do not need to describe the wanton theft and rape of life that I saw, for the Poets have already told it better than I could ever hope to; but I feel that you will be able to comprehend the impact that scene had on the mind of a naive Village priest. A moustachioed Sergeant led me to the corrugated shack that was to be my quarters, and feeling no guilt for the other men who went immediately out to fight, I locked the door and began to mourn instead the death of God, and of the world I had known. And it is for this reason that what I am about to describe to you was not wholly seen by these eyes—but I feel qualified to tell it, if you will allow me, for I heard it afterwards from a great many of those who did.

The battle, I am told, had raged on that strip of land, as wide as a Cathedral is long, continuously, for two months previous to our arrival. Small gains were won, but yards only, and quickly lost again. Artillery and tanks were brought by both sides, but nothing it seemed could break the stalemate. More men died there than ever lived there, and every pair of ears within a ten-mile radius became deaf to the sound of shelling.

Tanks trundled steadily across no-mans' land in one direction or the other but always towards death; and so no-one initially paid any attention as one more burst over the German fortifications like some surfacing Kraken and crawled over barbed wire and the dead towards our defences. Some would hit a mine and explode spectacularly; others emptying themselves of smoke through the blow-hole roof-hatch, machine gunners targeting the heads as soon as they appear, coughing; but one kept on coming, oblivious to shell and crater, shooting all the while. As a flock of birds, turning by some unspoken command, the Allied guns all trained on it and let fly the entire force of their righteous artillery. When the smoke cleared, they saw it advanced still.

Close to Allied lines now, it began to fire upon the heavy guns. The infantry responded by closing ranks around it, and when the word came, close to two hundred barrels were emptied, loaded, and re-emptied. They continued firing as they closed in further, only stopping when they became so close that the bullets might ricochet back at them. It seemed for one impossibly long moment that every Allied man was either firing at it of holding their breath as they stared; and when it seemed that nothing could prevent the defences from breaching, the tank stopped firing, rolled to a gentle halt.

A full quarter of an hour passed in silence, the circle unbroken, before one brave officer approached the still, Achillian machine. His pistol in his right hand, he used the tread to hoist himself onto the roof. There, trembling visibly, he twisted the handle, flipped open the hatch and took two steps back. He raised his gun, but nothing emerged. The big German guns even seemed to have stopped their sounding so as to better hear. After a minute he approached the hatch again, and there was a collective intake of breath as everyone realised the possibility of a shot ringing out from within. He took a sly peek, then a more confident look, finally dropping to his knees with his head just above the hole. Finally, he stood up, removed his helmet, and scratched his head. Shrugging, he said, 'I think someone better fetch the Chaplain.'

A rap on the door broke my prayers, and the Private responsible led me in silence towards the defences where the tank, eerily silent, stood. The moment that I saw the Panzer, with its black swastika clear upon the drab grey body, a shiver ran up my spine like an inverted lightning bolt. I did not need to be told that there was no soul in it; I ran back to my quarters and emptied my kit bag out across the floor. From among the underwear and sundries I picked up the olivewood crucifix that I had shunned only a few hours before. The fog upon my heart and mind lifted.

For this was not some petty squabble between nations as other wars have been; but a reprise of the original war, of Good against Evil as was fought in Heaven, that echoes eternally in our souls.

I took my cross to the tank, and in the name of the Lord I laid it across the swastika, which mocked the symbol of my faith in crooked reflection. And I realised why ME, HERE, NOW—for Satan was already well represented in this battle, and we had better make sure that God stayed on our side. I placed my left hand upon the warm, dusky metal.

'*Exorcito te*,' I enunciated; the words seemed to spread out, rise and dissipate like incense smoke, wisps travelling Heavenward. I fell to my knees in prayer, but not in sorrowful solitude this time; for every helmeted head bowed and prayed with me, and we felt that God was truly among us.

After we had all trooped off, the blue-grey tank remained, silhouetted by explosions in the rosy twilight. I do not need to tell you, I am sure, that despite the guard, no one in the camp got much rest. But the damned thing was there when the sun rose, and there still when it went down again. I had much to do that day, despite my exhaustion, as one by one the soldiers who had witnessed the event came to me to explain it to them, and to thank me. From some deep recess of my being, I found the strength to carry on.

But when dawn came around again, it had gone. Our commanding officer told me that it had been taken to Washington for study; American Intelligence had to be sure that there was no German technology involved. I noted that they had not returned my crucifix. I went back to work, and thought of it no more, except in my dreams.

When the wintertime came, I fell ill with pneumonia, and like so many others, I was recovering in a French hospital when we took Berlin and the war started to end. As that evening fell, sitting on the veranda, I allowed myself to remember that unholy vehicle for the first time. My mind's eye glided through innumerable sterile corridors, taking this turn and then that, until we finally reached a closed door. As it slowly opened I realised that we were deep underground, in the catacombs of American Military Intelligence. Within sat the tank; still decorated with its powerful symbols, the swastika and crucifix, the whole thing contained within a further symbol, that curious construction that they call the Pentagon. In the beginning was the Word, I thought; but whence came the symbol?

I knew then that they would never understand just what happened that bright still afternoon, nor I; but I thanked God in my prayers all the same.

TONIGHT I SING MY BLUES FOR YOU
J. Newman

I.

'Wake up, man. Wake up! You're never gonna believe this.'

Two o' clock in the frigging morning, and I'm jerked awake by my so-called friendBuddy, rocking me like an overeager child nagging at his father on Christmas morning.

'Dammit, Buddy . . . what the hell are you doing here?'

'Get up, get your clothes on. You are never gonna believe this, David!'

If you saw Buddy and I on the street, you'd never expect us to share anything in common. Where I kept my hair styled neatly these days, never allowed it to grow past my earlobes, where I wore khakis and nothing more exciting than the occasional too-loud tie to work, Buddy was my complete opposite. His dirty-blond hair, done up in those 'white-boy dreads,' fell just past his shoulders, and on the night in question, he wore his Mojo Faction T-shirt, a psychedelic explosion of colors around a portrait of that local blues band we liked to go see at the clubs. Buddy was still in college, where I had graduated two years before, and he seemed doomed to remain there forever. Not that you would ever catch Buddy complaining. Didn't matter we were both in our mid-twenties, and I had long since fallen into a comfortable job at the local elementary school, teaching fourth grade and living a 'responsible lifestyle' (as we used to sarcastically call such a thing when we were both long-haired party animals), Buddy was content with remaining the eternal college-boy, claiming when someone called him on it that he was still 'unsure of exactly what he wanted to do.'

To each his own, I guess . . . the guy may have been directionless, carefree, and—admittedly—more than a tad irresponsible, but he had also been my best friend for as long as I could remember.

'*Some* of us have to work in the morning, Buddy,' I said, frowning as I pulled on my bedroom slippers and a pair of sweatpants. 'Not that you would know anything about that.' Still, my tone betrayed my lack of any true anger at my friend. Buddy had that effect on everyone, even if he did look like a greasy hippie—something in the guy's face, I suppose, an inherent kindness that was instantly infectious. It was hard to stay angry at Buddy.

'You're never gonna believe this, man,' he said again. As if he hadn't made that clear already.

I yawned. 'You wanna tell me where, exactly, you're taking me?'

Two words rolled off my friend's tongue then, slowly. A melodramatic whisper: '*Sleeping Meadows.*'

II.

'It was like this when I found it. Contrary to what you might think, David, I *didn't* break in.'

'Uh-huh,' I said, still rubbing gritty sleep from my eyes.

Buddy referred to the fact that the cemetery's massive, spire-tipped gate—the only way into Sleeping Meadows other than the gravel service road at the opposite end of the property—stood wide open when we got there. This despite the sign: **NO TRESPASSING—GATES CLOSE NIGHTLY 9PM-8AM.**

'It's almost as if I was . . . *expected*, you know?' Buddy said. 'Like the gates were open just for me.'

* * *

Sleeping Meadows—nine sprawling acres in the very center of our city—was the final resting place of hundreds who had once walked these streets as far back as the late-1800's. Several skeletal black oaks, their naked autumn-branches reaching heavenward like gaunt fingers, loomed in no particular pattern throughout the cemetery, as if they were God's sentinels randomly placed there to guard the souls He would one day return to embrace. The jutting silhouettes of monuments, tombstones, and cherubic statuettes scattered throughout the place resembled odd-shaped pebbles sunning themselves on the bed of some shallow, moon-swept stream. The night's cool breeze kissed my face, slid through the trees, and whispered against those cold gray stones like voyeurs discussing our every move. The cemetery's grass had been recently trimmed, seemed to shine silver beneath the night's full moon, and that summery mown-grass smell assaulted my nostrils as I followed Buddy through the place. It reminded me of backyard barbecues back home—of childhood innocence, somehow, of a time when the world seemed so much larger.

As we made our way down those winding paths, sometimes across the blacktopped road that snaked through the cemetery then back into the sea of graves again, I asked my friend several times, in hushed tones, just where the hell he was taking me.

'I couldn't sleep, man,' Buddy finally began. 'Had a dream about my mother.' Tears glistened in the corners of his eyes, but he never stopped walking, never slowed down. I had to pick up my pace, in fact, just to keep several strides behind my friend. 'Dreamed she was outside my window, right? Singing.'

I understood Buddy's pain. It had only been a month or so since the accident. A drunk driver, head-on collision. It was bad, I'd heard—very bad. The mortician had done all he could, Buddy was told, but the wake had still been a closed-casket affair. My friend was entitled to his grief.

'I dreamed she was *singing* to me, David . . . dreamed I went to the window, and there she was, floating *two stories* off the ground outside my dorm-room. She was playing this old battered guitar, a blues song. Man, it was the most beautiful fucking thing I've ever heard!'

'Hey, man—' I started. I reached out, gently touched his shoulder, but he kept walking.

'I woke up . . . I mean, I *really* woke up this time. This part was real, I know, 'cause I was sweating all over. And guess what?'

He looked back at me, pausing only briefly before continuing on into the heart of the cemetery. To dark places that the full moon's alabaster glow could no longer quite reach. 'I could still hear that music, David. Swear to God, man . . . just this simple three-chord acoustic number, very sad, but it was the sweetest damn thing. At first, I thought I was imagining it . . . it sounded as if it were several blocks down the street . . . but there it was, plain as day. And . . . crazy as it sounds, man . . . it's like I *knew* . . . *that song was playing just for me.*'

'So what's all this gotta do with me?' I asked, my brow furrowed.

'I couldn't go back to sleep, after that. I had to come see her.'

Again I touched my friend lightly upon the shoulder. 'Hey . . . I'm here for you, Buddy. Anytime. You know tha—'

'Here we are,' he said suddenly, not really hearing me, and he stopped above a grave.

I looked down.

And I frowned. This wasn't Buddy's mother's grave.

I had been out here a couple times with Buddy, however, and I knew this gravesite just as well.

It was the grave of one Joseph 'Blind Dawg' Melton.

III.

'I don't get it, Buddy. What's Blind Dawg got to do with your mom?'

Buddy knelt before the modest marker—not much more than a flat, cheaply inscribed rock, really—at Blind Dawg Melton's final resting-place. For several long, awkward seconds, he said nothing. He just sat like that, brow furrowed, the tips of his fingers gliding across the late musician's chiseled stone (**1905-1999** was all it said below his Christian name, with a crude etching of a guitar beside that).

'Where'd they all go?' he said, more to himself than to me. 'They were right here.'

I just stared at him, uncomprehending.

'There were people here, David. Gathered around Melton's grave. They were standing here. Listening.'

'Listening?'

'Yeah. I'm over there—' Buddy gestured toward an off-white crowd of marble tombstones about a hundred feet away (the area, I remembered, where his mother had been buried)—'visiting with Mom, and I see them over here. Just staring down at Melton's grave. It really creeped me out at first, till I realized what was going on. A couple of 'em, I can see their shoulders hitching. You know, like they're crying.'

'Buddy,' I said softly, 'I know your mother's death hit you pretty hard . . . it hurt me too, man . . . but I think maybe we should—'

'No, David!' Buddy shot back, in a tone harsher than any he had used with me in quite some time. 'No! I saw them. They were here! They were listening to his music. I know, because I joined them. I'm not crazy. I stood *right here*. And I listened, too.'

A tear ran down Buddy's face, silver in the moonlight like mercury.

'Blind Dawg was playing. Down there. Never in my life have I heard anything so beautiful.'

IV.

Perhaps at this point I should fill you in on a little history. Joseph Seymour Melton—better known as 'Blind Dawg' Melton—had been a native of the city in which Buddy and I lived. Up until his interment in Sleeping Meadows, the old bluesman obtained little more than a small cult following despite having—in my opinion—deserved so much more. During his career Melton recorded only a dozen or so records, and all of those had been on a small label run out of Mississippi, a less-than-reputable outfit by the name of Sharky Records (which, last I heard, ended up on the losing end of a class-action lawsuit engineered by several other artists who never saw the money owed them by the company). Buddy and I often discussed, on those long nights when we would sit in my apartment or in his cluttered dorm-room listening to Melton's scratchy old records, why a man like 'Blind Dawg' Melton should live in such obscurity despite the inimitable talent God had given the him. Buddy and I owned every recording Blind Dawg ever cut, some of which cost us a pretty penny. Not that we cared. Because Blind Dawg Melton—who was truly blind, by the way, supposedly since childhood, at the hands of an abusive stepfather—was worth so much more. Guy had *soul*, lemme tell ya. Everything he sang came from the heart . . . and his guitar-playing, well, it was simply out of this world.

Buddy and I had attended Melton's funeral ten months before that night my friend claimed to hear Blind Dawg singing from beyond the grave, and—while it may sound silly, as we never knew him *personally*—it hit us hard. The guy was nothing less than a hero to these two blues fanatics, an idol no less revered than others in the genre who built their careers upon albums surpassing gold status the world over.

Blind Dawg Melton didn't just play the blues, he *lived* them. As the story went, he had been an alcoholic in his younger days, a troubled, bitter man with various mental problems. But Melton fought his demons and won. He battled racism through the forties, fifties, and sixties (hence his most-remembered, if not altogether *financially*-successful song 'We All Bleed the Same'), and had just barely made a living with his music in a world that seemed to desire screeching rock n' roll over the very heartfelt rhythm which inspired that genre.

Joseph 'Blind Dawg' Melton was one-of-a-kind. A beautiful man, in my opinion, who made music that was the closest thing to heaven Buddy and I could imagine.

We still visited his grave once or twice a month (more often than not leaving a rose upon his modest stone, just to show someone still cared), we still played his records faithfully and sometimes shed a tear or two as we listened, but we went on. Because, well . . . for God's sake, the man was ninety-four years old! He had to go sooner or later, right?

However, on the night in question, I seriously began to wonder if my friend Buddy was truly over it at all. If he would ever be. Because now, after losing one of his greatest heroes *and* his dear mother less than a year apart . . . I feared the poor guy had completely lost his mind.

V.

'He was playing, David. It was beautiful. He was playing from beyond the grave.'

'Okay, Buddy,' I said softly, conflicting emotions roiling within me. 'I think we should go home now . . . I think you should get some rest.'

"Don't cry for me . . . I'll see you on the other side."

'Hm?'

'That was his song, David. So perfect. And it was like . . . he was playing it just for me.'

'Come on, Buddy . . . come on.'

'You don't believe me, do you?' my best friend sobbed as I gently led him away.

And I honestly did not know what to say.

VI.

Buddy and I parted ways that night shortly after four a.m. He headed back to his dorm, and I to my apartment, confused as all hell and wondering if my friend was really going to be okay. I wondered just what the hell he had witnessed out there at Blind Dawg Melton's gravesite. I knew that my friend would not lie to me. Even so, if only in the spirit (excuse the pun) of some harmless prank, there was no way Buddy could have pulled it off so convincingly. Tears and all.

Still, I refused to entertain the notion that he might have actually heard . . . for Christ's sake, *a phantom bluesman working his mojo from beyond the grave?*

Something really *had* happened out there at Sleeping Meadows. Buddy *did* believe what he told me, that he had heard the late bluesman playing his sad song out there . . . my shirt, still moist with my friend's tears as I returned to my apartment that night, was ample proof of that. However, the question now was . . . what was wrong with my friend? Had my old pal been indulging in a little too much of the 'wacky weed?' Or was he into something much deeper?

I would know soon enough.

VII.

After that night in the cemetery, Buddy and I sort of . . . drifted apart. While Buddy never strayed too far from my thoughts, and I worried about my old friend every day . . . the truth is, I made no effort to contact him. Once upon a time, Buddy and I would never allow more than a week to slip by without getting together, never more than two or three days without calling one another just to touch base.

However . . . I must admit I was a little fearful of Buddy's sanity after that night. I didn't call him. I didn't visit him up at the college. For that, I will never forgive myself. Likewise, Buddy made no effort to contact me. Perhaps, I thought, my friend might have been more than a little embarrassed by his actions, by whatever insane things he claimed to have seen. Buddy may have realized that he did need help. Professional help.

I can only guess, however. I do not know what went through Buddy's mind in the weeks following our nocturnal visit to Blind Dawg Melton's grave. I guess I never will.

Because that night was the last time I saw my best friend alive.

VIII.

Three weeks after mine and Buddy's bizarre little *adventure,* if you will, I awoke in the middle of the night, a Friday night, and couldn't get back to sleep. I'd been having that problem quite a bit lately, plagued with some rather disturbing nightmares (which was odd because I hardly ever dream anything worth remembering). Buddy had filled my mind with some rather morbid images, and now I was suffering for it.

So I decided to take a walk. Through the city. This was something I used to do quite often back in my college days, take long walks at two or three in the morning just for the time alone, to think clearly about whatever was on my mind without the chaos of daily life getting in the way, yet after I graduated, fell full-swing into that 'responsible lifestyle' I mentioned earlier, I could no longer find the time for such soul-searching ventures.

Sleeping Meadows was most certainly not my destination that night, yet somehow I ended up there all the same. I turned the corner, and there it was.

The gate stood open, again.

Without even consciously thinking about it, I entered the cemetery. And headed straight for Blind Dawg Melton.

IX.

I heard them—faintly, in the distance—before I ever saw his grave. The sound of gentle sobbing, of several different whispered conversations spoken in breaths thick with snot and tears. Two or three people, their depressed conversations intermingling with one another.

I knew before I saw them that the people who made those sounds would be gathered around Blind Dawg Melton's grave. However strongly I wanted to deny that there could be any validity to Buddy's insane story of a ghost guitarist and his midnight graveyard gig . . . I knew they would be there. Indeed, three people were gathered around Blind Dawg's tombstone. Two men and a woman, seemingly oblivious to each other as they carried on like the world was falling apart all around them. One man stood, tallest son-of-a-bitch I've ever seen, gazing heavenward as moon-streaked tears trailed down his face. He was bald, dressed entirely in black, a yellow ribbon pinned to his lapel. He held his skeletal arms around himself, trembling slightly as his lips worked in a silent conversation with God . . . with Melton . . . with somebody. Strangest thing of all, though, was that—even though the big guy bawled his eyes out—he was smiling. *Smiling.*

Likewise, the man and woman on the ground—she sat cross-legged, Indian-style, also gazing heavenward, while the middle-aged black man beside her was on his knees, gazing down as if he could see all the way through the earth and into Melton's casket—wept as I had never seen anyone weep before, though all the while undeniable smiles kept creeping through their anguish.

It was the most bizarre thing I've ever seen, let me tell you.

I stayed out there for well over an hour, approximately a hundred yards away behind an immense oak tree, watching them. Wondering just what the hell was going on here.

Yet whatever these people carried on about so . . . whatever bled such raw emotions from them . . . not once did I see or hear a goddamn thing.

And, for some strange reason, I found myself oddly *depressed* by that. By the fact that, for whatever reason, I was not allowed to share in this.

X.

Six days later, after my own bizarre encounter at Sleeping Meadows, I was awakened by a phone call from Buddy's sister, Kara. Kara lived in

Atlanta, and I hadn't spoken with her in almost a year, so I knew right away something was wrong. Why else would Buddy's sister be calling me?

'He's dead, David,' she sobbed into the phone. 'They killed him.'

'Kara? Killed who? What are you talking about?'

'Buddy.'

'Whaaaat?' A lump formed in my throat. My heart began to beat faster than would seem humanly possible.

'Gang-bangers jumped him on 42nd. You know Buddy, stubborn S.O.B. that he is, he'd never let them just take his wallet. I always knew that mouth would get him in trouble some day.'

With that she broke off into a fit of sobbing. I felt myself heading in the same direction, but I had to keep my composure.

'Oh, my God. Where was he?'

It took her a minute, but finally she answered. 'He'd been staying down here with Donald and me the past couple weeks. I told him Atlanta wasn't a good place to be, out on the streets alone late at night. He'd been having trouble sleeping, and I guess he wanted to take one of his midnight walks. The police said those bastards stabbed him *twenty-eight times!* Why, David, why?!'

'Jesus, Kara. I'm sorry.' It was all I could think of to say. 'I'm so, so sorry.'

One of the last things she said to me then, during that unforgettable phone-call, hit me right in the gut. A stinging punchline to a very unfunny joke . . .

'He said he missed you, David. He told me that the other day. Said he hoped you were okay. Did something happen between you two?'

Another question I did not know how to answer. I left her with her tears then, and she with mine, and we parted with little more than a final 'I'll see you at the funeral.'

Two days later, beneath a sickly gray October sky, I watched the cold ground swallow up my best friend.

My brother.

Forever.

XI.

Buddy was buried in Sleeping Meadows, next to his mother. Just how he had wanted it.

It was the single worst day of my life.

Several days after the funeral, I pulled the worst goddamn drunk ever.

'Here's to you, Buddy,' I wept as I drank, screaming it out on more than one occasion until the guy below my apartment started pounding the ceiling beneath me.

'Lick my pole, asshole!' I cursed at the floor, grabbing my own crotch.

Didn't take long for Jim Beam to knock me flat on my ass. Everything went black, black as sin, and next thing I remember it's five in the morning.

Head pounding. Stomach churning. Blood rushing through my head so loud I could hear it, like ocean waves breaking on the shores of my throbbing temples.

To hell with it. I had to see my friend. I didn't care what time it was. I had to tell him good-bye one last time.

So I grabbed my jacket, shambled out of my apartment building half-drunk with anger at a God that could take my friend so abruptly, still half-drunk with the alcohol I had consumed earlier. I didn't care. I had to talk to Buddy. Tell him how sorry I was for doubting his sanity for even a second. *What kind of a friend was I, anyway?*

Once again, I headed for Sleeping Meadows.

XII.

The gate, once again, stood open. I remembered Buddy saying how it seemed as if it had been open just for him, welcoming him inside. Did the same hold true for me, tonight?

Maybe.

I shrugged off the thought, headed for my best friend's fresh grave, a tear already spilling down my cheek.

'I love you, Buddy. I'm sorry I wasn't there.'

In the moonlight—despite that fancy tombstone—Buddy's grave resembled little more than a nondescript pile of fresh soil. Even the veritable forest of flowers all around . . . their colors seemed so dull and lifeless in the night. Hard to believe that under all of this my dear friend, my brother, slept a sleep from which he would never awaken.

'You and me, Buddy,' I said to my friend, wherever he was now. 'It was all about you and me. I love you, you long-haired hippie freak.' I laughed at that, could imagine Buddy laughing along with me. Perhaps slapping me on the back like he always did when I got off a particularly good one.

'Remember our first year at UT, Buddy . . . we went to that Monica chick's New Year's Eve Party? Man, you got so fucked up, you couldn't remember anything that happened the whole night. Bobby Harwood and I had you convinced you'd spent the night with that gay guy who was always giving you the eye in Trig . . . . '

Again I uttered a sad little laugh, wiped tears from my eyes. 'You believed us, too. You were ready to kill me for letting you go home with that guy. I told you, 'Hey, it's what you wanted. You sure were horny last night.''

I bit my lip, fought back a new wave of tears. 'Man, that was the funniest shit.'

I sniffled, ran a hand across his tombstone, and it was like touching a block of ice. 'I'm gonna miss you, Buddy.'

And that's when I heard the music. About a hundred yards away.

Behind me.

XIII.

'Oh, Jesus . . . '

I didn't want to go over there. I was terrified. The eerie rhythm of that phantom blues shuffle made the hairs on the nape of my neck stand up. A chill ran down my spine like the frigid, undead finger of my late friend.

But I knew I had to. I had to go.

It was what Buddy wanted. What Blind Dawg Melton wanted.

I had no choice.

* * *

I turned, and my breath plumed forth into the night air like smoke. Either he had not been there before, or I had failed to notice him—though I did not see how this could be possible—but a man now stood over Blind Dawg Melton's grave. A man who at first appeared to be nine or ten years my senior, though once I saw him closer I suspected he was far younger than that. His eyes were very sad, glazed with recent tragedy. His clothes were wrinkled, his hair mussed and unwashed.

I left Buddy's grave behind, sat beside the man at Blind Dawg Melton's dusty stone.

I listened. And I felt it. At last.

As I approached the man, he did not acknowledge my presence. He dropped to his knees, listening to that phantom melody that I could finally hear. The man had been crying, I could tell, but now his face held a sad smile. A smile of hope. In his hand he clutched a wrinkled snapshot of a little girl, a toddler who so resembled him I knew right away she was his daughter.

Nearby, I spotted the fresh grave, about half the distance between Melton's and Buddy's. The grave of a child. Mid-sized stone carved at the top into the shape of a tiny angel, somewhere on there the words

CHERISHED DAUGHTER, GONE BUT NEVER FORGOTTEN, gigantic bouquets of flowers and several lost-looking stuffed animals propped all around the raised soil.

'Jeanie . . . my baby . . . oh, Jeanie,' cried the man, and I put my arm around him. He never seemed to notice, but that was okay.

I understood, then, who these people were. These troubled survivors who came to Melton's grave, who were drawn to hear his song of hope . . . the very thing they needed.

I understood, for now it was my song as well.

The sound of Blind Dawg Melton's guitar cut through the very marrow of my bones, bit deep into my soul. But it was not a song of tragedy, no. Alas, this was a song of hope, of new beginnings and peace. A warm song that brought new tears streaming down my face, though these were tears I wept with a smile. Tears born of something so much more than the tears one sheds for lost friends. Every word the bluesman sang from beyond this veil of mortality . . . every wailing note he played down there upon his ethereal guitar . . . each would instantly dry my swollen eyes . . . only to, seconds later, bring new tears of wistful happiness.

I understood now. I understood it all.

'Don't cry for me,' the bluesman sang. *'I'll see you on the other side.'*

'Yes,' I said, and the stranger beside me echoed my sentiments. The photograph of his daughter, which he so tightly held mere seconds ago, he now retired to his pocket. Gone, but never forgotten.

We listened. And we cried together.

We knew that life would go on.

And everything would be okay.

> *'Relax, I've only stepped out for a while*
> *You'll be here soon, you see*
> *And when your time has come as well,*
> *You'll be right here with me . . .*
> *One day you'll see I never left*
> *So don't you look so sad*
> *I'll just wait for you, up here*
> *And man, the fun we'll have. . .'*

> *'So when you feel you can't go on, just think of this, my friend*
> *'Long as love's inside your heart, there's no such as thing as 'the End'.'*

FATHER, SON
Geza Csath

One winter morning the head assistant of the Institute of Anatomy announced someone who wanted urgently to speak with the Director.

The Director sent back that he could see him for a few minutes only because he was on his way to his lecture. The hall was in fact already humming with students.

The visitor, a pale, well-dressed, tall man, entered, bowing deeply, and began talking excitedly, almost jabbering. One would have thought him a foreigner, seeing his clean-shaven face, though he had no accent. He wore a black-rimmed pince-nez, and was extremely myopic.

'Pardon me for bothering you, sir, but the matter is urgent—to me at least. My name is Paul Getvas. I'm an engineer and I got here from America yesterday. My mother met me at the train with the news that my father had died. The letter should have arrived the day I embarked . . . In short, I learned—no doubt of it—my father died in this clinic, this very one. My mother's been living in poverty, and couldn't afford to have him buried. So she left his corpse here because the clinic promised to inter him. I've checked up and learned yesterday that he was delivered here to the institute to be used for study by the medical students. I also discovered that the corpses are buried only after being cut to pieces and the shreds tossed all together into a coffin. I should very much like to know if this was my father's fate too, or what the orderly told me—that maybe his bones were boiled and assembled into a skeleton. I'd like to know, and I ask you, sir, if it's true, would you be kind as to let me have the skeleton, or the skull . . . but I'd rather have the whole skeleton, so I can have it buried . . . I beg of you, sir, have someone look for it, and find out if my father's skeleton still exists. The orderly said only the handsome, strong-boned cadavers are selected for that purpose and since my father had huge bones—he was as tall I am . . . I'll reimburse the Institute its expenses.'

The Director calmly stroked his beard through his long agitated speech. Then he said softly, 'Well, I could look in it. May I have your father's name, please?'

'Same as mine, Paul Getvas.'

'As a rule the Institute doesn't release the cadavers. But if the skeleton still exists, in the boiling-tank perhaps or assembled by now, I'm not against its being handed over to you.'

The Director rang. An assistant in white came in.

'Doctor,' the Director said, 'would you find out if a corpse named Paul Getvas was worked on last month, or the month before, and if so whether a skeleton was made for lecturing?' The assistant went off, and the scientist offered his odd visitor a chair.

After five minutes of silent waiting, while the guest's knees danced and the professor stared out at the rainy street, his hands in his pockets, the assistant returned hurriedly.

'The corpse is listed: we got it from Internal Medicine. It was dissected here in Room C. I had it given to the third year students because it was a fine skeleton. I had Matthias do the sinew work last week, and it was assembled the other day. We did quite a good job on it. We had it put in the dissection room, as you suggested, because the first year students broke one of the skeletons in there a month ago.'

The visitor made a sudden convulsive movement. Speaking as slowly as before, the professor said, 'Doctor, would you please have the skeleton we're discussing handed over to this gentleman? And please, pay the costs to me. I'm not certain as to the amount, Doctor. The maceration and assemblage comes to thirty-five crowns, doesn't it?'

The man immediately extracted his wallet and paid it out. Then, less agitated, in fact with some relieved cheerfulness, he said, 'Here you are, sir. And I thank you for your consideration. Pardon me for disturbing you. Have a good day, sir.'

The engineer was shown to the dissecting room, where the skeleton 'under discussion' stood in a corner. A huge, strong-boned skeleton with a fine skull, boiled to a china-white.

For a moment the stranger stared amazed at it. Perhaps he'd never seen a skeleton before. He viewed it before and behind; he revolved it on the stand; his fingers ran over its ribs; he touched the springs holding the jawbone in place. Then, awkwardly, he looked at the assistant and orderly.

The assistant praised the skull, and the stranger became curious about the rest of the anatomy. But the man in white left him hastily—he had his duties at the lecture.

Feeling he had to console him, the old orderly showed his knowledge off: 'What a handsome skeleton! We haven't had one like this for a long time. Even Peter—he's in Institute Two—said, 'Uncle Matthias, I sure envy you this cadaver.'

The stranger bent his head and began swinging the skeleton's leg. It swung rattling to and fro. Then he gazed into the eye sockets, biting his lip.

Even the case-hardened old Matthias, who had been tossing cadavers around thirty years and not much else, could see the tears in the gentleman's eyes, and so turned dutifully sentimental himself.

'Would you by any chance be this gentleman's relative?'

'He was my father!'

'Your father. Hm. Oh, well . . . '

He was promptly silent. They stood there like that awhile, looking at the skeleton. For some moments the skeleton's son felt he had to say something, felt he had to find some means of releasing that peculiarly mixed storm of emotions and thoughts that was building up in him.

But in that clean dissecting room glittering white as china the storm blew over almost before it came. In the strong light of the great windows the pain, the grief of death vanished, melting away. As though having suddenly changed his mind, the engineer seized the steel rod of the skeleton's stand and dragged it towards the door. He was hurrying his strange burden off, determinedly. But averting his eyes, as if blushing for his father.

He crossed the corridor, where some late-arriving medical students saw him lugging the skeleton—whose arms and legs danced grotesquely in the clumsy embrace of a cleanshaven man. Son, father.

BIOGRAPHIES

Hugh Lamb is one of the most respected editors and anthologists in the genre. His numerous books such as **A Tide Of Terror**, **Victorian Tales Of Terror**, and **The Taste Of Fear**, introduced rare and forgotten stories to the present day reader. He provided stories for *Enigmatic Tales*, and edits books for Ash Tree Press as well as working as a free-lance proofreader. He is a giant in the field of supernatural fiction.

Paul Finch 37, I'm a former cop and journalist, now turned full-time author. My bread and butter is British television's long-running crime series, **The Bill,** but I'm currently working on a movie screenplay commissioned from a short story of mine, "Our Hell", which originally appeared on the *Enigmatic Tales* website. Though my day-job is essentially television, writing horror and ghost stories, which up until recently has only been a hobby, is now becoming more lucrative for me. This is the second year running I'll have had stories recommended for Stoker awards, while I also have a full-sized collection due out very shortly . . . from Silver Salamander and my first collection **Aftershocks** is available from AshTree Press. Writing is a bug with me. It's now my entire life, and to be able to support my family through it is an incredible feeling. On the subject of my family, I currently live with my wife, Cathy, my two children, Eleanor and Harry, and a mischievous Labrador pup called Molly, in Lancashire, northern England.

Andrew Roberts considers himself a horror writer and is unconcerned at the negative connotations attached to this label (although he is glad book covers seem to have moved on since the 80s). By the time you read this, his published short stories will probably still be in single figures. He promises to try harder.

Jeremy C. Shipp's works have most recently been purchased by such publications as *Flesh & Blood*, *Voyage*, *3AM*, and *Whispers From the Shattered Forum*. Not only does he write fiction while basking in the warmth (both in weather and social atmosphere) of southern California, he also spawns comic scripts from the darker crevices of his mind. His graphic novel, **Beyond the Wall** (a story of conformity, individuality and the oppressive nature of the community mind) can be purchased at LoganEast Productions (**www.loganeast.com**). Also, his new mosaic of dark tales, "Self-inflicted Taxidermy", spawned of more than 60,000 words, has reviewers in an orgasmic frenzy! "Why'd you send me this?" —Maggie McHart, *Home Furnishings Magazine*; "Why Job and not this guy?" —Rev. Lincoln Homes, 2nd Magistrate Church; "This guy is sick." —Satan, Underworld Ambassador. Check it out for yourself at: **http://selftaxidermy.tripod.com/home.html** (But none of that is really important. What matters most is that he fears clowns dressed as ballerinas.)

Justin Stanchfield I'm a full-time rancher, part-time snowplow driver, sometime musician, and the rest of the time I write. My fiction has appeared in various publications including *Boys' Life* magazine and **The Bones of the World** and **Extremes IV: Darkest Africa** anthologies. I live on a cattle ranch in southwest Montana with my wife and daughter, and am a member of SFWA.

Robert Swartwood was born in 1981 and started writing fiction when he was in high school. Now he's in his third year at Millersville University and is still writing. His work has appeared in a handful of small press magazines, such as *Burning Sky* and *Black Petals* and in the charity anthology **Dreaming Of Angels**. He lives in Pennsylvania.

Stuart Young As a child I was the sole survivor of a plane crash in the African jungle. Fortunately I was adopted by an infinite number of chimpanzees. They raised me in their primitive ways—foraging for berries and typing out the complete works of Shakespeare. However, when they read the feeble literary efforts that came from my typewriter they disowned me and I was forced to return to civilization where I had work published by *Enigmatic Tales*, *Kimota*, **Nasty Piece of Work** and **Sackcloth & Ashes**.

Kevin L Donihe has been published in/accepted into such venues as: **The Mammoth Book Of Legal Thrillers**, *Eldritch Tales*, **Cemetery Sonata II**, **Darkness Rising**, *Crossroads*, *Enigmatic Tales*, **Nasty Piece Of Work**, *Frisson*, *Roadworks*, *Freezer*, *Burn Magazine*, *The Dream Zone*, *Rictus*, *Bathtub Gin*, *Vampire Dan's Story Emporium*, *Cabal Asylum*, *Frightnet*, *Penny Dreadful*, *Edgar: Digested Verse*, *Black Petals*, *Black Rose Publications*, *Goddess Of The Bay*, *Psychopoetica*, and many others.

William P. Simmons works as a professional fiction reviewer, journalist, author, and poet specializing in dark and fantastic literature. Holding a Cum Laude honors degree in World Literatures from Suco College at Oneonta, his first published short story, "The Wind, When It Comes" received an honorable mention in **The Year's Best Fantasy And Horror**. Writing the nationally published "Literary Lesions" column for *Gauntlet* magazine, which explores controversial literature, William also writes "Digging Up Bones," a column reviewing obscure horror fiction for *Hellnotes*. His reviews and literary criticism appear regularly in *Cemetery Dance*, *Mystery Scene*, *Rue Morgue*, etc. His fiction and poetry appear in issues #2-8 of the **Darkness Rising** anthologies, **Octoberland**, *Chi-Zine*, and *Gothic.Net*. As an interviewer, William has spoken with top names in the field, including T.M. Wright, Al Sarrantonio, Graham Masterton, etc. "That Terrible Freedom," a special interview chapbook interview with F. Paul Wilson, is available from Gauntlet with Wilson's **The Haunted Air** novel. His new series of interviews with female horror authors, "Our Ladies Of Darkness," will begin in issue #40 of *Cemetery Dance*. Available in early 2003, his anthology **Vivisections**, a collection of emotional, spiritual, and physical pain, featuring Ramsey Campbell, will be available from Catalyst Books.

Mark R Kehl. Mark comes from northwestern Indiana, where his story is set, though these days he lives in Bethlehem, Pennsylvania. He's the author of four young adult mystery novels and four collections of short stories for middle readers. Another short story of his appeared in a recent issue of *Futures Magazine*.

Pierre Louys (1870-1925) see **Darkness Rising 4**

G. Durant Haire lives in North Carolina with his wife and daughter. His stories and poems have appeared in *Redsine, Horrorfind, Burning Sky, Black Petals, Sinister Element, Mindmares, Frisson, Welcome To Nod, Parchment Symbols, Whispers From the Shattered Forum*, and *Edgar:digested verse*, among others. Visit him online at **www.gdhaire.f2s.com** He is also an Associate **Editor for** *Twilight Showcase.*

Charlie Williams lives in the badlands beyond North London. He has had a few dark stories published in places such as *The Dream Zone, Dark Horizons, Time Out Net Books, Mindkites*, and **Darkness Rising 3**. He has written a novel, which maybe one day—if the stars allow it—will be on a bookshelf somewhere. Other than that, he makes a living staring at a computer screen, moving a mouse around, and mumbling occasionally into a phone.

Spencer Allen lives and writes in the Midwest. His story "Hard Candy" took 1st place out of over 230 entries in a Writer's Weekly short story contest, and his fiction has been published with several professional and small press publications, including *Fangoria* and *Flesh and Blood*. Currently, he is looking for a publisher or agent for his three finished novels. If you want to drop him a line, Spencer can be reached at **spencer@midamerica.net**

Kurt Newton has had over 200 stories and poems published in anthologies and magazines, receiving six Honourable Mentions along the way. His collection from Delirium, **The House Spider and other Strange Visitors** has been well received, as have his three poetry chapbooks. Kurt is also editor and publisher, and has a new fiction collection coming in March 2002 from Delirium Books called **Dark Demons: Tales of Obsession, Possession and Unnatural Desire.** I've just finished my first novel, **The Wishnik,** and I'm hard at work on a second.

Jason Brannon. To date I have had stories published in more than sixty markets including *Twilight Showcase, Electric Wine, The Edge: Tales of Suspense, Nemeton, The Witching Hour, Foxfire, Peridot Books*, and *Black Petals*. I have also had stories accepted for upcoming publication in *Alternate Realities, Black Rose, Black Days*, **Denizens of the Dark**, *The Dead Inn: Volume 2, Black Petals, Dark Realms*, and the **New Traditions in Terror** anthology. In addition, my short story collection, **Puzzles of Flesh**, has been recently published by Silver Lake Publishing and my novel, **Rusty Nails**, is due out in the near future from The Fiction Works.

Paul Edwards I'm 25 years old and I live with my wife Mandy in Gosport, Hants. I've been published in *Peeping Tom, Kimota, The Dream Zone and Tales of the Grotesque* and *Arabesque*.

Mark McLaughlin My fiction, non-fiction, poetry and artwork have appeared in more than 325 magazines and anthologies worldwide. These include *Galaxy, Ghosts & Scholars*, **100 Wicked Little Witch Stories, Best Of The Rest 2, The Best Of Palace Corbie,** *Enigmatic Tales*, **Bending The Landscape, The Last Continent: New Tales Of Zothique,** and **The Year's Best Horror Stories** (DAW Books). I am the author of the story collections, **Zom Bee Moo Vee** and **Shoggoth Cacciatore**. Also, I am the editor of *The Urbanite: Surreal & Lively & Bizarre*.

Michael Kaufmann writes in USA.

Darren Speegle A resident of Germany, Darren Speegle is the author of numerous short stories, nine of which are collected in his book "That Old World Gothic." Among the magazines where his work has appeared are *Chiaroscuro, Writer Online, Blue Murder, Darkmuse, Electric Wine, Infernal* and *3AM*. Darren may be reached via his website at: **www.geocities.com/koobie2stoobies**

Christian Westerlund I was born in 1981 and I spend my days daydreaming and writing, somewhere in a small and strange city called Enkoping in Sweden.

Paul Kane is a freelance writer and artist from Derbyshire in the UK. Since turning his hand to horror fiction in 1998 he has had numerous stories published in magazines and anthologies on both sides of the Atlantic. His first collection **Alone (In the Dark)** was very well received, with favourable reactions from journals such as *SFX* and *Writers' News*. He has been called 'One hell of a talented and visionary writer' by **Night of the Triffids** author Simon Clark, and Tim Lebbon has marked him out as a name to watch. Paul is co-editor of *Terror Tales Online* (**http://www.terrortales.co.uk**) and his own website can be found at **http://www.shadow-writer.co.uk**

David Robertson is a writer, composer and chef, living in Edinburgh, Scotland. He is a member of the group *Magicdrive,* and is working on his first novel. Contact him at **david@adamkadmon.co.uk**

In the last year **James Newman** has been rapidly making a name for himself in the small-press with stories published in various 'zines and the anthologies **Nasty Snips, Rare, The Asylum 2,** and **Son of Brainbox**. His work will also be visible soon in **The Dead Inn (Volume 2)** and **Tourniquet Heart**. Newman's debut novel **The Wicked** is due out very soon.

Geza Csath (1887-1919) see **Darkness Rising 4**

Len Maynard & Mick Sims By the end of 2002 Len Maynard & Mick Sims will have been responsible for 40 books in the genre, as well as having numerous stories published in other people's books. Details can be found at at **www.maynard-sims.com** Active Horror Writers Association members, their collections, **Shadows At Midnight**, 1979 and 1999, and **Echoes Of Darkness**, 2000, were followed in 2002 by their third collection, **Incantations**, and two retrospective collections of their stories, essays and interviews, **The Secret Geography Of Nightmare** and **Selling Dark Miracles**, one introduced by Hugh Lamb and the other by Stephen Jones. Novellas, **Moths**, and **The Hidden Language Of Demons** have been published in 2001 and 2002 respectively, and the latest novella, **The Seminar**, is completed and accepted for 2003 publication by Sarob Press. They have worked as editors, with **Darkness Rising** the USA anthology series, and as editors/publishers they ran Enigmatic Press in the UK, which produced *Enigmatic Tales*, and its sister titles. They have in the past written essays, but currently they are writing novels. Their first novel, **Shelter**, is completed and being considered.

Amanda Sutton, this UK based artist has provided evocative cover art for both this volume and Volume 5.

Rhys Hughes. We are delighted he took the time and trouble to research and unearth stories from two lost writers (Louys and Csath) and to find out the stories behind the writers themselves.